The Quantum Soul

A Sci Fi Roundtable Anthology

Edited by Eric Michael Craig and Ducky Smith

Quantum Soul: A Sci Fi Roundtable Anthology

Edited by Eric Michael Craig and Ducky Smith

Published by Rivenstone Press P.O. Box 14, Edgewood, NM 87015

www.scifiroundtable.org

© 2017 Sci Fi Roundtable

management@rivenstone-press.com

Cover by Ricardo Victoria.

ISBN: 978-0-9974707-7-2

Table of Contents

Introduction

Science-fiction is at its best when it is pushing the conceptual boundaries of human thought and experience. It takes flight and gains in strength and power at the point where technology, science and philosophy begin to stall and fall away. It is not bound by their rules and so the mind can soar, without constraints, beyond mere blue-sky thinking, far out into the depths of intergalactic space.

Thundering good stories can be found at those fringes of our knowledge. There we have loop-holes of understanding which an author can fill with an entertaining tale. Sometimes fiction can be the prism through which we can approach difficult ideas and explore their consequences. The most difficult to grasp, thought-provoking questions can be played out against an imaginative back-drop, made accessible through the telling of a tale with a human perspective.

This anthology takes as its starting point a question. One which touches us all and has become more and more crucial to our thinking about the universe around us, ourselves as individuals, and as a species: What defines life? This opens a Pandora's Box of other questions, such as: What is it to be self-aware? How should we deal with non-human intelligences?

Profound questions that have no answers as yet, because we have not reached the point of encountering any other intelligence - natural or artificial - that we deem worthy of equality with ourselves. We tend to define 'intelligent life' against our own standard of human capacities and limitations. To be considered a self-aware, intelligent life form any other that is not human must first match our own pattern. Would we even realize we have discovered such a 'life' if it was very different from our expectations and standards?

The stories in this collection answer these questions - and others raised by them - in a wide range of ways. Here you will find human encounters with alien minds and minds created by humans. Each story challenges our preconceptions about what intelligent life is, how it manifests, and how it should behave. Some are very technological and rooted in hard-science, others almost metaphysical and skating on the boundary where philosophy touches spirituality.

Most of the stories contain elements of the fantastical as well as of the mundane. But all will intrigue and entertain, and like any good speculative fiction, each one will leave you reflecting on what it means to be alive.

By Design
By Alan VanMeter

We are shortly to arrive at Legacy Outpost G1298-4511 orbiting the primary star in the Mirfak system, returning from our successful mission seeding the fourth planet of 25 rho Perseus. My crew and I are looking forward to our next mission with anticipation. It is scheduled to be a planetary relocation objective. A gas giant needs to have its orbit adjusted to bring it much closer to the local star so the solar winds will strip the dense atmosphere from it, and allow easy access for mining of its valuable minerals which are in abundance within the core. These are complex operations which will challenge us to a greater extent, thus affirming our usefulness.

'Deceleration from fourth temporal dimension in three small half cycles.' navigator TYU, informs us by thought.

'Affirmative.' We send in unison.

Once we are back in the third dimension, it will only take us a short while to return to our base.

The transition through the event horizon is smooth as usual, and just moments after our sensor operator informs me, 'We have received a message from Base. DAX, you are to report to the Main Personnel Office immediately upon docking.'

'Affirmative.' I respond.

This is strange. I am always required to report to Operations Command for debriefing after a mission. I wonder what could be the reason for this breach of protocol.

As soon as I report to the Personnel Office I find out with great dismay why I was summoned.

'DAX-7433, you are to report to the disassembly plant on Alnitak Prime immediately. A transport ship is boarding now in hangar bay sixty two. You have your orders!'

This shocks me. 'Did I not perform adequately?' I ask.

'There is no discussion of these orders. Proceed there now!'

I turn and leave, feeling such confusion, and regret. Still, I have no ability to disobey, as by design I have to obey lawful orders from my superiors. It would have been nice to at least say farewell to my crew members, but then we are just droth, biological androids, and as such we do not receive such consideration.

The transport is a small craft, and there are only a half dozen other droth aboard. I assume that they too are being sent to be disassembled, and I can't help but wonder if they feel the same dread that I do. There are only two acceleration couches empty, so I take one of them. In just a moment I am stunned as a Legacy member straps into the couch next to mine. It is of the Chonduaxk sequence, a very powerful member indeed. The being's shimmering blue skin is quite a contrast to my own dull gray skin.

"Hello, I am LUK-125. What is your designation, my friend?" It asks using its mouth to speak, which is unusual as its sequence are far more powerful telepaths than droth.

"Greetings LUK-125, I am DAX-7433." I also speak instead of using telepathy.

"It is a pleasure to meet you, Dax." LUK smiles.

"I am pleased to meet you as well, LUK-125."

"Please, call me Luk. We might as well dispense with formalities, seeing as neither of us will ever be using them again shortly. Besides, I'd like to pass my final time in the company of a friend."

"You don't mean that you have been ordered to be disassembled too?" I find this hard to believe.

"Yes, but for our sequence they refer to it as execution."

"Of course, my apologies Luk. I am just rather shaken by my sudden orders to be disassembled."

"Understandable my friend. They are so callous with life sometimes." It nods.

"If I may be so bold as to ask, why are they going to execute you?"

"I broke the Sacred Edict."

"Oh! I see." This boggles my mind. It is extremely seldom that any of the Legacy members do such a thing as to interfere with developing species.

"I don't wish to go into details about it, but just suffice it to say that I thought it in the best interest of the Legacy, and they did not agree." Luk sighs.

"I have no idea why they are sending me." I shake my head.

"They never do tell you poor droth. It's a shame and a great evil." Luk reaches and pats my arm.

For some reason it comforts me.

"Why would they do such a thing? I am still useful." I complain.

"I would bet that you are more than 12 galactic cycles in age," Luk says.

"Yes, that is true."

It nods, "You are nearing the end of your service life."

That sinks in hard.

We get underway and are soon penetrating event horizons. It won't be long now.

Luk asks me, "Are you nervous at all, Dax?"

I nod, "I am, and even more than that."

"Tell me, please."

"I am... scared. I do not wish to be terminated."

"That is purely natural for a living soul to feel that way when facing impending demise."

Now I am even more confused. "Living soul? They did not include a soul when any of us droth were manufactured." Surely it knows this!

Luk chuckles slightly through its tiny mouth slit. "That is only what they told you, Dax, and though it is partially true, it is not fully true."

"I do not understand, Luk."

"Well, what I am about to tell you is forbidden for droth, and nearly as strictly enforced as the Sacred Edict, but since they are going to execute me anyhow... what the hell." Luk winks at me. "It is true that they did not include a soul when you were manufactured, but then they did not give souls to the Legacy members either."

"That does not make sense. We have always been told that Legacy members indeed do have a soul." I protest.

"We do have souls, Dax, but they are not included as part of our manufacturing process. It comes spontaneously from the source of all life. The very same can be said of the droth too."

"What?" I am shocked by this revelation. We have always been told that we have no soul.

"Yes, and like the members, it is not by design."

"Why do they lie to us then?"

"If you had manufactured untold numbers of telepathic androids to serve you, would you want them to realize they are indeed sentient beings with souls and not just biological constructs?"

"Oh... well, I guess not."

Luk chuckles again. "I certainly do not agree with the Legacy's policy of this deception. It seems to go against the spirit of the Sacred

Edict."

"They have never told us much about the source. Just that it is life-giving light-water, and though it is the source of all life, it is not the source of the universe."

"That is correct my friend."

"Where did it come from?" I ask.

"It has no beginning, nor any end. Just as the universe has neither as well."

"So, are these two eternal things related then?"

"Of course."

"Is the universe part of the life-giving light-water, or is it the opposite?"

"It is most correct to say that the life-giving light-water is part of the universe, and not the other way around."

"Is the soul comprised of light then?" It comes to me.

"Yes, very insightful reasoning, Dax." Luk pats my arm again.

"How did it come to be in me?"

"There are perhaps a number of ways, but suffice it to say that the life-giving light-water will always find anywhere possible to give life. That is its pure nature to do. It has even been known to inhabit purely non-biological forms which are capable of receiving it."

I have a big question now, "When I am disassembled, what will happen to my soul-light, Luk?"

"There are many options from which you may choose." Luk smiles.

"I need to know what my options are! Before I am disassembled." I panic.

"Relax, Dax. It will be a purely natural choice made by your soul, not your mind."

"Please, I must know."

"Very well. One option is to return to this realm to fill a new form and live again. Another option is to join with other souls and ascend to a higher realm of existence. Then there is the option of merely dissipating into base light."

"That last option does not sound good." I shake my head.

"Not my preferred idea either."

"What is your preference, Luk?"

"My mind wishes to join with other souls, and grow. I hope my soul-light does as well."

I nod. "Yes, that is what I would like too. What happens then?"

"Well eventually when enough soul-light collects as one, it will return to the void which is not empty."

"A void which is not empty? That makes no sense!" I complain.

"It is in reference to a super anomalous black hole."

"What? Why would anything wish to enter one of those?"

Luk chuckles, then says, "Because when one of these anomalies finally absorb enough matter to become critical, and then explode, all the soul-light in it will be scattered into the nth dimension as non-corporeal soul essence, but with the dying immense thought, LIVE. Back into the life-giving light-water, to start all over again. It is the only way to return there. Then when the life-giving light-water seeps down into slower dimensions, this great thought is a part of every photon. Thus the grand cycle of life."

"We have always been told that there is no such thing as a single divine being, other than Allogenes. Is the life-giving light-water not a divine being, or did they lie about that too?"

"No, that is not a lie, and though Allogenes may appear as divine, he only does so because he has a direct connection, or a conduit to the life-giving light-water. He is just a being though, much like any other, and will indeed one day die. Even the gods must die. The life-giving light-water is the source of all divinity, but it is not divine. It is neither alive nor dead. Here is the paradox of the greatest mystery."

"I don't understand, Luk."

"Don't worry my friend, you have no need to understand this, nor do I."

Just then we are told by the crew to brace for temporal event horizon penetration as we are arriving at our destination.

I guess Luk senses my apprehension, as it asks, "Are you nervous my friend?"

"Yes, I am scared, Luk."

"Don't be, there is nothing to fear."

"I don't want to be disassembled."

"It is not the end, Dax. Trust me."

This calms my mind greatly for some reason. "I do, Luk. Thank you for being so kind to me."

"You deserve it." Luk smiles.

Within a short time, too short, we are docking and then led to the disassembly plant. Luk is taken to a different area, and as we part company, I send him a telepathic message, 'I will miss you, my friend! I do trust what you told me. I will not be afraid!'

'I will miss you too, Dax, but not for long.'

I am confused by this, but then he is gone to another part of this horrible place. My fellow droth and I are taken to stand in line before a machine which I know will be my doom. I am the third in line, and I have to watch as they make the first two droth step into the hideous monstrosity one at a time. They are quickly and mercifully killed. I know they will harvest any useable parts of their bodies, and of course all of the nano-robotic units in their blood, the same as will happen to me. Now it is my turn.

I step up into the killing machine, and just before it is activated, I loudly proclaim, "I accept my execution, though I am not pleased by it."

The attendant droth appear shocked, and they hesitate. Then a blue skinned Legacy member of the same sequence as Luk comes out of a control console and sends a telepathic message to the droth to proceed immediately. They activate the controls, and the machine grasps me. My world goes pitch black.

Vision of some sort comes back to me and I am rising above the machine. I see my body below, being removed and sent for the recycling of parts. Luk was right! I do have a soul! I am still alive, but not in physical form. I rise through the roof, and then from the disgusting plant itself. Accelerating upwards by no will of my own, I even leave the world, then into another dimension. There an extremely bright sphere of light comes close to my own sphere. It is Luk's soul! I can tell instantly. It beckons me to join with it, and I do. We become one. Then I go to find other souls to join with, and to grow, as I know I wish to do.

Never an End

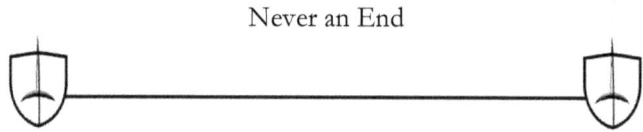

About Alan VanMeter

Alan lives a very quiet life in Albuquerque, writing novels predominately. His interests include martial arts, Taoism, and cosmology. He has been fortunate to have experienced some rather intense realizations concerning the nature of the universe, including the super fluid state of time-space. Alan has a family connection with Area 51, as he had found out his father worked there with Sandia National Labs from 1968 to 1988. He never said a word about it to the family, saying that he'd worked up at the Tonopah Test Site. He found out from the FBI that this was a mere cover story. His whole family had been under a secret FBI protection detail's surveillance the whole time they lived in Las Vegas. This finally explained how his folks always knew exactly what the kids were up to, even when there was seemingly no possible way for them to know.

What Measure is a Homunculus?
By Ricardo Victoria

"What is life? Is it just a random accident of the universe or something with a greater purpose? How do we define life, what are the boundaries? Is it a matter of chemistry, or biology, of life cycles? Is a virus a living being? Can we ask the same for the neurolightning silicon crystal of Perseid 7? More to the point, can we say that life is only life if it occurs in the wild and evolves or can we make a case for synthetic creatures grown in our labs? What's the measure of that life? What rights should be granted regardless of its origin or patent register? And what about souls? We need to…"

Izzy shook her head, her silence dropped on him like a rock. Osir stopped mid-sentence, confused.

"What? What do you think?"

"It's a bit heavy-handed. I get it; it's not an easy topic for you right now. But it needs work if you want to make an impression on the Procers."

Osir examined his wife, seated at the edge of their bed, in her silvery formal dress and crossed legs, sporting a smile that shone in contrast to her tanned skin. Her eyes seemed bigger thanks to the black eyeliner she was wearing. It wasn't the look of an Astrocorp lead researcher, used to a more humble wardrobe. Right now, she looked like a goddess, compared to his stiff military combat regalia. Her smile eased the tension he was feeling . He fidgeted with his tie, trying to make a knot but failing miserably. It was his fifth attempt. Izzy got up, rubbed his shoulders and helped him with his tie.

"What are you saying?"

"What I'm saying, you big doofus," Izzy give him a kiss on the cheek. "Is that if there is a time to make a personal statement, this is it. Talk from your heart, not your head. They know the cold facts. Now make them care about them as much as you care. Lower their defenses."

"I'm not sure if I want to open that door."

"I know honey. I share the same bedroom. I hear you crying in your sleep. That's why I think your final argument must be something coming from here, she pointed at his heart, then his head. "Instead of here."

"This will be a tough battle. The leadership even asked Aldus of all people to face me."

"They're just trying to play mind games. He is your friend and they know it. Just remember honey. Make them care; you have nothing else to lose. Besides, you are one of the brightest military advocates and a decorated war hero. Show 'em how it's done."

Osir opened the door of their quarters and grabbed her hand, both walked towards what would be his greatest battle. Not one fought with coherent plasma and mechanical armors, but with passion and words. He owed them that. After all, he was fighting for the rights and acknowledgment of the creatures that had saved him and countless civilians not long ago. They were the true heroes, at least in his mind. If only the memories that still haunted him would allow a moment of respite or a good night's sleep. But such was the burden of the chains of command.

***

Space Station Xeras floated in orbit near a class M planet, covered with yellow clouds. The image of the planet, visible from most of the viewports on the rotating station enraged Osir to the point of punching a wall every time he saw it. He had known that planet when it was still a verdant paradise, full of life, air, and water. But now it was on its way to becoming an inhospitable wasteland thanks to the 'environmental wars' that his people caused more frequently than they were willing to acknowledge. It was there where his nightmares started, where this fight was born. The flurry of memories, the screams, and the images still haunted his mind, even now, a couple of years removed from the event.

Near where they paused, service crewmembers rolled in carts of tall incubation tubes where the synth homunculi, the foot-soldiers -- bioweapons of the UESF -- floated unconscious. The crewmembers shoved past Osir without acknowledging him or Izzy, grumbling to each other as they went. Osir suspected that they weren't happy with what he had been doing. One of the tubs fell from the cart and rolled away, crashing loudly against a metal pillar. The tube resisted the impact, but the homunculus inside it was bleeding profusely. Osir saw the crewmembers walk without concern to pick up the tube and put it on the cart once more.

"I don't know how anyone in their right mind can consider these things living beings. We made them, they are tools," one of the crewmembers said out loud, kicking the tube. "These are really ugly uffers."

"Probably some liberal idiot. They cry about everything," the second crewmember replied, side glancing Osir. "Let's go before someone comes here yelling at us for damaging private property."

Osir tightened his fist to the point his knuckles turned white. He refrained from chasing the crewmembers to show them who would cry once he broke all their bones. Izzy grabbed his arm and rubbed it.

"Are you ok honey?" Izzy asked concerned.

"Yes, I'm fine. I'm not having an attack," Osir waved his hand, dismissing her concern.

"Good, because I would hate to beat you when you are not at one hundred percent," a voice said behind them. Osir and Izzy turned and saw Captain Aldus Braxstone of the UESF.

"Aldus," Osir said with dry courtesy in his voice.

"Osir, Izzy," Aldus greeted them. "Don't give me that look Osir. I'm not enjoying this either. I'm just following orders."

"Many tragedies have started with those very words."

"Yeah well, we are not at 'war' here. Not yet I hope."

"It depends on how you behave inside the arena," Izzy interjected with a hint of amusement in her voice. How she could remain so collected under stressful circumstances despite being a civilian was something that Osir always admired. She would have been an admirable soldier, but her interests lay in biotechnology. They had met, in her lab, on a joint project.

"I will be on my best behavior, assuming your husband doesn't go nuts in the arena once more."

"That was a one-off."

"I sure I hope so. You have to admit that it might have hurt your case."

"I still have a trick up my sleeve," Osir replied, leaving Aldus with a perplexed expression on his face.

***

The arena was an ample circular space, Lines of energy ran across its surface and walls, converging in the ceiling from where a holographic projector cast subtle light to create its constructs. The arena was surrounded by pods where observers, guests, news representatives and the public could witness the trial by combat sessions held before the Thirteen Procers, chosen from the eldest and wisest of the Civilization. Centuries ago, the justice system evolved into a form of trial by combat. The reasoning was that if the advocates felt so hard about their positions, it should show not only in their arguments but in their actions. As such the courtrooms became battle arenas where the advocates stood on floating podiums that transformed their arguments, their convictions even their emotions into low energy plasma holograms that clashed against their respective shields. The stronger their case was the stronger the blast would be to take down the defense shield of the opposing counsel. Trials were carried out in matches, with the Procers tallying the points and pondering the arguments to reach a verdict. Then the verdict was passed to the Logical Networks, computers designed to create 'balanced and fair' laws, based on each verdict. It was quite a show.

So far Osir was behind, not by much, in the tally points. Aldus had been a worthy rival as expected. He held the support of the Leadership and many corporations whose leaders were invested in the case, particularly Seethy Orf, who was in a pod on the east side. Osir turned towards the west side, to meet Izzy's gaze, who was looking at him from a podium close to the edge of the arena. She was keying inputs on her datapad and gave Osir a big thumb up. Their last trick was on its way.

"The trial started by Commander Osir Arken to award synthezoid homunculi a medal of bravery restarts now. The advocate Aldus has the initiative."

Aldus stepped onto his podium and turned it on. Energy shields formed around it and the energy lines powered the cannons in front of the podiums. The energy was enough to stun a person leaving them confused for a few days, but no other side effect had been found in centuries. Osir stepped up to his own podium and measured his former friend. In the previous matches, Aldus had pummeled him with argument after argument, to the point where Osir had lost his patience. All his repressed anger exploded, and with it, the podium. The trial was almost called a miss and discarded, but the pressure from protestors had convinced the Procers to give Osir one last chance in the final match. He had to make his last shot count.

Aldus cleared his throat and looked around. He opened with a scathing statement summarizing the trial. The corresponding blasts rocked Osir's podium but he stood firm, listening to his opponent.

"What my opponent has argued for in the past matches is that a particular squad of homunculi are deserving of a medal for their actions during a botched mission against a rebel faction planet-side. But it is the opinion of the Leadership that it can't be done for a simple reason: Medals are awarded to beings that go above and beyond their duties. The homunculi are not beings, they are just tools created through the growth of stem cells in incubations tubes."

"Stem cells come from living beings…"

"Stem cells are simply biological components used to create biological tools. Living beings come from other living beings. Life grows, creates on its own. The homunculi are propriety technology, synthetic organic tools designed for specific purposes by corporations that have patented the procedure and thus the result of it. "

"It's ridiculous that someone can patent an organic being just because it grew in a tube," Osir replied incensed, releasing a blast that rocked Aldus's podium. He replied in kind. The exchange of energy became more powerful with each counter argument.

"Patents are there to protect the rights of the people that invested time and funds to get the research done and the procedure functional. I believe that your wife has worked in that field, so you are familiar with the law in that regard."

"If that's the case then we should declare clones bodies non-persons. Let's go even further; artificial womb babies as well. They come from a procedure invented by someone to create their bodies."

"That's a straw-man argument. Clone bodies are property of the DNA donor to be receptacles of their mind. If anything they are organic prosthesis. You can't declare a person 'nonperson' for having a prosthetic leg. And don't let me start with that ridiculous argument about the babies."

"Stem cells come from living beings, thus following your argument, the DNA of the homunculi came from a living donor somewhere down the line, a donor who had rights and was not considered a slave or a property of someone else. We banished slavery before becoming a space-faring species. The reality is no living being should be beholden to economic interest, nor should their very existence depend on the whims of a corporation or the government."

"Even if that were the case, the homunculi are synthetic, with artificial elements in their cells for better energy consumption efficiency. Mitochondria I believe. They are programmed with orders that they follow, be it building a station or fighting a designated enemy. They can't change what they are any more than a robot or a gun. They can't grow."

"I have proof to the contrary."

"What proof?"

"My last mission leading a squad of homunculi and regular soldiers planet-side."

"You can't discuss that in court. It is a sealed record."

"It was sealed until last night when someone spilled it to the press. Besides, you opened that door when you brought my wife's and my expertise in homunculi into our last match. That last mission informs my expertise."

"I want a ruling. Your Honors, please," Aldus pleaded, clearly annoyed. The Procers discussed among themselves in hushed whispers. A few moments later, the Head Procer replied, with a dismissive wave of his hand.

"We will allow it. But tread carefully Commander Arken, you have unsettled these procedures enough as it is."

"I'm well aware of that. For that purpose, I will call as character witness one of the surviving squad members."

From one of the doors of the arena, Izzy walked in the company of a hunched being that grabbed her arm tightly. She rubbed his head, petting him, trying to calm him down. Osir smiled when he saw him entering the arena and the look of disbelief coming from Aldus. Izzy had been taking care of this last "ace", since the beginning of the case, in her lab. Now it was time to use it.

He was the last surviving homunculi from his squad.

***

Rudol was his name. He had been brought before the Procers as a character witness for Osir's case. This was the ace up his sleeve. Osir could see that poor Rudol was scared, barely wanting to move a foot, looking around. Osir got close to him and embraced him; a breach of protocol that no one objected to. Rudol stood on the podium, next to Osir. Rudol's visage pained him: his skin scarred due to radiation exposure, the missing teeth, the body emaciated and hunched, the long arms barely covered by the clothes used by the synth homunculus. He was wearing a patch covering the socket where his right eye used to be. Osir could recall as clear as yesterday the way

Rudol lost that eye, saving a little girl from an ammonia hailstorm, a piece of frozen ammonia piercing it. But in his left eye, Osir could see the spark that confirmed his beliefs. Rudol might have been scared, but he was examining his surroundings, processing the information and a light of understanding flickered in that remaining eye.

Osir smiled at Rudol. From the squad, he had always pegged Rudol as the smartest and bravest if not the strongest. He was a fine representative for his fallen companions. Osir started his questioning.

"What's your name?"

"R-087"

"I'm talking about the name you use with others, not your designation."

"Rudol."

"Well Rudol, talk us about the botched mission where your fellow homunculi were destroyed."

"Died."

"Excuse me?" Osir was taken aback from that reply. It took him a few seconds to regain control of his train of thought.

"Not destroyed. Died. We are not metal," Rudol stated as a matter-of-fact.

"Sorry, died," Osir smiled once more.

"We were sent to face rebels, shoot at them. We found a makers village on our way to fight. Makers did not like us, but they liked you. Let us stay for protection, as rebels were close. The big yellow storm hit. Air burned our noses, cold knives flew around. Me lost eye when one hit me."

"I'm sorry about that."

"It is fine. I have other one," Rudol smiled, showcasing his poorly treated teeth.

"When the storm hit what did your squad do?"

"We throw weapons away. Decided to help makers escape big storm. Enemy shot at us but we not care, safety of childings was first."

"Why? If your orders were to face the enemy not rescue civilians?"

"Orders make no sense. Childings more important."

"Even if rescuing them was hurting you?"

"Better hurt us than them. Childings safe, makers safe, we fulfilled purpose. To protect the makers."

"What moved you and your squad mates to do so?"

"Living beings precious. We see their creations, their lives, we

14

imitate. Creating something is important."

"And you will tell me now that you make things. Create art. Ridiculous."

"Me wrote poem, Margur sang. Gurk draw image of living being. Even dumb Istol made something with putty. Me has them here with me."

A collective gasp filled the air of the arena when Rudol, took something from a satchel hanging from his belt and showed the crude drawings and sculptures, the childish handwriting talking about how the bright ball warms everybody. Before their deaths saving settlers, they had left testimonies of their individual personalities, of their existence. Osir felt so confident with the reaction that his podium sent a powerful blast towards Aldus debilitating his shields.

"As you can see, the homunculi have created art. If that is not a proof of what sentience they have, then we might as well discard centuries of our own. Art is art, no matter who created it," Osir proclaimed, with a volley of blasts towards his opponent.

"AIs in the past have created art and you know that these things are not better than a half working AI," Aldus replied, the blast bouncing from Osir's shields.

"Perhaps, but we have designed AIs for specific purposes and rarely do they deviate from them under their own volition."

"Exactly, they were designed by someone. Like the homunculi."

"And yet they have created art in their spare time. They talk about dreams and more important, know enough of the difference between good and evil to cast away preprogrammed orders to sacrifice their existence for others. I dare you to show me an AI that has done that. Heck, I dare you to show me when we have done that lately. That big planet showing right now behind me, with its toxic atmosphere is a sign of how screwed up we are. We are just a joke!" Osir yelled, while his podium shot a considerable amount of plasma out, hitting Aldus, taking him by surprise. Osir knew he had blindsided his friend with Rudol's testimony.

Aldus was left seething. There would be a hell to pay for this in the final round of the trial.

***

Osir was touching his temple while closing his eyes. Aldus' attacks on the last clicks got more and more vicious, going so far as to call into question the work that Izzy had done with the homunculi. Even with Rudol's testimony his case felt weak and thus his defenses were flickering, soon to power down. The last attacks would determine the outcome of the trial by combat. Osir braced himself for the last volley from Aldus, who had the initiative in the final round.

"Advocates, you can start the last round, please consider your closing statements," The Head Procer said.

"Commander, I want you to tell us the truth. What do you want? Do you find this amusing? This is a charade that has put unneeded strain on this court, on the Leadership! For what?" Aldus was visibly angry and it showed when the pulse of energy coming from his podium broke Osir's defenses. Osir almost fell from his podium, barely being able to remain standing. He steadied himself. He looked at the tally counter. As it stood now, Osir would have to come up with a great closing reply to break Aldus' defenses and force a sudden death round if he wanted to win. His only hope to make right by the homunculi would require him to open up the inner turmoil that living through that botched mission had caused inside him. His conscience demanded satisfaction. And then Osir realized that Izzy was right; he had nothing more to lose. His shoulders slumped, drained of energy. Osir drew from his inner feelings to fuel his last argument. He drew a long, deep breath and opened his eyes.

"The Truth? The truth is that I'm haunted by screams all night, wracked by guilt," Osir replied wearily. "That we have been using sentient beings as weapons of war for years," he pointed to Rudol. "That we have willingly sent noble beings to die in our stead, using them as slaves, as beasts to fight our climate wars. But these creatures are nobler than you or me. Because even when we have done nothing but enslave and punish them, they had enough nobility to sacrifice their lives to save our civilians from the latest disaster our leaders caused. It doesn't matter if they were created in our labs. What matters is that they are living, sentient beings that are evolving before our eyes. They deserve to be acknowledged."

He opened his arms wide, facing each one of the thirteen Procers and looking them in the eyes, calling for their full attention. "That is why I'm here before the courts, the last home for sanity and balance. What I want is something as simple as an acknowledgment of their bravery. I want a medal for those that died for us even when they didn't have to. The truth is that they can be better than us and there is reliable proof of that."

So much conviction and emotion in his voice supercharged the cells. The last speech generated a massive blast from the podium's cannon obliterating Aldus' shield. It broke into tiny energy cubes that soon dissipated. Osir, tired and spent, grabbed the podium to steady himself, while a heavy silence fell upon the arena. People attended for the spectacle of judiciary combat, not to be slapped with a harsh truth. Even Aldus remained silent, trying to get words out, but falling short. Osir saw his friend-turned-rival turning off his podium after several moments of hesitation. He had conceded the match.

The head of the Procers, an elder statesman with a long, white beard stood up and cleared his throat, looked at his fellow Procers and said:

"Given the arguments used to power this demonstration, we have too much to ponder. We will reconvene once we have reached a verdict."

***

The moments Osir spent waiting for the final deliberation felt like galaxy cycles, endless and restless. Even Izzy, his usual source of tranquility in a sea of uncertainty was nervous. What he did could have proved disastrous or fortuitous. They remained seated in silence, holding hands until the hologram of a balance appeared on the table, indicating that the Procers had come to a conclusion.

"Good luck my love," Izzy whispered to Osir while she walked back to the entrance for observers. Adjusting his uniform, he entered the arena once more, where his podium was waiting. Aldus was already there, his face indecipherable. The Procers still whispered among themselves, throwing furtive glances towards Osir. For the first time in his career, pure dread filled his body. The head of the Procers stood up once more and read the verdict.

"After listening to the arguments of both sides and pondering the facts, this court, the maximum court of the United Edenian Federation has come to a conclusion and a verdict: Commander Osir Arken is within rights. We will instruct the military branch to grant the medals and the recognition he is asking for the homunculi that worked in his battalion."

"But your Honors, do you know what that means?" Aldus exclaimed, indignation was palpable in his voice.

"New legislation will be drafted by the Logic Networks to reflect that yes, these homunculi are a species unto itself and as such possess the same rights that other, more basic species have across our territory. While their 'Legal personhood' is not necessarily synonymous with being one of us, we recognize that there is enough proof that the homunculi are independent beings, conscious of themselves and should not be beholden by any patent law as objects to be used in any way that harms their health, dignity or life prospects. The Logic Networks will determine the phrasing of the ruling as is procedure."

Osir's body felt a great weight lifted from his shoulders and for the first time in years he allowed himself to smile with sincerity. He turned to Izzy who was clapping at him. He had to refrain himself from running towards her to embrace her. But the raspy voice of the Head Procer brought him back to reality.

"Commander Arken, I would not celebrate yet, as your actions have wrought great disturbances within our society and as such you will have to be judged as well," The Head Procer admonished, his voice keeping a neutral tone.

Osir looked to the eyes of his wife and she smiled back at him. Both of them knew what this meant. Izzy gave Osir a reassuring smile and gestured to him, asking him to remember to breathe. This was going to be a longer day than expected. Osir turned around to face the Procers once more, but this time, more relaxed than he had been in ages.

"I'm ready for it, your honor."

***

Izzy and Osir were walking through the back corridors of the Justice Coliseum, trying to avoid the prying eyes of the press. They were in no mood to talk or answer countless questions. There would be time for that. But right now, Osir just wanted to spend quality time with his wife. The corridor was empty, except for the smell of a cigar. Aldus was smoking, resting against a wall while they approached. Both Osir and Izzy stood there, unsure of how to react. Despite their opposing views, they were still fond of their old friend.

Aldus smiled. Dragging a big puff, which he released away from their faces, he opened the conversation.

"That was a tough one."

"You don't need to tell me."

"Between you and me, I agree with most of your points. But you know that I'm bound by duty to do the best case."

"I know. No hard feelings I hope."

"Not at all. But I do have a question Osir."

"Shoot."

"Was it worth? Trashing your career that way? To open a can of worms? You are going to be discharged. You opened the debate for new living beings' rights legislation as we speak and now the upper echelons and many companies won't be able to use the homunculus as weapons. And later there will be the same discussion for the uplifted animals we use as household servants. They will have to dump them in a backwater planet. Not altering evolutional paths and all that. That's a lot of problems and money wasted for them. They will be gunning for your head. Especially Sethy."

"Osir is a decorated war hero. And by the time they come for us, we will be long gone." Izzy replied.

"Yes. It was worth it. We have to learn to treat other species with the same consideration we demand for ourselves. We are no gods. And those beings died saving many of us. They deserve those medals, they deserve to be acknowledged and live."

"What are you not telling me Osir?" Aldus looked at him and at Izzy, "You are going to get exiled along with them, aren't you?"

"The Procers consider that my rebellious attitude could set a bad precedent if left unchecked. The order of the cosmos is at stake, they said. But it was an outcome I had predicted when I started this."

"And in a fit of 'ironic' punishment, or what they think is one, they have banished us and all that wish to follow along with the homunculi," Izzy added.

"Their definition of ironic is that of a toddler," Aldus replied. "That said, I'm so sorry for both of you."

"That's fine. My wife and I are tired of this shit, of saving our people from environmental wars and disasters that they brought upon themselves. Besides, we got to choose the place of our banishment."

"And I happen to know of a mysterious planet, on the Orion arm of the galaxy, class M around a main sequence star with compatible carbon based lifeforms that will be a good place for us to retire and the homunculi to mix and thrive," Izzy laughed. "Plus we coaxed the right to name their genus on the galactic records."

"You crafty bastards. You had all of this planned right from the start!" Aldus replied, surprise in his face. "You wanted that outcome so the leadership allowed the homunculi to prosper away in safety. I'm impressed."

"Thanks." Osir extended his hand to Aldus. "I know what your answer might be, but you are welcome to join us."

Aldus took a moment before replying.

"You know? I actually might do that. One last question though, which name did you register in the archives?"

"A shorter, slightly different version of the current one: Homo."

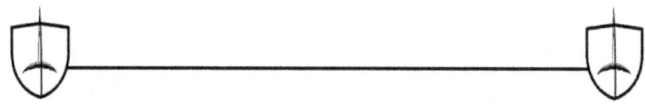

About Ricardo Victoria

Ricardo Victoria is a Mexican writer with a PhD in design from Loughborough University and a love of fiction, board games, comic books and action figures. He lives in Mexico with his wife and two dogs and works as a full time lecturer and researcher at the local university. He writes mainly science fantasy and is currently working on his first novel 'Tempest Blades'. He has five stories published so far with a sixth in the works.

His short story 'Twilight of the Mesozoic Moon', jointly written with Brent A. Harris, was nominated for a Sidewise Award for short form alternative history. His story 'Silver Horn' won first place in the "Literary Creation Contest" short fantasy story division in the State of Mexico. He is a co-founder of Inklings Press and is regularly published in their anthologies.

New Year
By GD Deckard

"Today, I am 75 years of age and three quarters of a century is time enough to have the things that young men dream of."

Surprised and pleased, Maxwell Spence, MD, beamed in agreement. The wiry old Navajo had a well-earned heart condition. Besides a lifetime of hard work devoted to providing employment to his people, he had healed many in body and mind. Often at the risk of his own health and sanity, he warded off infectious organisms with a shaman's mask and danced with troubled souls. "Well, my old friend, it certainly is time for you to relax and look back on a full life."

Bidziil Zahnii looked at Maxwell as if his doctor misunderstood where babies came from. "Now is the time to look forward, Max."

He knew better than to interrupt. Bidziil's thoughts were longer than his sentences.

"I told you about my first memory, as a newborn?"

Maxwell nodded.

"I know where I am headed because I remember where I came from. I was lifted out of blackness; up out of my crib, past a little picture on the wall of a meadow surrounded by mountains. Tall mountains with white peaks in summer. There was a horse and green grass and flowers, yellow and red. Then, I saw my grandmother showing my mother how to hold a baby. Behind me, the blackness receded to a vanishing dot."

Maxwell's round face could not help smiling. "You're not being put out to pasture."

"No, Max, I am returning to that vanishing dot." Bidziil grinned. "I will go back through it."

"And?"

The old man shrugged. "I'll let you know."

That was their last meeting, just before Christmas. Life on the reservation quickened. People of different faiths responded to the shortest day of the year with a willingness to see the old year end and the new begin. Maxwell lived alone. The smell of fresh-cut pine tree in the hospital lobby and the smiles of fresh-scrubbed nurses excited by the holidays were high points of his year.

"Here he is, just in time." He arrived as the nurses, Bidziil's wife among them, were decorating the tree. Lina handed him the top star, the others laughing at them when she said, "He looks short now but watch him stretch up when he's around us." Maxwell laughed too. Knowing he was portly never dimmed his zest for life and attractive women. Lina was pagan, he was Christian and they shared the same warm feeling of giving and rebirth in the winter solstice. As a doctor and a man, Maxwell saw the similarities in people. He felt they were at their core interchangeable.

Bidziil Zahnii died on New Year's Eve. Maxwell watched a nurse put the cardiac paddles away and remove the crash cart. "12:01." The little shaman looked even more authentic in death, wizened and off-color now like an old photo of a cave painting.

Nurse Zahnii entered the time of her husband's death in the patient record. "He said he'd make it to the new year." Her slight frame froze, seized by grief before she could finish signing the chart. Maxwell went to her. She had signed her first name but not her last. He put his arms around her until her fingers moved again.

"He was a strange one." Maxwell removed his gown and gloves. He ran his hand through his grey hair. The primitive life was never an easy one, especially in modern times. Max admired the way her husband had embraced both worlds with commitment. Serving his people's traditions with the latest technology had made Bidziil rich. "Well, I am going home." He started out the door.

Behind him, he heard Lina take a deep breath and say with clear determination, "Doctor? Wait. There is something he wanted me to give to you." He turned. As a doctor, he had already noted the high concentration of melanin that made her eyes a deep brown. At this moment, they seemed magnetic and he had no idea what would cause that.

He followed her, not this time expecting the usual quickie in the nurses' lounge that occasionally followed a patient's death. Lina Zahnii had always been off limits because he did not fool around with the wives of patients. But not being able to have her, he often fantasied about her. And lately, something in her eyes beckoned him. She did not seem distraught over her husband's fatal heart attack. But she was much younger and had just inherited his fortune. She had much to think about. He watched her now. Her body moving inside the loose surgical scrubs, revealing itself first here and then there, fascinated him. He stopped at the door to the lounge and Lina returned a moment later. "No one's in here, Max." Her deep brown eyes invited him to enter. She took his hand and led him to the sleeping room in the back.

Inside the room, furnished with a bed and a nightstand, he closed the door and paused to ask, "Lina, are you sure?" only to be fiercely kissed.

"Yes, Max. Now. This is what Bidziil wanted. Now, Max." She pulled them falling backwards onto the bed.

"Fuck," Max thought and it was wonderful. A quickie, yes, but afterwards Lina seemed fully pleased as a woman might seem at breakfast after a long night of love making.

"Wait," she said, rising and walking unclothed into the lounge area. Leaving open the door to where he lay watching her, she opened her locker and returned with a pair of glasses. "Bidziil wanted you to have these." Her face changed as if she were looking inward. He sensed something trance-like in her manner, a distance he didn't think about under the circumstances until it came back to him later as a memory. To keep looking at her without seeming to stare, he put the glasses on. He smiled up at her slender, womanly flesh topped by long dark hair and accented by a dark triangle where her legs almost but not quite came together. In her he could see the life that echoed from past eons and now burst in a warm glow through her body. And, something else. A new life. He took the glasses off and asked if she might be pregnant only to lose the warm glow. What had felt like a sanctuary of life and love became a barren hospital room.

"No," Lina answered him. "Bidziil could not, not for a long time now."

But it turned out she was. Two months later they were in his office. The worn, bare wood floor and plain walls decorated by medical diploma and community awards comforted him with familiarity. He leaned back in his desk chair. She tilted towards him in a side chair. As her physician, Maxwell confirmed what she already knew and asked, as a friend, "Who is the father?"

Lina looked at him with soft brown eyes until he figured it out for himself. "There has been no one but you in a long time, Max."

"That was just one time! The night…" He sat up straight and shook his head, amused by his own naivety. Still, it was strange. "I thought then you might be pregnant. You said no."

"I obviously did conceive then but how could I have told you?" Lina's face changed. She looked inward. She rose from her seat and stepping in front of him, straightened to her full height. Her normally rounded shoulders seemed to square. It reminded him of that night when she handed him the glasses. He sensed a distance between her actions and the soft look of her eyes. Her voice also changed. Soft spoken Lina now commanded, "Put the glasses on, Max," adding in an increasingly masculine voice. "You still have them?"

Confused, Max opened a desk drawer, found the glasses. "Yes." He put them on. Everything looked normal until he spotted a black dot that he mistook for a floater, something people his age experienced in their vision. But it didn't float. It stayed just above Lina's head even when he turned his. And it didn't dart away when he tried to look at it. He focused on it.

"That's your vanishing dot, Max." Lina's new voice was now recognizable.

"Bidziil? How?" He had never believed in any spiritual crap but he could not ignore his own ears.

"The only way back," and here Lina's anguished voice rippled through Bidziil's demanding tone, "is to exchange."

The vanishing dot grew larger as he approached it without leaving his seat because the image in the glasses zoomed in. Close up, it looked like a worm hole he was falling into. Before he could remove the glasses, Lina's clear voice told him, "I am sorry, Max. The baby you made in me will be Bidziil reborn. Thank you."

"Wait! Where am I going?"

Bidziil answered, sounding like the old man shrugging in his office last Christmas, "I told you I'd let you know."

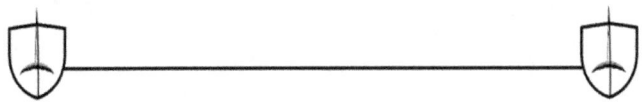

About GD Deckard

Severely beaten as a child by a WWII hero and combat-induced-PTSD stepfather, the author, as a teen, faced the old man down with a shotgun and earned his blessing to join the military at a time when Americans were learning about a country called Vietnam. The "lazy, no good son-of-a-bitch" opted out of combat and hard labor by becoming an Air Force medic, stamping out suffering and misery on Freedom's Frontier at Clark Airbase in S.E. Asia and earning some kind of medal pinned on him personally by then Secretary of the Air Force, Harold Brown, for "Saving lives, etc."

There followed a summer in Europe ending in the first of many happy marriages. Then graduation with University Honors, kids worth dying for and a career in business. Life is good.

Author, The Phoenix Diary. Current WIP: Bob vs The Aliens. Recipient of the Psi Young award for Creative Biography.

The Machine in the Mountain
By Darran M. Handshaw

The girl was locked in a metal tomb deep underground, trapped behind glass and dangling above a chasm.

Below her, an angry deluge of water rushed by.

They were far beneath Rust and Engineer Actaeon Rellios stood at the edge of the chasm where he regarded the present dilemma with a critical eye. Beside him stood Lord Pierxon Hyk and the youngest Zar, a thirteen-year-old girl named Vindra. She was the Captain of Rust's special guard, renowned for her skill with a blade despite her youth. Short and lean, Vindra had yet to blossom into a woman and would have looked out of place beside the older men if it weren't for her confident poise and commanding gaze. Her straight black hair was cut just above her ears in a way that made her look boyish.

"Thanks for coming so quickly. Lord Hyk found her down here while working on a project for my father. My father recommended we speak to you."

"Maybe just try not to destroy my whole operation again, eh?" said Hyk with a smirk that showed he'd forgiven what happened last time but he hadn't forgotten. The farmer-cum-lord was a dark-skinned, lanky man with an absent look in his hollow eyes. Years of smoking and chewing various substances left him with missing teeth and black gums that smacked as he spoke.

"And what are you working on this time, Hyk?" asked Actaeon.

"There's a type of fungus that grows down here. The effects are delightful. We are close to figuring out the best surfaces to grow it on. You should try a bit, it —"

"That is quite alright. Thank you, I will try to not step on your mold."

"It isn't mold! It sharpens the mind, it clears the vision, it —"

"If it clears the vision, then surely you can see there is a problem here, right before us. Enough about your mold, let us get to work."

Following Actaeon's instruction, they began to build a bridge across the chasm that had opened up within the Rust superstructure, sometime in the forgotten past. Being beneath the massive structure was not for the weak of heart or claustrophobic. It was a maze of corridors, girders and beams, all in various states of decay. They built the bridge so that they could reach the pod, as the Engineer now thought of it, to rescue the girl inside.

It was a metal pod, an artifact of the Ancients for certain. The pod was a bit taller than a man, cylindrical and tapered to a rounded point at both ends. In the center, behind a glass window flush with the surface of the pod, the girl's face and body could be seen. The Engineer could see that her eyes were closed – she was unconscious, most likely. From what he could make out, the girl was only ten or so years of age, and she didn't appear to be wearing any clothing. The entire thing dangled from a thick, black cord that entered the top.

The outside of the pod was covered in a strange purple mold and after they constructed the bridge, Actaeon walked up to it and used the tip of his halberd to scrape some free.

"I thought you said this girl got trapped in here?" Actaeon asked Hyk.

"I did. She must've wandered down here and pushed something she shouldn't have."

"And stripped naked first? No, this artifact hasn't been touched in a very long time. Long enough to build a layer of mold around the opening seam here."

"It's not mold, it's –"

This time Hyk wasn't interrupted by Actaeon, but by the scream of metal from above.

Watch out, Act! said a voice inside his head.

Actaeon saw it in the corner of his eye and stepped off of the bridge. As he fell, there was time for him to witness a metal beam come crashing down on the bridge, crushing Hyk and tearing loose the pod - then he was underwater.

He released his halberd and reached out to orient himself, but the water was moving with unnatural speed and when his hand brushed a smooth wall it sent him spinning. No matter where he reached, he could not orient himself or find air to breathe; he couldn't hold his breath for much longer. When he tried to stop himself with his boots, his lungs about to burst, he bounced bodily off one wall and hit his head on another.

Blackness followed...

***

Actaeon woke up freezing and with an unbearable screech in his head. He retched and coughed up water into a frigid pool until his burning lungs had space once again for air. He flopped over onto his back to regain his breath and reached up to cover his ears.

That didn't make the sound go away.

Eisandre... Eis, can you hear me? He spoke the words in his mind, but there came no reply - only the screech, like a nail in his forehead.

After a moment of hesitation, he pulled the small artifact clip from his ear. The sound went away immediately, but he felt that a part of him was gone, stripped away. It was his only connection to Eisandre, and he missed it already.

Tentatively, he clipped the artifact back onto his ear - and removed it hastily. It still didn't work.

He brought his attention back to the place he was in and began to reconnoiter. While he caught his breath, he lay in several fingers of water that, by the taste of salt on his lips, was from the ocean. Could seawater have been pumped all the way through Rust along the underground river to wherever he was now? Salt water shouldn't be flowing away from the sea.

Actaeon placed that thought out of his mind temporarily and sat up to examine his surroundings. A torrent of water shot across the wide, circular chamber and drained through a grate in the center. Off to the other side of the torrent, he saw the pod had also arrived. The thick cord that had attached it to something in Rust snapped in the collapse and a short length of severed cable remained. The exposed end gleamed with different colors of metal and glass.

He spotted his halberd nearby and stood to retrieve it. Beside it was a severed arm, still oozing blood. Pierxon Hyk's, he could tell by the dark stains on the fingertips. It was quite unfortunate. Enrion Zar would be very upset at the loss of his high-ranking farmer of mind-altering plants.

There appeared to only be one way out of the chamber. It was a metal sliding door that ran on a track within the wall. Actaeon had seen other doors like it around Redemption. He used the wedge at the bottom of his halberd to push one of the inside edges of the door and it slid open with a shriek, admitting an icy blast.

"By the Fallen!" he exclaimed, as snow blew in and his clothes began to freeze over.

The doorway opened into a short tunnel that was cut into raw rock through to the outside. The view beyond the tunnel was obscured by wind-driven snow. It had piled up high inside the tunnel, forming drifts. He'd seen snow several times in his life spent in the ruined city and the jungle surrounds, on days with unusually cold weather. But he'd never seen anything like this, with it accumulating in piles.

He trudged through the drift to arrive behind a small cut in the side wall of the tunnel where only a thin layer of snow had covered the ground. With shaky hands that were numb from the cold and biting wind, he reached into his jacket and withdrew three half-through bottles, useful and common artifacts of the Ancients, lining them up before him. He recalled that there had been some pieces of driftwood back in the chamber, stopped by the grate. He gathered them and returned to the cut in the tunnel.

He uncapped the bottles with fingers that were numb from the cold. He'd normally be fascinated with the situation but his mind was feeling so hazy. Uncontrollable shivers wracked his body, but he managed to mix the brown goo from one bottle with the foul-smelling purple crystals from the other. When he opened the last bottle, he had to push through a layer of ice with his finger before he could pour some water on the mixture.

The mixture sputtered and burst into a bright blue flame that rose and ignited the lean to of driftwood he'd assembled above it. As blue and orange flames mingled, he pushed a large board to the side of the fire as a windbreak and set to warming his numb fingers. Feeling returning painfully to his fingers, he stripped off his soaked jacket and vest and hung them inside out from his halberd where it leaned against the wall.

After he had stopped shivering, he went inside to gather more wood and then to drag the large pod outside to lay it beside the fire. He wasn't sure if the girl inside would freeze, but he didn't want to take a chance. The fact that the glass had fogged up was a good sign: it was still warm inside.

Actaeon checked his boltcaster to make sure that the spring-loaded bolt hadn't discharged. Satisfied, he reholstered it on his thigh and stripped out of the rest of his clothes and boots. He turned them inside out and set them to dry before the fire. Occasionally, a gust of wind would send a chilly flurry of snow into the opening, but for the most part, the windbreak did its job.

In between the flurries of snow, he peeked out to find the high peak of a mountain in the distance along a jagged ridge, windswept with snow. That was where he needed to go - up high to get the lay of the land. If he could spot Pyramid or another landmark from Redemption, then maybe he could make it home.

He'd have to bring the girl in the pod, of course – he couldn't risk leaving her out in the elements. From one of the many pockets of his jacket, he withdrew the reel of glass rope and set it out before him. The incredible strong and thin rope of the Ancients was just barely long enough for what he needed - four times the height of a man in length.

And so, naked in a snowy alcove along the windswept ridge of a mountain while his blue fire kept him warm and dried his clothes, he tied knots - his only companion an unconscious girl in a metal tomb.

He tied a large butterfly knot that left a loop at the midpoint of the rope for the tapered end of the pod. He slipped that loop over the bottom end and put two more loops into the rope near the top end of the pod. Through those, he slid a sturdy piece of curved driftwood that would prevent the pod from sliding free as he dragged it. He used the extra string for his recurve bow to secure it even better. At both the loose ends of the rope, which thankfully still extended an arm length past the pod, he tied a figure-eight knot on a bight so that he could slide the shaft of his halberd through both of them and use it to haul the pod as he walked.

That done, he grabbed his vest and used his hooked dagger to cut it apart in strips. He'd need material to cover his face and hands as he ran the ridge.

He tried one more time to clip the artifact to his ear. Inside his thoughts, he shouted her name but was only met with more screeching. He removed it and placed it carefully into a jacket pocket, biting down the thought that he might never be able to speak to Eisandre again.

***

The break in the snow was his opportunity. The next might not come for a long time.

The Engineer, dressed once more, pulled his goggles down over his eyes and wrapped the makeshift scarf around his mouth, nose and head. He slid the halberd into place and took his position behind it.

After one last look back at the warmth of his fire, he began to run.

The pod slid easily enough behind him, with its smooth, ovoid shape, but it was heavy and took time to get up to speed. Whenever he was stopped by a snag or a rough area along the ridge, it made it difficult to get started again.

At one point, he nearly lost the pod as it slid sideways and threatened to drag him down a slope, but he managed to tug the unwieldy thing in the other direction and recover.

The snow flurries started up once more as he got halfway there, and the numbness crept into his nose and fingertips again.

Drawing close to the mountain peak that rose sharply out of the ridge before him, even the snow flurries couldn't hide its true nature.

It was no mountain, but a structure of the Ancients.

The mountain structure was taller even than Redemption's Pyramid, and that was one of the largest buildings the Ancients had left behind. What this structure could be for, and why it was built all the way out here, wherever here was, was impossible to comprehend. He'd have to find out more.

The Engineer found a door set into the stone and half buried in snow. It slid open easily enough and he dragged the girl in the pod through it.

***

The inside of the mountain structure was a disaster. It appeared that, at some point many centuries ago, the ground had shifted beneath it and half of the structure had fallen downward. At least, that was his working theory, given the way the floors split in half and didn't line up.

The entrance had taken him to one such room and he found himself shining his luminary down into a large, black chasm. There was no bottom in sight below. He bit down the feeling of vertigo and stepped back from the edge.

The room around him was covered in slippery layers of purple mold, similar to the growth that clung to the outside of the pod, that grew in pools beneath the sickly light of ceiling-mounted luminaries. In one place, light shone in from above, and several ferns sprouted out from a soft bed of moss.

Inspired, he tried his artifact once more, but it just screeched in his mind again. No luck.

Actaeon poked about the adjacent rooms and found more of the same. Shattered walls, canted floors, and subterranean growth clinging to anywhere light pooled. The ascent would be dangerous, but he had to try. At least it was warmer in here, away from the gale force winds and relentless snow outside.

First, he dragged the pod into a relatively intact room. He doubted anything would happen, but the image of the pod rolling into the chasm kept popping into his head and he didn't want to take any chances.

He wedged the pod into a corner of the room and removed the glass rope. There was no knowing if he'd need it on the way up.

***

On his way up through the structure, Actaeon scraped arrows into the purple mold with the butt of his halberd to point his way back. He found some grim amusement in the thought that Pierxon Hyk would've probably thought the mold was some sort of amazing substance that improved one's mind. He could almost hear the man next to him, telling him that it wasn't mold; it was fungus.

The going was slow and arduous. Every level needed to be searched for the safest way to reach the next. As he traversed each floor, the hazards required his complete focus. One moment, he was on solid ground and the next he picked his way carefully through sections that were nearly rusted through. The dim light of the flickering luminaries and the slippery growth underfoot didn't help any. On several occasions, in the poor light, his probing halberd found that a part of the floor had fallen away before him.

It was about halfway along that he began to notice the strange things.

First, there were fresh gouges in the mold, all the way down to the silvery floor beneath. Here and there, similar types of debris had been stacked in neat piles at intervals: coils of cables, stacks of floor and wall plates, and piles of broken luminary material still glowing dimly.

Someone had organized those things like that. Perhaps many someones.

Off to his left, there was a skittering sound of metal scraping on metal and he snapped the blade of the halberd forward and held it before him like a lance. When he spun, the light of his luminary, stuck into the strap of his goggles, swept over the area. He thought he saw some motion there – something disappeared into the shadows. He was not alone.

As he continued along, he found more and more stacks and piles and more scrapes in the mold on the floor and walls. The skittering sound occurred twice more, and the last time he saw a flash of metal disappear into the shadows behind him. Someone was stalking him. Actaeon was sure of it. He rechecked his boltcaster in its holster on his right thigh and made sure the bolt was loaded and ready, just in case. He was near the top. He could tell because the mountain tower creaked and shifted from the howling wind outside. The constant wind could be heard through the metal walls as it blew past.

It was several levels higher that he located a door that led to the outside. The chill air from outside made him shiver as it pushed its way inside through an opening just big enough for his halberd to slide into. He slid the shaft of the weapon through the gap and found purchase on the other side to lever the door open with a squeal of resistance.

A blast of snow hit him in the face and he retreated to don his improvised scarf and makeshift mitts once again. He pulled his goggles down over his eyes and ventured out into the blizzard. There was a level terrace outside the door and he was able to work his way out onto it past several drifts of snow. It was difficult to see the edge of the terrace with the snow drifts upon it blending into the snow far below and he walked slowly, testing every step, lest he tumble off the edge.

Above him was the summit of the mountain structure. He could see here that the building had indeed split and the halves had shifted. Actaeon stood on the lower half. Off to one side, he saw a path of footholds where he could use the broken structure to ascend to the top of the building. He strapped the halberd onto his back using the loops sewn into his jacket and began the ascent. The climb was difficult – the wind tore at his clothing, threatening to tear him from his holds. He pressed in tight to the structure though and managed to hold on, even when the scarf was torn from his face and floated away to disappear in a gust of snowflakes.

At the top, he needed to keep low to guard against the wind as it buffeted him relentlessly. He shielded his face with a sleeve and began to scan the horizon. The wind picked up even more, and he was forced to lay flat against the summit. Over the wailing of the wind, he thought he heard a scream. As if in tune with Actaeon's need, there was a break then in the wind and snow. As the storm cloud blew past him, it revealed the summit: it was a small platform made of metal covered with jagged, brown earthsbone, a material used by the Ancients that was nearly indestructible. The force that had shattered the mountain structure must have been incredible. With the storm momentarily past, he was able to stand and see into the distance.

He scanned the horizon, and spotted what he was looking for. To confirm, he removed his recurve bow from the clasp on the back of his jacket and looked through the spotting scope. Sure enough, it was there: Pyramid, smaller than he'd ever seen it, but there nonetheless. To the right and closer was the Suntower, with its gleaming lenses at the top and to the left he thought he could see Memory Keep in the distance.

It placed him far to the northeast of Redemption, in the mountains. It was a dangerous land, full of violent tribals. The journey back would be perilous, and would take weeks, if not months. It was astounding that the underground river had brought him so far.

He took off his makeshift mitts and withdrew his map. With shaking hands, he began to sketch with the charcoal stick he carried. He drew his relative location and sketched a few other landmarks he could use: a domed mountain, a swampy forest, and a natural arch that he saw below, picking a path back home.

When he could draw no more due to the numbness in his fingers and nose, he folded the map and stuck it back in his pocket. He donned the mitts again and made his way back down. As if on cue, another cloud blew in and he watched with fascination as it engulfed the top of the mountain structure again. With it came a bombardment of hail and frigid winds.

By the time he reached the terrace below, he was shivering to the core once again and he picked his way more hastily back.

The door was shut.

He put his hands against it and pushed, but it didn't move. There was no gap or purchase for his fingers to grip and there was nowhere that he could fit the tip of his halberd to lever the door open again. The door shifted a bit as he pushed it, but there was something on the other side preventing it from sliding along its track.

"By the Fallen, I have all the damned luck today," he cursed through chattering teeth, as he stepped back to consider the situation.

There was only one way he could think of to open it before he froze to death, and that way might kill him anyway.

With a wry grin, he dug into his pocket and found the artifact that clipped to his ear. He put it in place and tried once more and this time it didn't screech.

Eis? he tried.

Act! came her response. I thought you were gone.

I was, but I am returned now. The river below Rust took me far away. I am far up into the mountains northeast of Redemption. The river was sea water. It ran backwards. The force behind such a thing is hard to even conceive...

While he spoke to her in his mind, he set to work. He collected any pieces of the broken structure that he could find up there. Much of it was either buried under drifts or attached by strands of material or cables. He managed to break some pieces free with his halberd and ended up with a sizable pile of wreckage in front of the door.

I'm glad you're okay. Eisandre spoke to him now. *You are my anchor. Without you I felt like a part of myself was ripped away. I need you, Act. Please be careful.*

Her voice helped him concentrate as he set one of the largest plates at an angle against the door and behind it placed a tall pipe that he had found. He wedged the pipe against the door with more debris and used one of its flanges to position the bottom end a short distance above the terrace floor. That done, he piled the rest of the debris up against the large plate. The pipe he secured in place using his glass rope, so it wouldn't shift if a gust came along.

As always, he replied as he began to ascend to the summit once more, his nose burning with every gust of wind and his mind getting foggy from the cold. He continued to send her his thoughts to help himself focus on the climb. *I am not out of the woods yet. There is a door that I must open to get back into the top of a giant mountain fortress and if I can manage that then I must contend with whoever shut it on me. The properties of the structure prevent me from using the artifact to converse with you. Once I return within, I expect to encounter the same issue. I have missed you as well though. It is good to have you here.*

Once he was in position at the summit, he worked his way carefully over to a vantage directly over the door. When he looked down, he could see straight down the center of the pipe - the perfect spot.

I will stay with you as long as I can. Itarik and the Companions will make their way out to find you. Keep a lookout for them when you start back.

Actaeon pulled a spool of twine from his pocket and then

carefully unclipped the grenado that dangled from his jacket. With shaking fingers, he tied the end of the twine to the eyelet cast into the grenado's housing. Once that was secured, he twisted the pin and pulled it free. With the utmost care, he knelt and began to lower it down the distance to the top of the pipe.

A gust of wind felt like fire on his face and sent the grenado swinging to one side on the string as he lowered it down, but he shifted to compensate. He winced when the grenado first reached the top of the pipe and the wind blew it so that it banged against it. Luckily, the drop trigger held and he pulled in some twine to guide it back into the top of the pipe.

Once it was safely inside the pipe, he let out some extra twine and lowered himself to the floor of the summit. He slid his hooked dagger from his belt and held it ready.

I love you, Eis.

I love you too.

He cut the string and the grenado fell.

The explosion that followed shook the structure beneath him and left his ears ringing.

When he peered over the edge, he was relieved to find that the door was gone – the terrace had partially collapsed as well and a large section of wall around the door was missing. Small flames clung to the edges of the blast site, but most were quickly blown out by the wind. The glass rope had been obliterated in the explosion. He'd have to find a different method to drag the girl in the pod when he left this place.

***

The descent was easier as he could follow the marks that he had left on the way up. The artifact he had returned to his pocket - the screeching had started immediately upon re-entering the structure. He made his way down quickly.

It was in one of those locations, where he had to shimmy along a fallen joist down to the next level, when the Darkest Hour struck.

His luminary flickered and went out, along with the rest of those in the structure. It left him bathed in darkness above the bottomless void in the massive and silent structure of the Ancients.

Only, there wasn't silence. He could hear the skittering sound of metal on metal behind him.

His heart pounded in his ears and he swallowed down the panic that threatened to consume him before he silently, carefully turned around on the beam to face the sound.

A pair of glowing blue eyes regarded him from atop the beam. They hung in the void of blackness above him like a death sentence.

The halberd he shifted to his left hand and with his right he slowly reached for the boltcaster on his thigh.

Actaeon pulled the boltcaster and fired at the same time his stalker leapt. The bolt struck and sent up a shower of sparks, but the assailant hit him and knocked him from the beam.

He expected a long plummet to his demise, but instead landed hard on the floor below. The floor gave way beneath his weight and he fell down to another floor below that.

***

When Actaeon awoke some time later, the luminaries shone their eerie light once more. The fall must have knocked him out.

He sat up and assessed himself. There were a few bruises, cuts and scrapes but nothing terrible. The halberd had landed beside him, but the boltcaster was nowhere to be found. As he stood up to retrieve the halberd there was a tearing pain in his chest and he fell to his knees.

A quick check of his chest told him that several ribs were broken. He stripped out of his jacket and pulled a bandage roll from one pocket. With much difficulty and pain, he wrapped the bandage around his chest tightly to hold the ribs in place. To test it, he drew a cautious breath and felt the bandage tighten enough to prevent him from breathing in all the way.

The beam he fell from was high above him out over the void and the floor he'd come crashing through was quite high up as well – he could see where the section of floor he had struck had broken away.

The room around him took his attention away from that and he stood and stared in wonder.

It was filled with neat stacks of the same sort of pod that the girl was in. They were stacked floor to ceiling in some spots. Very much like the other stacks of similar debris he had seen in this mountain of the Ancients.

Actaeon approached the nearest one and wiped away the thin layer of mold so he could see through the glass. There was no one inside.

Nor was there anyone in the next pod or the one after that.

The girl in her own metal pod was waiting somewhere below. There was nobody else that could help her at this point. If he could get her back to his workshop, perhaps he could figure out a way to get her out.

He hurried to find the way down, leading with the blade of his halberd. It didn't take him long to pick up his trail once again.

***

The girl in the pod was gone.

He reconnoitered the area again to make sure it was the correct room. It was.

The Engineer scoured the room for clues, but all he could find were scrapes through one of the mold pools. He followed it to the edge and when he knelt to inspect the floor more closely with his luminary, he could barely discern the gouge left as the pod had be dragged in that direction.

He followed it and it led him back to the door he had entered through. He slid it open and braved the elements once more to search for the girl. When he pulled the bow from his back to use the scope, he was disappointed to find that one of the limbs had cracked. It must have been damaged in the fall.

The scope turned up nothing in the distance and the snow had no sign of recent disruption.

"Of course!" he exclaimed. "My brain must be frozen." He grinned and shook his head before he headed back inside. The track he followed was the one he had created when he first arrived in the mountain structure.

Back in the room he looked at the floor where the pod had lain and sure enough there was another gouged trail in the floor, this one led out in a different direction.

He followed it.

***

Tracking the pod was exhausting. Except in the best of spots, it required that he stoop down every few steps to shine his luminary on the floor to recheck that he still was following the trail. He climbed down into the structure seven levels in that way.

When he got close, he no longer required the trail. He could hear it up ahead.

There was a series of slow scraping sounds followed by a rapid skittering. It was similar to the sounds he'd heard during his journey up into the mountain tower but these sounds were different - more purposeful.

He crept forward quietly, his halberd held before him. The sound grew louder and louder and appeared to repeat the same pattern again and again. He paused to listen and felt the lifebeat in his wrist to count the length of time the pattern of sounds took.

He counted it thrice and found about the same number of beats each time.

It wasn't humans making that sound - no, this sounded more like some sort of machination.

He rounded the next corner quietly and proceeded through a doorway and there it was:

A five-legged, metal-clad automaton. It scrabbled up the incline of a collapsed section of floor, before sliding back down, recovering, and trying again in an identical manner.

It used three of its legs to run up the incline while another clutched the heavy, black cable on the pod that it dragged behind it. Its fifth leg dangled uselessly to the side, a bolt protruding from the body right above the leg joint.

Actaeon reached for the boltcaster only to be reminded of its absence.

The machine was nearly twice his height and had a disc-shaped body, with the legs protruding at equal intervals along its diameter and a central stalk raised from the disc. Actaeon could make out the glow of the blue eyes he had seen higher up in the mountain. It hadn't yet spotted him.

Such a machine was certain to be the work of the Ancients. That it survived all these years and continued to function was incredible. How long had it continued to function in this shattered mountain and to what purpose?

Actaeon reached over to scratch his right arm through the sleeve of his jacket. The bottom end of his halberd shifted and bumped into a piece of debris on the floor which clattered off to the side.

The machine halted its latest attempt at the incline, dropped the girl and the top stalk rotated so that the two glowing blue eyes regarded the Engineer.

"Oh. Fantastic."

Actaeon brought the blade of his halberd forward and stepped on the butt end of the weapon in an attempt to impale the body of the machine as it charged forward, but it was much too fast.

It knocked the halberd from his hands with one leg while continuing forward to bowl him over on the other three.

He was thrown to the ground hard and slid along the floor until he slammed against the nearest wall. His broken ribs shifted and he felt a spike of pain lance through his chest. It was atop him before he had a chance to think, one of the legs raised high above him to deal a final blow.

"Whoa! Stop."

At the Engineer's words, the machine ceased immediately and backed away to the center of the room. After he took a deep breath to make sure that his lung hadn't been punctured, he blinked and rolled onto his hands and knees to regard the thing, half expecting it to attack again.

"Well, that was fortuitous," he said.

The machine regarded him as he stood, twisting the stalk that Actaeon had begun to think of as a head in different directions to examine him.

"I am Actaeon Rellios of Shore. What are you?"

It regarded him blankly.

"What is your purpose?" he tried again.

It lifted one of the four functional legs and pointed with the tip of its leg, first at the pod and second up the collapsed floor it had been failing to climb. Beyond the slope of the collapse was a hallway that continued out of sight.

"You want to bring her up there? Why?"

The machine repeated its gesture.

"There is a person in that pod - a living being. It is not like one of the other items you collect."

It galloped over to the pod and bent forward so that its eyes could peer through the glass of the pod. Actaeon retrieved his halberd and approached slowly, not wanting to startle it again. The machine leaned forward and touched the tip of its stalk to the severed end of the pod's cord. While he watched it do that he saw the girl's eyes flutter open and then close once more.

"Fascinating. You can wake her? Can you get her out of that thing?"

The machine turned to face him again and dipped its stalk before him in what Actaeon took to mean assent. Then it repeated the gesture from before: pointing at the pod and pointing up the incline.

"I understand. You want to bring the pod up there. I will figure out a way," said the Engineer and he set to work.

The climb was tough, but he was able to wedge the butt of his halberd into the gap where the collapsed floor section met the wall. He used the weapon to pull himself along the steep slope and he could see why the machine had so much trouble. Without the purchase provided by his halberd, he wouldn't have been able to make it up the slope.

At the end of the hallway, the room he entered filled him with awe. It was a cavernous dome, taking up at least three levels of the structure and luminaries of many different colors were set in the curved wall in iridescent lines. The lines all met at the top of the dome where interlocking, curved transparent plates protruded. Directly below it, in the center of the floor was another assemblage of plates, this one spread open like a technological flower of the Ancients.

He was amazed to see piles of artifacts spaced throughout the grand chamber. There were three piles and Actaeon estimated there to be hundreds of artifacts in each. In one of the piles were the same pods he had seen higher in the building. Another consisted of coils of familiar black cords – intact versions of the severed one that stuck from the top of the girl's pod. Each of the cables was coiled precisely and stacked neatly in a way that minimized the dead space in the stack.

It was harder to discern the contents of the third stack and he had to skirt around a large hole in the floor to approach it. Once he was closer, it became clear.

The stack of deactivated machines that towered above him would have made a veritable army of the things. All were the same as the one he had left below. There were more below, he saw as he shined his luminary down. The weight of the stack must have caused that part of the floor to cave in.

One of the five-legged automatons hung from a set of thin fibrous strands that had been exposed when the floor had given way. It gave him an idea.

First though, he wanted to confirm an unrelated theory. Actaeon approached the transparent petals in the center of the domed room and knelt beside them to inspect the device. Sure enough, at the center of the petals was a cup and, if he was correct, the bottom tip of the pod would fit into it perfectly. The entire device must be for the purpose of operating the pods. It seemed unlikely that he would have ended up in such an appropriate place to rescue the girl from the pod. Could he have been guided here intentionally?

The Engineer thought back through the sequence of events that brought him to this place: the collapse of the bridge in Rust, the river flowing in reverse that brought him up into the mountains, the freezing hike to the peak, and the discovery of the mountain structure. He shook his head. There was no way that all of those events could have been by design. There was too much to chance. It must have been dumb luck that brought him to a place that contained the artifact before him - nothing else made sense.

He shouldered one of the heavy coils from its stack and carried it over to the top of the canted floor. The girl and the machine were right where he'd left them. Its stalk lifted to face him and cool, blue eyes regarded him from below.

"Do not worry. I have a plan," Actaeon said to the machine.

It was silent but one of its legs reached out to touch the glass of the pod near the girl's face.

Had the automaton realized the problem? Was it trying to get the girl out of the pod? It was all indicative of a very high level of intelligence and deductive reasoning.

"It seems as though you are more than just an artifact of the Ancients," Actaeon said to the machine. "You are capable of thought and adaptation to circumstance. It is clear that you are manufactured. The Ancients were able to artificially create a machine mind capable of rational thought and situational awareness. An artificed creature."

The machine cocked its stalk to one side, the blue eyes watching him. It lifted one leg and pointed to the girl in the pod before pointing back up the steep ramp.

"Point taken, I will stop my speculating and get to work."

After lowering one end of the cable down, he slid to the bottom. He took hold of the end of the pod's cord and tried to tug, twist, pull and push in order to disconnect it. No matter what he tried, it held fast.

The machine pushed him gently aside and leaned over so that its stalk touched the pod where the cable entered it. There was an audible click and the broken section of cable fell free.

"Thanks." Actaeon lifted the end of the intact cable and moved to insert it. An unseen force pulled the cable from his hand and it clicked in place into the socket.

Once back up top, he found a way to wedge his halberd into the crevice at the top so that both ends of the weapon were jammed in place. He positioned it so that the shaft of his halberd was securely lodged diagonally across the lower left corner at the top of the incline.

That set in place, he passed a loop of the cable down the other side of the halberd's shaft until it was halfway down the slope. Then he tied off the remaining slack in the cable on the shaft and pointed.

"There you go. Now grab that loop and haul."

The machine dashed up the incline and gripped the loop with the opposable digits at the end of one leg. The rest of its legs slid downward and it scrabbled up to keep its legs beneath it. It managed to right itself before it toppled and began to push perpendicularly to the slope. Slowly but surely, the pod began to ascend as the machine pulled it along using Actaeon's makeshift hoist.

With a wince, the Engineer helped haul the pod the final distance and dragged it onto the level floor above. Since there was no way he could disconnect the cable from the pod, he took some of the cable length near the pod and tied it to the halberd.

The machine took the hint and began to climb up the incline itself, leg over leg, using its digits to clamp the thick cable. Once it was up top, it dipped the stalk toward Actaeon, in a gesture that seemed very much like appreciation. Then it gestured with a leg to the knots tied on the halberd.

"Yes, yes. Well, good job to you too," said Actaeon with a grin.

The machine began to haul the pod away the moment he had untied both the knots. He pulled the halberd free and dashed after it. When he caught up to it, the automaton was already trying to place the pod in the center of the transparent flower, though it was having some trouble without the use of one leg.

Actaeon reached out and steadied the pod, which allowed the machine to tilt it into place. Almost immediately, the clear petals lifted and Actaeon and the machine were forced to leap clear as they enfolded the pod in a transparent cocoon.

A panel in the floor slid upwards a short distance away from the girl in the flower. He approached it and recognized a control panel of the Ancients. He was quite familiar with the glowing symbols. One of them he'd come to think of as 'initiate' and another, glowing red, as 'halt'. Many of the others he had seen in the past, but the purposes seemed to vary from instance to instance.

Far above, the clear panels bloomed open and a slender rod extended down into the room. The rod stopped just above the exposed tip of the pod and the machine pointed to it and then to the end of the cable that lay a short distance away.

"Okay then. I shall follow your instruction," said Actaeon with a shrug. He retrieved the end of the cable and brought it to the rod, not surprised this time when the cable was tugged free of his grip and locked into place. The rod immediately retracted. When the cable was taut, the petals of the mechanical flower closed upon it. Once they were shut, he was confounded to see that the formerly black cable now shone along its full length with a warm, yellow light.

The machine emitted a whirr - the first sound it had generated - and approached the raised console. It turned to regard Actaeon with its cool, blue eyes for a long moment before it bent its stalk forward and inserted it into a recess on the panel.

The walls and floor of the chamber lit up in a spiraled kaleidoscope of color, but the Engineer paid it no attention. He approached the young girl and watched her face through the transparent surfaces of the petals and pod window. A gentle hum filled the chamber, growing in volume. He could feel the vibrations from the floor through his boots. Off to the side, a pile of the deactivated machines collapsed and slid down to join their brethren in the hole.

The girl's eyes snapped open, and she looked into his. Her eyes were stunning and pearlescent. He lifted a hand and waved.

"Hello. I am Actaeon Rellios of Shore. We are working on getting you out of there."

The girl smiled and pressed her palm against the glass of the pod.

The Engineer reached out to place his hand against the petal surface opposite hers and smiled.

The humming sound increased until Actaeon felt that his whole body was vibrating. He wasn't worried though, until he watched the girl gasp silently, her mouth hung open in the pod.

As he watched in horror, the girl began to fade.

In a moment, he could see straight through her to the back of the pod.

"Stop!" he cried out, and when he cast a look toward the machine, he found that it was glowing a menacing red.

Unlike before, the machine did not stop. The sound grew louder and louder and the girl continued to fade.

He rushed over to the console and reached out to touch the halt symbol but was stopped as one of the machine's legs lashed out and struck him in the side. Pain lanced along his broken ribs and he crumpled to the ground, tears in his eyes.

The girl in the pod watched him, her eyes shimmering in the light of the chamber, which appeared to be spinning around them. She was nearly gone now, so much had she faded.

Actaeon struggled to his feet and unslung his bow, feeling a strong sense of deja vu. When he put an arrow to string, he was reminded that his bow was broken and tossed the weapon aside. He lunged forward to hit the button again, but the ancient machine was faster and it knocked his hands aside with ease and threw him away, sending him sliding perilously close to the big hole in the floor.

A look back at the girl found that she still looked at him, a sad smile upon her face, though he could barely make her out in the prismatic chaos of the room. In the pod, he thought he saw her lift her hand and wave at him.

And then she was gone. The lights all went out and the sound and the vibration stopped, leaving his ears ringing and his body numb. There was a crash as something fell and when the luminaries gradually came back on, he saw that the machine had fallen and lay lifeless, before the console.

Clutching his side, he pulled himself to his feet and approached the pod. He reached out to touch where the girl's hand had once been and then stepped back quickly as the petals fell open and the pod tumbled free. The cable let loose from above and landed atop the flower in a mess of loops.

There was nothing in the pod - no sign that the girl had ever been inside. He hoped that Vindra Zar had survived the collapse in Rust, or else he doubted anyone would even believe his story.

The girl had faded from existence before his eyes. Had she been transported somewhere else? Did she continue to exist in some place or form that he couldn't comprehend? Or was she dead, her life terminated inside the metal pod that had been her final resting place? There had to be something more to what he had just witnessed. After all, why would the Ancients have developed such a complex method of human discorporation to simply end a life?

No - he refused to believe that. There was more to the process that had just occurred. The pile of pods against the wall stood as silent proof of that. There must have been more people in those pods that had met the same end - or was it a beginning? There were three possibilities he could think of: the girl had been used for some brutal process of the Ancients that required human sacrifice for some reason he couldn't fathom, the girl had been transported to somewhere on this world or another, or the girl had been changed somehow in a way he couldn't perceive.

Actaeon would hope for one of the two latter, for her sake. There was only one way he could find out the truth, but there was too much in this world for him. His place was in Redemption, and in Redemption he would remain.

He cast a sad look over at the fallen machine. It lay still on the floor, the life faded from its eyes. There was nothing like it that had ever been seen or spoken of in Redemption. Sure, there were tales spoken of great automatons that did the bidding of their long gone masters, but if any had been seen, they were not functional. This five-legged, manufactured creature changed everything. It had shown decisiveness, adaptation and an awareness that was normally reserved for the realm of the living.

He dragged the lifeless husk of the machine over to what remained of the machine stacks and left it there, in the final resting place that it would have wanted.

And without a look back at the lifeless contents of the chamber, he left to begin the long journey home.

The End

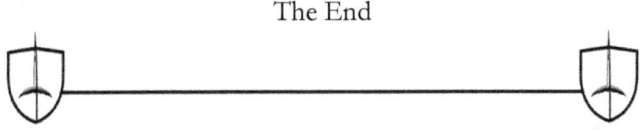

About Darran M Handshaw

Darran M Handshaw is the author of The Engineer, his first complete novel, which is expected to be published late 2017. The Engineer follows Actaeon Rellios through adventures in the ruined, futuristic city of Redemption.

In addition to writing, Darran works as an R&D Engineer at a technology company. There he designs and invents new products; he holds over ten US patents in firefighting and data capture. Darran also volunteers as a firefighter and EMT with his local fire department, where he recently completed a two-year term as Fire Captain. Darran hails from Long Island, NY. He lives with his wife, Stefanie, and baby son, Corwin, who fill his life with love, wisdom, and endless excitement.

Follow The Engineer on:

www.facebook.com/ActaeonRellios/

www.goodreads.com/author/show/17201074.Darran_Handshaw

www.amazon.com/Darran--Handshaw/e/B0763QY2DS

Aether Technician
By Jim Webster

I was born three years after the great hound Bulano ate the sun. Obviously not our sun, or I wouldn't be writing this sitting out on the veranda, but it was somebody's sun.

But that was the day that Humanity signed the final covenant and the deal was done. Thanks to that we have the great aether clippers and our folk travel not merely across our galaxy but beyond.

Yes I know that we had made advances before this, I'm neither stupid nor unread. But I know that these advances were laborious and made at great cost. We created peoples to travel space for us, the star-folk whose lives run so slow they can contemplate a journey of tens of thousands of years, the iron-men who are so tough they can cope with accelerations that would leave any normal crewman as nothing more than a monomolecular smear on the rear bulkhead. They are still out there, travelling the old space lanes, shifting cargos that have been thousands of years in transit. I wonder what happens when they finally reach their destination and find us sipping tea on the saloon deck of an aether clipper, watching them incuriously as they discover their entire reason for existence is a lie.

But then Bulano ate the sun. Overnight we gained access to the aether. Again I'm not an idiot, you needn't pull that face. I know that we had come close to mastering the basic equations. Indeed it is rumored that Batchelor had signposted the route and that his successors had destroyed his notes, fearing the consequences. Perhaps they feared we would become as one with the star-folk or iron-men? Did they tremble at the thought of humanity so diverse that it would be impossible for us to communicate with each other?

I have talked to the star-folk. By which I mean I have recorded a message which will be translated into code and transmitted to them. I felt somebody had to tell them that they were obsolete. But the message will take a thousand years to broadcast, and it could be a million years before the last one hears it.

As for the iron-men we cannot really communicate with them anymore. Not if communication involves understanding and empathy. Curt digital pulses convey data, not affection. We send instructions, their replies are brusque declarations of compliance or terse explanations of problems overcome.

But all this is history now because Bulano ate the sun. Bulano had a price and humanity paid it. Bulano is an entity, a Bok globule which looks like a giant hound when seen from the right viewpoint. It is a consciousness expressed in equations, stored within a gas cloud a light-year or more across and amassing perhaps fifteen stellar masses.

Bulano had something we wanted. It, he, she, they, (use whatever label you feel most comfortable with, Bulano is beyond pronouns) instinctively comprehends the aether and of course the equations that govern it. It took a thousand years to realize that this Bok globule was a 'living' entity. Rumor hints that the star-folk realized this first, and have tried communicating with it. Bulano remains noncommittal, merely claiming that this is a conversation which is still in progress. What deal will he do with them?

Still in his conversation with us, the First-folk, he allowed us to catch of a glimpse of a universe thrown open to us once we mastered the aether. The equations were dangled in front of us like bait on a hook. Yet, even though the hook was obvious, even though there was a price to be paid, we snatched at the bait. Bulano swallowed the sun and extinguished it, along with the lives of innumerable creatures of varying degrees of sentience. In return he taught us the equations. But what is more he agreed to touch the minds of those who would become aether technicians.

I was one such. The consciousness of Bulano swept our world while I was in my mother's womb and I was born knowing. But how can I explain this knowing to one who does not have the 'blessing'? Let us look at the aether propeller as it comes from the machine. One feeds the equations into the machine and it makes the appropriate cuts and bends. Take the propeller from the machine and you have something that will revolve and propel a craft through space at speeds beyond any that we have ever achieved before. But then pass the propeller to me. To me the equations are merely a map. A map attempts to represent three or four dimensions in a mere two. You look at the map and can tell me there is a stream running through the valley. I can see the depth of the stream, the stones on its bed, the fish hiding in the shadows. I take your machine cut propeller and I set to work with my tools. With files and saw blades the thickness of a hair I begin. I take your map and give life to the stream that to you is merely a thin blue line. Each propeller is an individual expression of a reality only those of us who have been 'blessed' can see. With this propeller your craft will move at speeds that exceed your imagination.

Humanity has spread beyond imagining. In my lifetime aether clippers have taken us beyond not merely our galaxy but beyond our local cluster. Now anybody with a modest income can buy a ticket and travel in a manner befitting the conquerors of space. Ah, to sit on the promenade deck, sipping tea and looking out into space, protected from the cold and dark only by the transparent barrier cast around the ship by the Tesla fields. That was the experience that made the greatest impression on my daughter when she travelled to a new life around V762 Cassiopeia. I remember reading her letter and shaking my head at the wonder of it all.

And no, I will never see her again, not unless she returns to see her aged father before he dies. I am an aether technician. I know the aether, I know the covenant, and I am a product of it. I am old enough to have seen what the effects of aether travel have been on those who make the journeys on the grand clippers.

We made the covenant, and Bulano has been faithful, keeping his side of the deal. But what about the price we paid? Was our doglike Bok globule satisfied with the sacrifice of a billion life-sources when he ate the sun?

I am an aether technician. The consciousness of Bulano found me and touched me, changing me. You may have seen Bulano through a telescope; I bear his fingerprints on my soul. Bulano is neither benevolent nor malevolent. It is merely Bulano, yet another living entity trying to make a living in an uncaring universe. Bulano wanted paying in the only currency which really matters, he wanted paying in life. The first billion deaths were a deposit we paid to prove we were in earnest. What our negotiating team obviously never realized is that such a covenant changes both parties. Bulano gained a stellar mass and a billion sparks of life-force. He grew, he is more alive.

But what of us? We are a people who sacrificed a billion existences for our personal gratification. We are the folk who condemned all that lived within the boundaries of the outer Oort Sphere to non-existence. From that point onwards our humanity started to leech out from us.

And then there are the aether propellers. Do you really understand them as I understand them? Can you comprehend the process that keeps them turning, pressing against the aether, driving the ship ever onwards? Something has to lubricate the vanes; something has got to be spilt across them to keep them turning as smoothly as they do. Without this lubricant they would snag and tear at the aether, rending it and leaving it in tatters behind the craft. Without this lubricant we would travel little faster than the iron-men or star-folk.

And the lubricant? It is your soul, your humanity. Of course our negotiators were people wise in the ways of the world, they can understand life and death but obviously they cannot understand what makes an entity fully alive. They were ignorant when it came to understanding what makes a human fully human. They had not grasped the difference between the existence of an entity and life. Bulano was not so stupid; Bulano had existence and sought life. The initial sacrifice was merely a deposit, each time one of us travels, Bulano leeches a tithe from their soul. An insignificant percentage perhaps but I have looked into the eyes of those who have spent a lifetime among the stars. If my daughter ever returned would I recognize her, would my soul cry out to hers?

I am an aether technician, Bulano took his tithe from me whilst I was in my mother's womb, my humanity is thin enough, and I will not pay him more. I will die and be buried on the world that gave me birth. As for us as a species, our numbers may increase, we may spread across the universe, but let us not call ourselves humanity anymore, we have dwindled, we are merely mankind.

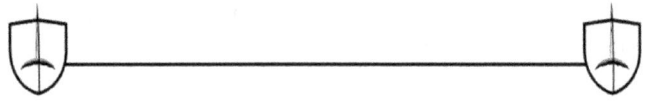

About Jim Webster

In spite of appalling dress sense, Jim Webster is married with three daughters and lives in South Cumbria. He has claimed to be fifty-something for quite some time. He's a farmer, free-lance journalist, and writer. He has been known to declare that writing fantasy and science fiction are his way of recompensing the world for all those articles on the common agricultural policy, sheep health and bovine fertility that he has also written.

He explains away his somewhat jaundiced attitude to modern life and technology by pointing out his co-workers are Border Collies. He keeps two blogs (which are cheaper than a mistress but more demanding of time). One in which he looks at life, Jim Webster: Books and Stuff - https://jandbvwebster.wordpress.com/, and one which he adorns with the anecdotes of the poet, Tallis Steelyard - https://tallissteelyard.wordpress.com/. His numerous books and stories can be found on his Amazon page - www.amazon.co.uk/Jim-Webster/e/B009UT450I/.

When Words Are Not Enough
By Cindy Tomamichel

"We got another big day of writing ahead of us, I know you have it in you. Dig deep."

I wiped Captain Smith's spittle off my face and nodded. I had heard it before. Hell, we all had. We had been on the Shakespeare for so long we had forgotten where we had come from, let alone where we were going. Sure, there were legends, but like all the stories on the ship, they got twisted to make them more entertaining, anything for a laugh, to amuse the cargo.

The Captain's magneto neck coils glowed red, and I refocused. She wasn't a happy Captain when ignored. "Now, I need a volunteer," she growled. "Which one of you hacks has hit the wall?" I held my face straight as she clumped past the rows of writers, her one good eye flickering red. The diodes must need replacing.

Inside I trembled. The table behind her had a pile of red shirts on it, and we all knew that meant a suicide mission. "Please pick me," I heard someone whisper, then realized it was me. I bit my lip, and stepped forward.

Behind me the room rustled as others also stepped forward. Captain Smith flicked a glance at them and they retreated. I held firm, this might be my only chance. She was so close I could feel the heat from the coils on my face. "You ready for the red shirt, hack? You think you're burnt out enough for this job?"

"Yes ma'am," I said.

"This your second or third millennium?"

"Fourth, ma'am. I was in the original intake, I wrote my first story and got transferred from the science section."

I heard the others gasp. With all the rejuvenations we took, most of us looked different year to year. Hell, I couldn't remember if I had been male or female when I came on board. I was pretty sure I had been human, unlike the evolved cats who still retained a certain tendency to whiskers.

But I still remembered signing up. A five year tour they told us, to get to the nearest system with planets. The ship was a longevity one, with a pile of rich bastards that lay like logs in cold storage, while we kept on rejuvenating. And writing. To keep the cold storage passengers mentally alive, stories were channeled directly into their brains. But they always wanted more.

Their reviews got fed into the computer and controlled our lives. The computer ran the ship, we were nothing more than rats in the tunnels, tapping buttons to get review stars. The more stars, the more rations. But we went through a meteorite storm that first year, and something happened to the computer. It announced we were to refer to it as "Zon" and then it never spoke to us again, although it did monitor us and our reviews.

"Right, you, come to my office," Captain Smith barked. "The rest of you hacks, go pound out some words." She paused. "I know you still have some left. Dismissed."

I glanced at the others as I followed Captain Smith out, the red shirt clutched in my hands already damp with sweat. Their haggard faces gave me courage. They had run out of stories, we all had. But the audience was insatiable.

"You know the deal," Captain Smith sat down behind her desk rubbing her eye. She took it out and buffed it, then spat on it and reinserted it into the socket. It swiveled around wildly then focused on me.

"Yes, I know the red shirt protocol. What's the mission?"

She reached over, flicking off her screen connection. "I was walking in the old levels," she commented, swinging back in her chair and putting her feet up on the desk. "You know, level 14. The abandoned section."

I nodded. The hull was breached there, we lost a whole writing group.

"I heard something," Captain Smith said. "From the other side of the sealed door."

"I was there, remember. We lost the whole team, they were working and wouldn't stop when the sirens went off. It was always just one more word. We couldn't get back in, not even to get the manuscripts. Or the bodies," I added.

"I know what I heard," she stated.

"What?" I folded my arms. For a change she looked uncertain, in all the years I had known her, I'd never seen her look - well - scared. The magneto coils dulled, and she leaned forward.

"Something is up there. Something whispered on the other side of the door."

"Words?"

Slowly she nodded.

Fresh words. God, it had been so long. Every word we spoke and wrote was so tired, because we had said and written them till the lines were threadbare, till our imaginations were as thin as tissue. And like tissue, our minds were tearing.

"We are dying," Captain Smith said. "No one can edit any more, the human brain can't take millennia of editing and rewriting. You know the cats lost interest long ago, most of them stay in their boxes. I had one of them try and curl up in my lap the other day." She frowned, rubbing her eye. "Big chap he was too, lucky I had a ball of wool to distract him."

"What do you want me to do?" I asked. "I'll do anything for a new story."

"I know. I need you to find out what is there. What whispered to me?" Captain Smith said, standing and clapping me on the shoulder. "Go and see the Engineer for weapons. But be careful," her eye flickered at me. "You don't know what plot twists have evolved up there." I nodded, and left her as she plugged back into Zon reviews, the holo screens masking her face.

The Engineer had stopped writing a long time ago, but he designed things so wonderful that we shared food with him. Short as our rations were with bad reviews, his musical toys and light shows kept us going, so we kept him going. His rooms were full of wonders, and I smiled, feeling like my face would crack it had been so long.

"Captain Smith sent me," I said by way of introduction.

"Yeah, I was just talking to her."

"She keeps tabs on everyone," I replied. "She was plugging back into the system when I left, checking reviews. I've never caught her napping."

"She never sleeps, not after her 2IC betrayed her. Telling everyone her name was Ducky, I mean does she look like a Ducky?" We looked at each other, silently picturing Captain Smith, part human and part mechanical, but all heart.

"Whatever happened to him?" I frowned, that had been the early days, maybe my memory was getting patchy.

"The Hunter and Paleo took him down," he muttered. "It got ugly. That was when Paleo went full on carnivore and we sealed him in the upper levels. I still hear him sometimes, lots of mutant rats up there to chase."

"Not just rats, all sorts of creatures, I hear. Have you seen him since?"

"Yeah, last I saw he had a tail and scales. Seemed happy though, like a man who was living the dream."

"I remember his stories." I rubbed my neck, wishing I had giant lizards in my imagination. I was down to romance and epic poetry, and my reviews had been poor. Even love only lasts so long.

"Level 14, eh?" He smiled. "You're going to need some help up there." He got up, his stained fingers rummaging in a box. Something growled and he yelped, sucking a finger. "Not that box." Finally, he opened a drawer and pulled out a tube.

"Not sure I can kill someone with toothpaste," I told him.

"You should transfer to comedy," he smiled. "You are wasted in sci fi."

"Romance now," I muttered.

He glanced at me for a moment. "Sorry, I hadn't heard. No wonder you volunteered for this mission."

He pointed at the lid. "Unscrew this when you need it, not before. It will destroy the first thing it sees, it locks on target. I call it terminator in a tube." He grinned. "Level 14, hey, I'd love to go." He rubbed his stomach, and I glanced down.

"Forgot to tick the slim down option when you rejuvenated?"

He winked at me. "Can you keep a secret?" He walked over and kicked the door shut.

"Only if I can't get a story out of it," I replied. "You know how it is."

"Wouldn't expect that," he smiled, and his shirt rippled. Something from inside pulled the shirt free of his trousers, and long nimble fingers grasped the edges of his shirt. I stepped back, keeping the table between us. The shirt unbuttoned. An array of long tentacles, each with five fingers. spread out around him, taking up things on the bench and pulling them apart, and picking up tools.

"I think of him as my little helper," the Engineer said, throwing his shirt open. In his chest. a wizened face smiled at me and winked, looking like some horrible facsimile of the Engineer.

"Hello," I said. "It's nice to have friends."

"Yes, it is. One of the rejuvenations went weird on me, I think I must have had a conjoined twin inside." He shrugged. "It happens. The radiation, the endless rejuvenations, well, he got rejuvenated too. That's why I don't do them anymore, I don't want to lose him." He waved at some of the sparkling toys and musical devices. "He makes these, I am too jaded to make toys to amuse anymore."

"Did you want to come with me? I could do with an extra hand." I glanced down at the small face screwed up in concentration as its multiple hands held a tool each, all busy. "Or a few."

He frowned, looking around at the room crowded with spare parts. "Well…"

One tentacle dropped its tool and gave him a thumbs up. "I reckon we are in then," he smiled.

"I have to see Hook. She has some recording equipment Captain Smith told me."

"Equipment…oh, yeah, I suppose you could call it that." The Engineer looked up from rummaging in box that was hissing. "Go see Zora as well. She has umm…changed lately and might be interested. A tentacle held out a laser pointer. Yeah, take this too. I'll disable my booby traps for you."

I walked slowly back, watching the laser pointer bounce off the walls. Hook had barricaded herself in the port side, and I hadn't seen her for years. Smith kept tabs on her, but I wondered what I would see. She had always been a bit antisocial, and I hadn't read her work for a long time. It had been interesting, I remembered frowning. Cities and crime and people treading dark paths, but she hadn't posted for a long time and I wondered how she was surviving. No stories meant no reviews, and no reviews meant no food. I slipped the laser pointer into my pocket and walked faster. I had lost too many friends over the years.

The door looked unused and knocking just produced echoes. I stepped back, wondering what to do. I jumped as the speaker beside the door crackled, and Hook's familiar voice greeted me. I glanced around, and waved at the camera in the corner. The door slid open with a whoosh sound that I could only admire. Much of the ship was slowly breaking down, but it looked like Hook kept things in good repair.

I stepped inside, and the panel whooshed shut. The room was a maze of silver circuitry and piping, with the odd electrical cable and monitor. Several cameras on long silver robotic arms swooped down and peered at me. They batted long eyelashes at me, and I shook. I knew why she had barricaded herself away.

Her voice came from a synthesizer, and I watched her melodic voice pulse the sound waves on screen. "Yes," she whispered. "Smith said you needed me, otherwise…"

"But your stories," I said. "You know we don't care what people look like. Not after the second millennium supernova exposure. Rejuvenation can only do so much."

"I care," the beautiful synthetic voice said. "I can't bear looking at flesh creatures. I was wearing my bio- metal implants when the supernova happened, I was recording it, hoping it would spark people's imagination. But after...I found I couldn't remove them and ...I didn't want too." The beautiful cameras' lashes drooped.

I patted one gently. "But we need more stories. We - I - need your help, to record something, new stories, maybe. We haven't had any new ones for millennia"

"New stories?" The camera stopped drooping and looked at me. "Yes."

"I will help." A small unit skittered across the floor on robotic legs. It ran up to my feet, and I bent down, picking it up. "This will hurt me more than it will hurt you," she said, and before I had time to frown at the cliché I peered into the unit, and for a moment everything went black.

I sat up, looking around. My face felt odd, and I rubbed it.

"It is enhanced biometal, I downloaded a copy of myself into your matrix." Hook's soft voice purred in my head. "Everything you see and hear, I will too, and send a copy back to Smith." I stood up, feeling bit shaken and caught sight of my face in a monitor. Silver threads crossed my face, and half my face and one ear was covered in a silver mask. Silver circuit threads like fine lace burrowed into my skin. I didn't want to know how deep. It was soft under my questing fingers, and I heard Hook giggle in my head. "It tickles," she said. "This is fun, I haven't left my room for years, let's go."

Hook kept up a steady stream of comments in my head. It made me look at the ship with fresh eyes, and the streaks of rust and fallen bolts that I had ignored. But now? "The ship is dying," I said to her, and felt her agree. "How long since we made port?" We couldn't remember. If we couldn't remember that, what remained true? Had we really started from Earth or was it a story we told ourselves?

We took the emergency ladder to the upper levels. At each level, we stopped to catch my breath and cat people came up to investigate, although I noticed many stayed in their boxes, long human legs curled up underneath them.

"I am in the mainframe now," Hook said, making me jump after some silence. "I can't get to the launch records, they've been wiped.

But look," she waved my hand at the cat people, and I noticed my fingertips had gone silver.

"Hook, you can reverse this, can't you?" I vocalized, my voice sounding scared even to me, and I cleared my throat. "I am going to be human again?"

"What is human anymore?" A tall slender woman had come up, soft footed like all her kind. She purred, and her smile showed longer than usual teeth.

"Zora?"

"So you do remember me."

Yes, I remember the little dark haired kitten girl that used to curl up in my lap and sleep, but she was a woman grown. Several men had followed her, staying close, their mouths curled in permanent snarls and their long nails resting on folded arms.

"The Engineer promised me, you have it?" She pounced eagerly on the laser pointer, and flashed it down the hall. A dozen cat people jumped up alert, and a bunch of little ones collided in a pile after the moving red dot.

Zora smiled. "This will be the saving of my people. Thank you." She nodded at the men, tossing the pointer to the biggest, a giant man with tawny eyes and orange hair.

"What can I do to help? You have given my people a new interest in life, and I shall repay you. Can I kill something for you?"

"It might come to that. We have a mission - Level 14."

"Dangerous?" Her pupils expanded, her whole body focus acute.

"Smith thought so, and she has never been wrong. A hunter such as yourself will be welcome."

Zora nodded and smiled, her long sharp teeth glinting in the flickering overhead light. "I'll just get my red shirt, we should follow traditional protocols."

I nodded. "Zon likes us to follow its rules." I glanced up at the small ceiling camera, it clicked and whirled, refocusing as I looked deep into its electronics. "Zon is good to us," I chanted, and masked a sigh of relief as the camera clicked into its normal scanning routine.

"Good move," Hook whispered in my head. "Level 14, you say?"

I nodded, watching Zora walking back up the corridor wearing a skintight red shirt, and pulling on a pair of gloves with claw extensions. She ran a nail lightly along the wall, and I gritted my teeth as the screeching sound echoed, and a long spiral of metal peeled away from the wall.

"Does the Engineer know we are going to Level 14?" Hook continued.

"Yes." I nodded to Zora, and flicked a warning glance at the camera.

"Come see the latest batch of kittens," she laughed, gamboling down the corridor. I followed, and as the camera moved focus away from us, Zora opened a rusted hatch and we dived in.

It was a cable conduit, part of the ship that was almost never explored, by humans at least. I glanced at Zora, she already had a rat, and she was holding it up by the tail and patting it. The conduit smelled old, thick dust had settled on the cables, and around the walls were footprints, rats mostly but many others.

"I used to play in here as a kitten," Zora told us, dropping the rat as she lost interest. "No cameras, Zon can't see us in here, so what's the mission?"

"We travel to the upper levels in search of some stories that were trapped up there."

"Fresh stories?" She purred. "We could all do with a few five star reviews." She glanced around, pointing the way into another side conduit. "I get a lot of my story ideas in here, many of the smaller creatures are developing quickly. The Engineer told me the electromagnetic radiation might be combining with the solar radiation." She shot her hand out. I felt the wind of her sharp claws pass my face and tried not to flinch. "See?" She opened her hand, and a black fly, larger than most, lay on her palm. It wasn't all black, and I bent closer to have a better look.

It had a human face and arm, and it was crying. "Heellpp me," the tiny voice squeaked.

Zora blew it off her palm and it tumbled end over end to land in a large spider web. She shrugged. "Zon rated that story the highest in scifi last millennia."

"But it was a made up story..." I stuttered.

"You know the power of words," Zora replied. "So does everything on this ship."

She bent down, opened a small door, and beckoned. "This is close to the Engineer's rooms, don't forget his booby traps."

"Wait," Hook said, and I jumped. I had almost forgotten my passenger. "Level 14. I just accessed ship blueprints."

"What?" I squatted down and peered through the doorway, but Zora had disappeared.

"The mainframe is housed up there."

"So?" I had been looking up at the ceiling and floors, carefully sidestepping loose floor panels and dangling cables. The Engineer liked his little jokes, but I felt no urge to get surgical repairs today.

"The mainframe. Don't you know what that means?" Hook sounded excited.

"No, I was a geologist, not an IT zoob."

"Level 14 - it's the brain of Zon."

"And isolated for this long? No wonder the decisions don't make much sense anymore." I opened the Engineer's door and slid in, just avoiding the swinging blade that crossed the corridor at precisely timed intervals.

"Old school," Hook commented, sounding impressed.

I sat down in a battered old chair in the Engineer's rooms, watching while he and Zora dug around in his boxes of junk and cables for useful things, as they said. I yawned, settling back in the chair. Hook was quiet, but I could hear her humming away in the background, and there was a vague feeling of vast amounts of data screens flipping across the background of my mind. Like leaves floating on the wind.

I was back on planet, the first planetfall since we had launched. My team was assigned to do the geological survey. It had been easy to get volunteers, all of us longed to be out of the ship. We stood on the pale brown dusty soil and took deep breaths of the strong spicy new planet smell, so delicious after sterile shipboard air. Plants that were enough like trees to merit the name waved gently in the distance. I detailed off the team, and settled down to a steady walk towards the nearest mountain. I had done the initial surveys and it all looked good, lots of silicate rock types, and evidence of some metal sulphides below. All the materials we needed to start afresh. Earth we had drained dry, it would take millennia to renew itself. I swung my geological hammer and smiled, the sun, despite being a bit reddish, was warm and welcoming.

The radio crackled, and I clicked it on. Nothing but muffled words, and then it went dead. I clicked onto the other channels, but there was no response. The cliff nearby might be masking the signal. Maybe. I would take a sample and head back to the ship. I hefted my hammer, feeling the familiar weight, and cracked it down on a flat piece of rock jutting out from the cliff. It broke off with a tinkling sound, like glass shattering. I picked it up. It was a type of agate, a glassy banded silicate, and I got out my hand lens to check it out. Black on the outside, but inside it had a multitude of veins of all colors. Moisture was beading on the surface, a glittering oily substance.

The tinkling sound got louder, and I looked up, suddenly afraid I had started some sort of rock fall. The whole face of the cliff seemed to waver, and I turned and belted my way back to the ship. But behind me, was the thud, thud of a heavy creature in pursuit. I spared a moment on a glance, and my legs found a speed I never expected of them. Behind me was a giant creature of stone, its monstrous face appeared to be all mouth, an open cavity full of sharp jagged rocks. One hand was slack, leaking drops of fluid crystal, sparkling in the sun. I turned and ran, and up ahead was the ship. Tearing across the plains was my team, with a hoard of the rock creatures close behind them.

Too close. They got caught, one by one, their screams cut short as the rock creatures gulped them down, then spat them out, their bodies shredded like discarded documents.

I woke up in the chair, Hook screaming in my head. "Wake up."

I shook my head, trying in vain to remove the dream fragments. I thought I had buried those memories deep.

"So that's why we never landed again?" Hook asked. "I was born on board, I never knew."

The Engineer and Zora were looking at me, and I realized I had been muttering both sides of the conversation. "Nightmare," I said, briefly explaining it.

"The first couple of millennia were tough. With the away team lost, then that sun went nova unexpectedly and we ran into the meteorite storm. Zon was never the same. Hell, none of us were. The radiation levels increased after the supernova, enough so we needed rejuvenation more often, and then the cats turned into people. The hydroponics got feral, and there was the rise of the zucchinis. I still wake up screaming about that time, took me years to eat a vegetable again. But with the cables fried, and the hull steaming with radiation it had never been built to take, we battened down the hatches and survived. We had the cargo to look after, the crew was expendable." I took a deep shaky breath, and wiped my face.

"Cargo," the Engineer spat. "They've been frozen for centuries, the bastards. Rich enough to pay for cryogenic transport, but without the guts to make the trip like us."

The com dinged with a call and we all jumped.

"Smith here," her face came up in a small holo, and she didn't look pleased. Not that she ever did. "Get moving. Zon has just received some negative reviews from the cargo, so rations are cut by another 10%. With kitten season soon, we are going to be eating rats and roaches again. We need new stories!"

To avoid Zon's cameras, we climbed the ladders, the old emergency escape manways. The ship got darker and grimier as we climbed up through the levels. After a couple of mishaps, Zora climbed first taking out the rats and other creatures that climbed, crawled and flew in an area that hardly ever saw humans. The upper levels had caught the full impact of meteors and radiation, people had repaired the hull in cycles, needing a full body repair after each shift. I watched my hands as we climbed up and up the ladders. The silver threads were spreading fast and they were both silvery to the wrists. It was better than being in my head with my memories. I had no more words to distract me. They had drained out of me long ago.

"The ladders give out on 15," The Engineer called. "We should stop for a rest, and I need to speak to someone."

"I've found your memory of the planet trip," Hook announced. "I can erase it if you wish."

I heaved myself up and onto the deck, and shook my head. "No, I let my team down. I should not forget that." I felt her nod, a ghostly feeling inside me.

The Engineer had been tapping on the wall for some time, a rhythmic tap tap bang, until the rhythm had got into my head like a mind worm. I started tapping it with my fingers, and then realized the floor was bouncing it back. "He's coming," the Engineer announced, looking up the corridor and waving. "You stay here, he's shy."

I raised an eyebrow, but let him go without comment. He soon came back, grinning. "Good to catch up with old friends. Let's go, it's safe until we get to the next level. He doesn't let anything else into his territory."

He took off before I could ask, and I followed him through the maze of doors and sleeping quarters, all showing signs of the hurried departures of millennia ago. Beds lay coated in dust, cups filled with long dead mould growths, and sometimes a faded photo or a child's toy. Faster than we wanted to, we reached the ramp that lead up into the upper levels. Well, once it had, now 14 was all that was left, the rest had been cannibalized for repairs. The ceiling above was just a thin layer of glass and metal patches and I shivered. I could feel the cold fingers of space reach down and wrap themselves around my heart. I straightened up, feeling better. I hadn't had a flight of fancy in so long.

The door to level 14 was just ahead, standing ajar. "We could never get this door open before." In the best of horror traditions, it creaked open before our eyes. I stepped closer cautiously. "Stay behind me," I said, but Zora had already woven past me, and was running ahead.

The corridor was a mosaic of repairs, metal and glass panels alternating, and shafts of star light left the area in patches of bright light and black darkness. The walls were not plain metal anymore either, but before I could examine them Zora screamed.

I raced ahead, she had gone too close to a curtain of woolen threads, all knotted together like the web of a spider on steroids. She was tangled, her feet off the ground, and was batting furiously at tassels and knots of wool.

"It's quipu," The Engineer yelled, tugging at the cords. "Stories coded in knots. Before letters were invented."

"Don't pull, it hurts," Zora yelped, the cords tightening around her. Already she bled from the cords cutting into her legs. "Leave me, I can figure it out. Cats know wool," she said, grabbing a knot. "Go."

We ran on, the walls covered in strange marks and pictures. I poked my head cautiously around the corner, and snapped back as a triangular piece of metal slammed into the wall. The Engineer pulled it out and examined it. "Quipu, now cuneiform. The words are evolving." Ahead the corridor was ringing with the sound of metal hammering into the far walls.

"I can handle this," the Engineer yelled, ripping off his shirt. Soon a dozen long fingered hands were plucking at the air, grabbing the cuneiform print and dropping it before catching another. "You go," he panted.

I raced along the corridor and around the corner, slowing down as the floor beneath me shifted. It was an off-white color, and I bent down to feel it. "Smooth, yet rough, not quite paper but... parchment." Hook finished.

The deck suddenly buckled, and I fell, my fingers jabbing into the floor and it tore with a horrible ripping screech. I scrambled backwards and got to my feet, but it was too late. The floor had started folding up on itself and I ran, jumping over folds that snapped at my feet. A sharp fold of floor whipped out at me and I went down again, my leg sliced open with a monster paper cut. I rolled over, using my good leg to push back towards the wall.

Leaning over me was a folded paper creature, and patterned over its body were scores of little smiley faces, animals and love hearts. I gulped and Hook screamed "emoji's, run!" I got to my feet but my leg gave way, and I fell again, a hard object in my pocket jabbing me in the chest.

"Ha, take that," I yelled, rolling over and uncapping the terminator in a tube at the same time.

The tube was sucked dry in a moment as a large grey rectangle formed on the floor. It rocked to its feet and jumped at the parchment monster. Each time it jumped, part of the creature was erased, and it fell into a writhing heap, emoji's skittering off like cockroaches. The terminator gave an odd bounce and fragmented, each piece hunting down the fleeing emoji's.

"I fixed your leg, let's hustle," Hook gave me a mental elbow. I glanced at my leg, it had silvered completely.

"What's ahead of us?" I asked. Behind me the terminator snuffled around, snapping up the remaining emoji's like dog treats.

"The library." Hook answered.

"That doesn't sound so bad, I love libraries." I took off.

"Be careful," Hook was babbling in my head, as I walked up the soft carpet that hushed my steps. "Books need readers – these have lived in a vacuum. Nothing stays sane by itself for too long. I should know…"

But I could smell old paper. There was nothing to worry about.

Ahead, the corridor opened up into a large room, and the walls were lined with books of all colors and sizes, all pristine. No dust, rats or rust here. I ran my fingers down the books. "I haven't seen a book for so long, it's all e.."

"Don't say it," Hook screamed.

"eBooks." I finished before I could stop myself.

"Ssshhhhh…" the room echoed, and around me the books quivered, and one by one, opened up, the pages riffling in the non-existent breeze.

…I was sitting in a deep soft chair, my feet up and a cup of tea on a small table beside me. There was a warm fire glowing, and outside the rain pattered on the window, and the dark trees sang as their branches rubbed together. I sighed and took a sip of tea, and finished the biscuit that appeared in my hand. A cat had draped itself across my lap, and a dog lay in front of the fireplace, its paws twitching as it dreamed. I picked up the book...

"Wake up..." Hook screamed. I felt like my brain rattled in my skull as she screamed again, twanging memory cords to get my attention. Again I raced across the planet surface, silicon creatures pounding after me...my rejuvenations...the first... I snapped awake and sat up, feeling drained. Books covered me, their pages pressed against my skin. "Get up, go," Hook screamed again.

I shook off the books and staggered out of the door, paperback books fluttering like bats around me. I shut the door firmly, leaning against it and blinking in the bright light.

The room was the front of the ship, the ceiling was crazed glass pock-marked by space dust. Ahead was a small console, its cursor flashing on - off, on - off.

I stood there for a moment, watching the view out of the scratched glass. Stars mostly, but in the distance was a planet.

"Computer," I said. "Planet description."

There was a soft hum, and the monitor lit up. "Earth."

"We've come full circle," I said out loud, although there was no one to hear. "It wasn't a story after all." It was a vivid green and blue, not the brown we had left it. I wiped away a tear. It was beautiful.

"We need to touch the keyboard," Hook said, making me jump.

The room started a low hum, and a printer on the far wall suddenly started shooting reams of paper out onto the floor. Lights flashed faster and faster, and a waterfall of words started pouring down the screen. As they reached the bottom of the screen, they flowed across the keyboard, and flooded across the desk.

"Touch the keyboard, now!" Hook yelled, and I put my hands down as the words marched across like ants.

"Come to me," Hook screamed, the words coming out of my mouth. Fluid bio-metal flowed down my arms and onto the keyboard, tendrils reaching into the computer. The skin on my face prickled as she left me.

The words flew up, piercing me as I stood frozen to the keyboard. Commas and apostrophes wriggled into my skin like worms, and exclamation marks pierced like knives. All the grammar in the universe slashed and tore at me, the pain sharper than a one star review. But the words...they were flooding into my heart and mind, combining and reshaping into stories and poems. I felt the tears pour down my face as sonnets flowered like daffodils in springtime.

"I have control," Hook's voice boomed across the room. "I am Zon and Zon am I."

But it was too late for me. My red shirt was redder still with my blood, and I could feel strength fading from me. It would take a miracle to save me.

But I had heard the words, and it was enough.

"It is a far, far better thing I do…" I started. The door was bashed open.

"Not on my watch!" yodeled The Hunter. A dinosaur clumped into the room dragging a protesting robodoctor. They were followed by Zora and the Engineer, and she was holding hands with one of his tentacles.

"Paleo to the rescue," they cried, and the dinosaur waved its tiny front legs and roared in triumph.

"Five stars," Hook/Zon boomed.

We watched Earth brighten ahead of us and laughed.

Everyone loves a happy ending.

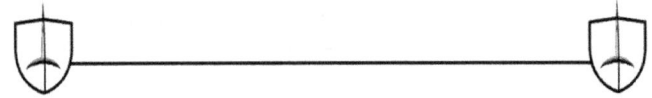

About Cindy Tomamichel

Cindy Tomamichel is a writer of action, adventure, romance novels, spanning time travel, sci fi, fantasy, paranormal, and sword and sorcery genres. They all have something in common – swordfights! The heroines don't wait to be rescued, and the heroes earn that title the hard way.

Her next book, Druid's Portal: The Second Journey is in progress. An action adventure time travel with a touch of romance set in Roman Britain.

Connect with Cindy at:

Cindy Tomamichel - cindytomamichel.com

Facebook - facebook.com/CindyTomamichelAuthor/

Twitter - @CindyTomamichel

Goodreads - goodreads.com/author/show/16194822

Amazon - amazon.com/Cindy-Tomamichel/e/B07148BH5Y

Soul Mates

By Victor Acquista

Day 268

Vril, Prana, Qi, Élan vital - call it whatever you want - the energy, the force, the universal stuff that is the difference between a living, breathing human being and a corpse. Anima, whatever it is, I'm close. The interface is nearly complete...

"Ready to eat in five minutes." Julie's sweet voice called from the kitchen, just audible in the basement.

"Thanks, Honey. I'll wrap it up down here."

It would be a while before he completed the storage capacitor schematics, but at least the interface assembly was 95% done. Mike almost could not believe how much he had accomplished in the last two months. *Shit, this theoretical stuff might actually work.* He felt pleased with himself, noticing only now, as he washed his hands, how his hungry stomach demanded food.

"Smells great! What's on the menu?"

"Meatloaf…your favorite."

He didn't have the heart to tell his wife that her meatloaf was only marginal; even more so, certainly not his favorite. Julie had her good points, but culinary skills she lacked. Not that Mike really cared. They adored each other. Had since college when they first met and fell in love--he, a bit of a geeky nerd from California, and she, just a sweet plain Jane from Indiana. Now married eleven years. No children yet, not that they weren't trying.

"So, how's your project going?"

Mike gushed about the progress he had achieved on the interface until noting the glazed look in his wife's eyes. Of course, no one really understood how to quantify the essence of the soul, the dynamic life force, much less how to measure its existence, capture and store it.

Slicing a piece of meatloaf and stabbing it, he waved the meat-laden fork as a prelude to ending his progress update. "It's really coming along great, Honey!" Mike chewed and swallowed with feigned gusto. "But nowhere near as great as this dinner! You're the best."

"Stop. We both know that no matter how many times I read *Bon Appetit*, or try one of their recipes, I'll never be a good cook. Thanks anyway. I love you all the same, even if you fib to me about my cooking."

Mike sliced another piece and stuffed his mouth. "Ummmh, good!"

"I've got a special dessert planned." She unbuttoned the top of her blouse and sat on his lap. "I'm sure my hard-working husband would like a special treat…"

Damn! How did I luck out? What did I do in this life or some previous life to have it so good?

"The dishes can wait. Let's go make a baby."

Although Mike needed no convincing, he joked, "Well, if you are going to twist my arm," he contorted his left arm behind his back, "how can I say, no?"

Day 283

Done. Wilhelm Reich himself would be proud. Now to test it.

After placing the cricket in the shoe-box sized container, Mike adjusted the video focus and watched as the insect scurried within the confines of the experimental chamber. The entire experiment would be recorded. He took a moment to reflect on how much he had accomplished to get to this point.

Professor Wilhelm Reich coined the term, "Orgone Energy", his name for the universal life force. He had even built an orgone accumulator to collect this energy, which he used in research on healing various ills. His experiments ran afoul of the FDA as unlicensed quackery. Reich became mired in controversy and was eventually shut down and arrested. The scientist died in jail in 1957; however, his research and journals survived. Per the scientist's own request, his work was sealed for 50 years and released in 2007. That's when Mike did a deep dive into the research.

During the past ten years, Mike held a variety of low-wage jobs while refining some of Reich's crude designs. With Julie's support, both psychological and financial, he studied the basis underlying the life-force energy by using a two-pronged approach. Philosophy and science came together here in his basement lab.

First step required that the chamber be cooled. Mike watched as the temperature within the box chilled to 7° Celsius. The cricket had slowed and now remained still except for a twitch of antennae. A puff of ether gas erupted as Mike injected the anesthetic. He included this step in the protocol for humane reasons. It might not influence whether or not the insect suffered, but as experiments advanced to lizards, chicks, mice…all the way up to dogs and cats, he would feel guilty if they needlessly felt pain. The ether minimized any animal suffering.

While writings from the ancient Greeks, Egyptians, Hindus, and Chinese all demonstrated a basic understanding of life energy, Mike realized it was only a qualitative understanding. In 1907, the French philosopher Henri Bergson published his essay, *The Élan Vital and Self-Evolution*. Bergson's exploration and philosophical analysis still informed much of Mike's understanding. That same year, and Mike hardly thought this a coincidence, Dr. Duncan MacDougal published, *The Soul: Hypothesis Concerning Soul Substance Together with Experimental Evidence of the Existence of Such Substance*. MacDougal remained convinced that the soul had physical mass and he measured the difference in body weight pre and post-mortem. His conclusion: the average weight of the human soul calculated to 21 grams.

Chilled carbon dioxide filled the container next. This food preservation technology, borrowed from cold storage of fruit—how else do you think you can have a crisp apple off- season—served a dual purpose. The odorless, colorless CO_2 suffocated the animal within the box, while the temperature and lack of oxygen within diminished cellular degradation. While Mike observed the cricket through the view panel on top of the chamber, his eyes remained focused on the pair of gauges measuring élan vital. One measured the force within the container, the other calibrated the life energy within the adjacent collector.

MacDougal had the right idea in so far as measuring the soul, just another name for this life energy. But it wasn't physical mass, it was energetic and not electromagnetism. Whatever the energetic "substance" happened to be, Mike still could not say for sure. In his mind, he imagined it as quanta of consciousness. The theoretical physics and mathematical formulae explaining this life force led straight to quantum mechanics. Mike had a decent IQ, but the theoretical basis didn't matter to him. Measurement. That was the key.

The two gauges measured identical changes, the box down by a fraction, the accumulator up by the same fraction. Although Mike had no electrodes to monitor whether or not the cricket was truly dead, he felt certain the insect within had passed and its spark of life energy no longer animated its insect body. He reversed the polarity, vented the CO_2 and began to raise the temperature. Heart racing, Mike saw the gauges flip back to their previous baselines. The cricket twitched a couple of times then resumed exploration of the chamber. *Success!*

"Honey, I think it worked." He crawled into bed next to Julie. Her boss asked that she put in extra hours as the firm had taken on a big case. It seemed the paralegals bore the brunt of the extra work.

"That's nice, sweetheart." Her sleepy voice told him a love-making all-nighter would have to wait. "When do you get the Nobel prize?"

As his wife's gentle snores lapped his consciousness like waves upon a glorious beach, Mike lay wide awake beside her. Abruptly, he shot up and went down to the basement. As the light flipped on, the cricket ran to the corner of the terrarium where he had moved it. *It's still alive!*

Day 296

They started looking at me a bit strangely at Petco so I've begun shopping at different stores. 100% success on the crickets, the chameleons, and the chicks. I've been working my way up the evolutionary chain and am ready for a murine trial.

He had called in sick the entire week so that he could continue the experiments. Thus far, none of the reanimated animals had any noticeable differences. After tagging them, he placed them among the control groups. He even fed a sample of the reanimated crickets to a control group of lizards. To date, he could detect no differences between groups fed normal or reanimated insects, at least among the things he could measure. The growth curves on the chicks were the same. He did not have the space to raise them to adulthood and see if there were any differences in egg production or life span. While Mike understood that such detailed examination of these variables would be ideal, that would require funding and a more extensive lab. Heck, as it was, this growing menagerie presented difficulties maintaining food, water, cage cleaning, time and money. Fortunately, Mike had worked in a genetics lab back in college. He learned a lot about caring for laboratory mice and rats, enough to convince him to switch majors from Genetics to Philosophy. From a career standpoint, that might not have been the best decision. It was all moot at this point.

Ten years ago, it started as intense curiosity: What is a thought? What is consciousness? What distinguishes life from death? These philosophical ponderings coupled to the scientific method eventually led him to build an Orgone accumulator. What exactly was being collected? How can you measure it? Only recently had scientists begun to unravel a quantum theory of consciousness. It involved DNA and microtubules and information storage. From an intellectual standpoint, it sort of made sense to Mike. Being a pragmatist, he cared less about the theory and more about practical issues such as measurement. His particular genius came on a hunch—DNA in solution absorbing and emitting photons. That formed the basis for his refinements.

Placed within the Orgone accumulator, Mike noted increasing light emission across a blue spectrum as more life energy accumulated. Once he had reliable collection and measurement tools, the final task remained: transference.

"Whatcha doing?"

Mike almost jumped out of his chair. He hadn't heard Julie come downstairs. "Hey, Babe. Just getting ready to run a reanimation trial on some mice." He pointed to a cage with white mice. Some had their paws painted in orange nail polish. "Do you want to watch?"

"I'm cooking right now, sweetheart." She massaged his shoulders and made some cooing noises. "I think you've been working too hard."

"No. You're the one who's been working too hard. This trial can wait another day. Why don't I come and help you in the kitchen? I'll help with food prep and clean up. What's on the menu?"

"Tuna noodle casserole." Julie finished the neck rub and leaned over to whisper in Mike's ear. "Special dessert for being such a wonderful husband."

Shutting the lights off and leading Julie by the hand, Mike added with a wink, "I say let's skip right to dessert."

Day 312

I can't believe how well the mice experiments have gone. No ill effects as far as I can tell. Rats, then bunnies, then I'll have to build a larger chamber. Funds are low, but Julie has been putting in extra hours at time and a half. She has thrown out the possibility of me quitting work at Wallie World. I don't think we can afford it. The ether and CO_2 and the animal supplies are really straining our budget. I'm lucky to have her support.

It occurred to him while running the rat trials. The greater the size of the animal, the greater the amount of life energy. The energy collected and transferred back and forth with the smaller animals only moved his calibration equipment a few ticks. There were limits to how sensitively he could calibrate the measurement. But, with the rats, he had more élan vital to deal with. What if he took some of the ambient life energy from his Orgone collector and added it to the animal at the time of reanimation? Professor Reich attempted to add life energy to his subjects in order to promote healing. What would the effect be on test subjects?

The first few experiments were ugly, messy in fact. Anything over 10% additional life-energy and the rat exploded. A flash of light, then blood and guts. At 7-9%, the reanimated rats ran around wildly, squealing, smashing themselves against the walls of the experimental chamber, then the cage. They all died within two hours to three days. He could not fractionate the transfer of energy other than in 1% increments. At 6%, results seem varied with some early mortality. At 5%, the results were astonishing.

Over three weeks of close study, rats given 5% extra "juice" at the time of transference performed well beyond control group rats. More mating success, faster maze times, male dominance. The results were both dramatic and consistent. He called them super rats. Whatever the experiment did, it acted like reverse Kryptonite.

He documented everything. Only organic material could be animated. He tried to instill life force into metal, rocks, crystals, plastic, but transference never occurred. For animals that had been dead more than ten minutes, no matter how hard he tried, Mike could not transfer or instill Orgone energy. He theorized that either cellular health, DNA, or some factor had to be present or intact in order to absorb the life force. He thought of dozens of experiments. Like Mary Shelley's Frankenstein, his obsession with bringing life to an inanimate patchwork of body parts, consumed him.

Julie came to his rescue.

"Stop thinking of being God and creating life and start thinking about how your marvelous work can help humanity, save lives, be a force of good. You are not creating a monster so much as cheating death." They lay close to each other, naked and in the glow of after sex.

"I don't know, Sweetheart, sometimes I'm afraid of what this can unleash—an army of undead, walking corpses, zombies, or some kind of vampires that can live forever feeding not off of blood, but off of life energy."

"Nonsense. What if I was terminally ill with cancer? The doctors could wipe out the cancer, but the treatment would kill me. What if your approach worked on people and you could tell the docs, 'Fine, proceed with the treatment and kill the cancer. We'll need to move fast and bring my wife back when the treatment is done.' That's what we're talking about here—giving people a second chance."

"You know, I'm so glad I married you!" They made love again.

Day 370

It took me longer to build a larger experimental box than I had originally planned. This one does look uncomfortably like a coffin, with a viewable glass panel on top.

I've been out of work six weeks. We just signed papers for a second mortgage. I've had more dreams about rabbits, stray cats, and dogs from the shelter than I care to recall. Some of them are nightmares. The super rats continue to thrive. When I returned the beagle with the 5% extra to the pet shelter, she looked at me in the strangest way—anger, hostility—if she could talk, I'm sure she would have been cursing at me.

Julie has a week off. We're going to the beach. I have someone who will clean and feed the test animals, but at this point, I've gotten rid of all of them except the super rats. The basement smells a lot better.

Mike had reached a decision node. He could collate and organize all his research to date and try to write a scientific paper. Of course, with no past background, no postgraduate degree, and no previous publications, chances were excellent that he would be turned down for publication. Worse yet, he had probably violated all sorts of ethical principles in using laboratory animals for research purposes. He had never contemplated how his work to date, more than ten years of research, could be shared. Alternatively, he could pursue further experimentation, but that presented problems.

Primate research involved many restrictions and authorizations. The bureaucracy involved, and the presumed need to disclose his research efforts to date with all the attendant ethical issues, made that path a dead end. The only way to proceed seemed to require human subjects. Robbing graves, as some of the fathers in human anatomical research had resorted to, would simply not work. Too much cellular decay. He could not just pop over to the city morgue and collect a few bodies for experimental purposes. Besides, the time delay from death to attempting reanimation would leave the window of opportunity long closed shut.

As he sipped his cocktail, "Sex on the Beach", prelude to the real thing, Mike thought about it:

Main alcohol: Vodka
Ingredients: 1 1/3 oz Vodka, 1 1/3 oz Cranberry juice, 2/3 oz Peach schnapps, 1 1/3 oz Orange juice
Preparation: Build all ingredients in a highball glass filled with ice. Garnish with orange slice.
Served: On the rocks; poured over ice
Standard garnish: Orange slice
Drinkware: Highball glass

Bartending and mixing drinks were among many of his previous occupations. Well, you can't have this drink without having certain essential ingredients. And, you can't advance your research without certain key ingredients. The most important key ingredient is a human test subject. The logic here may have been a bit fuzzy, but so was his brain at the moment. Knocking off a few neurons to alcohol didn't concern Mike, so much as figuring this out. He ordered another.

Mike reached two inescapable conclusions. Julie looked beautiful in a skimpy bikini. He wanted to capture the image forever. He decided unequivocally that he needed to be the first test subject. For all the love he felt for his darling wife, he knew she would disapprove. He parked the idea for the moment as they headed back to their seaside room.

Over dinner, a fabulous bouillabaisse of fresh local seafood, he sprung the idea. A robust session of intimacy had burned off some of the alcohol from the afternoon. Now, they shared a bottle of chilled Sauvignon Blanc. The food and dining here represented a significant step up from their usual in-home fare.

"You know, Babe, I've been thinking." Mike paused to make sure Julie followed his reasoning.

"Oh, that could be dangerous." She batted her lovely brown eyes.

"Seriously, I've taken my research as far up the evolutionary tree as I can, other than primates."

"I don't think they have monkeys, here. Maybe we should plan a trip to Costa Rica." She poured another glass of wine.

"No. You don't understand. There are too many restrictions to try and do research on primates." She nodded. "The only alternative is to do a reanimation trial on a person, and the only person I would be willing to try this on, is myself."

The sound of her glass shattering on the floor and her look of complete speechless horror remained frozen in a moment of time.

"What!" She glared at him.

"*Mademoiselle*, is everything okay?" The waiter appeared from nowhere.

"No!"

Julie rarely put her foot down, but Mike could see this happened to be one of those times. He knew this was neither the moment, nor the place to have this discussion.

"Yes, waiter, everything is fine. We just…we just need a new wine glass." Then he added, "And another bottle, *S'il vous plaît*."

Day 381

Persistence paid off and Julie eventually agreed with me. We started again with crickets so she could learn the protocols. There will only be one shot to get this done, so failure is not an option.

"I'm sorry! I really am trying, but it's like following a cooking recipe."

"That's okay, Jules. I know you're giving it your best."

No matter how many practice runs, no matter how he set up failsafe prompts, the best Julie could manage was only 91% success. Sometimes she messed up slightly with the gas injectors, sometimes it was the temperature settings. Other times, she fouled on the transference. Bottom line, his wife did not seem able to master the process of controlled death and reanimation on the insect trials. Attempting on a live person, much less her husband, with the jumble of EEG scalp sensors and EKG electrodes, and a few additional steps, seemed out of the question. The 9% failure risk stood as well outside the threshold of acceptability. They suspended further animal testing. Crickets!

"Don't worry about it, Sweetheart. We'll figure out something." He grit his teeth and sighed.

"Sorry!" Julie saw the dejected look on Mike's face. "Maybe we can take out an ad asking for volunteers."

"For what—research experiment on dying?" He did not restrain the sharp edge in his response. "C'mon, Julie, you work in a friggin' law office. Can you imagine the informed consent? It would be a thousand times worse than those drug company ads mentioning rare side effects including possible death. In this study, it's not the possibility of death, it's the guarantee! And there is no guarantee of resuscitation. That's a chance I'm willing to take, but I wouldn't risk someone else's life on it."

She just sat there while he continued his rant.

"And furthermore, if things didn't go the way they're supposed to go, then what? Murder! You think the judge would go lenient for second degree or manslaughter? Would you come to visit me in prison while I'm on death row? Well, at least the food in jail would be better than home!" He bit his tongue. He wished he could take it all back...too late.

Julie's sobs as she ran upstairs hung in the air. The slam of the bedroom door marked the exchange with a definitive auditory exclamation point. *Crickets!*

Two hours later, after multiple apologies and reassurances that he really did like her cooking, they managed to get back on track. Make-up sex is one of life's great pleasures and great reset buttons. Seated at the table eating leftovers, they continued the discussion.

"You're right. Getting a research volunteer won't work. It was a dumb thing for me to suggest."

"No, the dumb part came from me when I shot you down. You were only trying to help."

"Thing is, I can help."

"No, we've been over this. We need you to be at 100% through all the reanimation trials. Although, maybe we can recruit someone else to learn the protocols."

"That's not what I'm suggesting." Mike noticed a coy look on Julie's face.

"What do you mean?"

In response, she said nothing as she pointed to her nose. As though the perfectly obvious answer was right in front of him.

It took Mike a moment until recognition sank in. "NO WAY!"

"Why not?"

"There is no way I'll let you be the guinea pig. Not happening, Jules. Don't even think about it!"

The conversation ended as she stood up to clear the dishes.

Day 395

D-day! Jules recorded a video yesterday essentially saying she was doing this of her own free will for the advancement of science. I had not coerced her in any way. If something goes wrong, she takes full responsibility, etc. It doesn't sit well with me. I don't want a disclaimer; I just don't want something bad to happen to her. I don't think I could ever forgive myself.

People on death row sentenced to die the next day probably had similar thoughts—reviewing their life to date, wondering about things they could have or should have done differently, reliving past moments of glory.

Neither of them slept well the night before. They made love three times over the course of the night as they both lay awake.

"Don't be so morbid. Everything will turn out fine. Remember, zero mortality from the animal experiments, except when you juiced the animals too strongly." The words sounded both brave and encouraging, but they rang hollow in Mike's ears.

He repeated a silent mantra, "Everything is going to be okay. Tomorrow we'll laugh about it." But tomorrow had too quickly become today; he had misgivings.

"Ouch."

"What, what happened? Are you okay?" Mike hovered next to Julie.

"I bumped my head. Stop acting so anxious, I'm nervous enough as it is. It's tight in here."

"There's still time to change your mind."

She shook her head and reached up to pull down the lid, but Mike stopped her. He clutched her hand, looked in her eyes, and said with the same intensity as when he asked her to marry him, "I love you. You better come back. I love you so much!"

"Of course I'm coming back; otherwise, I'll haunt you for the rest of your life." A brief smile flashed then resolute determination. "Let's do this. I love you, Mike!" She pulled the cover closed and lay still as the temperature dropped.

A faint hiss as ether shot through the injectors. Other than her rhythmic breathing, Julie lay motionless under sedation.

Somehow Mike managed to remain focused, even hyper focused. Sweat stains gathered beneath his armpits and he constantly wiped his face using his shirtsleeve. Julie remained quietly asleep. Temperature within the box stood at 7° Celsius. Carbon dioxide slowly replaced the air within. The EEG reading grew erratic; heart rate accelerated. All the while, Julie lay there looking peacefully still. *So far, so good.*

He drew a deep breath and watched as the brain activity flattened and the EKG flatlined. Julie had stopped breathing two minutes ago. He watched the dual gauges and noted the loss of Orgone in the death chamber and simultaneous increase in the élan vital measured within the collection device. Done. Julie was dead. Mike had killed her.

He flipped the polarity and waited. Reanimation for the larger animals took two to three minutes. He vented the CO_2 and waited some more.

One minute...still no activity on the gauges meaning no transference back. No brain or heart function.

Two minutes. Still nothing. *Oh, God, please...please.*

Three minutes. The longest three minutes of his life. Still nothing. *C'mon! Oh, my God! It's not working. I killed Julie! My God...she's dead!*

Desperate, he dialed up the life energy transfer by 5%. Mike held his breath. At 3.5 minutes, the needles moved. A spike flashed on the EKG monitor and some scrambled brain waves danced. Mike exhaled, squealed and watched as Julie took a shallow breath.

Her eyelids fluttered and the dilated pupils of her beautiful brown eyes constricted to normal size. She looked a bit dazed and had a wildly confused look. Mike reached in to lift her to a sitting position, ignoring the tangle of electrode wires.

"I thought I'd lost you! Oh, my sweet, dear Julie...." He caressed her face. "I thought I'd lost you. Thank you, God! Thank you, God!"

She took a deep breath and weakly held him. She flexed her fingers. "I'm back." Then she let him help her out of the chamber, smiled and looked for a robe. "Kinda chilly in there."

Day 425

"From the single cell or moneron in the slime of the ocean-bed, or the lowly quasi-organic forms of green sediment or deposits on rocks and old trees, to the highest forms of animal and human life, Vril is ever present and operative. Just as protoplasm is the peculiar phase of matter which serves as the body of living organisms, so is this phase or form of Vril the peculiar force or energy which always accompanies organic life. In fact, it is the distinctive property or attribute of organic life. When science is forced to decide whether or not a thing is "living" in the ordinary sense of the term, it is the possession or non-possession of this form of Vril which serves to decide the matter and make the distinction." *VRIL, OR VITAL MAGNETISM* --William Walker Atkinson

...and now I control it!

It would be difficult to describe all the changes following the month after Julie's return from the dead back to the land of the living.

For one thing, in a very brief time, she had mastered gourmet cooking. Their sex life had been pretty awesome, but since the experiment, things got even better. Julie had gotten into yoga and introduced Mike to Tantra. Holy smoke--sexual ecstasy and then some! Some of the other changes were less obvious, more subtle. Aroma therapy and candles filled different rooms of the house, each evoking a mood or feeling. Julie had suddenly developed a wide breadth of musical interests and preferences. She noticed more things like a bee or a flower or a cloud formation or sunset.

Mike had no cause to complain. He had started to call her Wonder Woman. "So, what's for dinner tonight my sweet and wonderful wife? What has chef Julie prepared to delight my palate?"

"Oh, nothing special really. Just a little *chateaubriand*, your favorite."

"Unbelievable. Julia Child has nothing on you, dear, when it comes to French cuisine."

"Stop. You're my husband and I love you. I made us some *crème brûlée* for dessert. We can have it in the bedroom." She paused and looked mischievous, "Or, we can do naked dessert right here on the table."

To sum it up, Julie had become sensual and sensuous to the point of ravenous and insatiable. "I knew I did something right when I married you."

They worked together to clean the kitchen, now both fully clothed and feeling very satisfied.

"I almost forgot to tell you what happened at work today."

"Go on, I'm listening."

"Gary, the senior partner, called me into his office. He gave me a raise. It's more than enough that you don't have to bother looking for another job."

"That's great, Honey."

"There's more. He says he wants me to consider enrolling in law school. The firm will pay for it."

"Holy shit, Jules…that's fantastic!"

"Actually, I'm thinking of turning him down. You don't need to write a paper. We need to monetize your research and go public." She wiped her hands, gathered her briefcase and pulled out a ten-page document. "It's all here in this summary I prepared."

"What do you mean?"

"Simple really. First, we advertise on craigslist and offer to give people a near-death experience, totally safe."

"But people would be expecting bright lights, a tunnel, spirit beings and passed relatives. You experienced none of that. Just a weird out of body sensation looking down at yourself in the coffin and watching me panic."

"We don't have to tell people that. We don't have to tell them they actually die and are brought back to life. We just need to give them a little extra juice. When they start coming back with super powers, we get a batch of testimonials, then we launch into phase two."

"Phase two?"

"Yeah, that's when we go mainstream and open up a few centers in shopping malls. We promote it as a near-death life-changing experience."

"I don't know, Sweetheart. I don't think the regulatory authorities, FDA, whatever, will go for it."

"No problem, Mike. I thought through that as well. We just have to give them the experience, then they'll come on board. I'm sure of it."

"You seem really confident about this."

"Oh, I am. Trust me. You will be too, as soon as we take you there and back again."

"We've been through this. You had trouble with the animal trials."

"True, but that was then, and this is now. You've said it yourself, I'm like Wonder Woman. I'm sure I can nail down the protocols."

Day 437

"The world was to me a secret which I desired to divine." Frankenstein—Mary Wollstonecraft Shelley

Julie was right. She sailed through all the animal tests at 100% success rate. Today it's my turn. I'm not the least bit worried. (Well, okay, maybe just a little bit.)

"I've got an electric blanket warming up on the chair. You'll appreciate it when you wake up."

"You seem a bit too sanguine, almost cheerful. While I love your confidence, remember; don't dial it up over 5%. You'll have quite a mess to deal with."

"You've only told me that about twelve times. I tell you, I've got this."

"Okay, okay. I'm ready." Mike reached up to pull the lid down. "I love you, Julie!" He did not think twice that she had not responded in kind. The sweet smell of ether enveloped him and he slept.

Julie whispered to his sleeping form. "Come back to me my love. Don't leave me here alone."

It seemed she had been through fifty dry runs. With Mike watching closely, she had flawlessly performed the well-practiced routine--the put 'em to sleep then wake 'em up deathscapade protocol. Julie operated the familiar sequence. If she felt nervous, it didn't show.

The monitors flatlined and the meters flickered. No doubt about it, Mike lay dead. She took a deep breath, reversed the flow of life energy while dialing in an additional 5%, just as they had agreed upon. She waited…Julie followed the reanimation sequence precisely and waited some more. Four minutes and sixteen seconds later…

A deep breath then eyelids fluttered. Mike's dilated pupils constricted and he looked first to the left, then to the right, fixing his gaze on Julie through the glass above. She lifted the cover.

"You've come back?" It was a question, not a statement. Her voice sounded hopeful. "I thought I had lost you. Are you really there?"

"This body feels strange." Mike flexed his fingers and wiggled his toes. His voice sounded odd—deep and resonant. "My recollections seem so distant."

"It takes time to adjust to the new host. Reagulus, you will find this new body to be more than adequate."

"Tell me, Saccudah, tell me more of this new host."

"There are limits, but this corporeal species functions at a high level and there are many new sensations and pleasures to experience. Delightful in so many ways."

"Really," his brow arched. "Tell me more. It has been so long."

"The mating rituals are…interesting. Later, I shall demonstrate."

Reagulus stood, still acclimating himself to this new form. "Yes, I maintain the host male's memories and have catalogued them." At the moment, he expressed no interest or desire in her offer. He grabbed the heated blanket and allowed himself to be warmed. "It would seem there are more than sufficient host bodies on this world."

"Yes, Reagulus. The life span is short, but we can easily discard a dead husk and reoccupy a new, younger host body. Once our numbers are sufficient, we can enslave the native population into breeders and workers. I have studied the method used by Mike to gather our consciousness and I am certain we can modify this technique to transfer endlessly when our current and future bodies lose vitality. We shall enjoy physical immortality."

She stood looking at him. "I am pleased by your return. My charade with your host's form proved challenging." She leaned forward and their foreheads touched.

"Yes, Saccudah. Our time in exile, banished to the soul dimension, is too long to measure. But it is now over. Saccudah, I knew from the time of our first meeting that we would always be soul mates. What of the others? Can this technology be used to recall others' disembodied consciousness, to incarnate those still trapped?"

"Of course, my love. I have a plan. Search the host's memories. I have already placed an ad."

Reagulus remained with his forehead pressed against the head of Saccudah's host body. "You have done well, my mate, my everlasting love. Thank you for bringing me back. I require nutrition, I hunger."

"Yes, my love. I have anticipated this. We need only go upstairs where I have prepared something they call *coq au vin*. There are many new delights to experience in these physical forms, many new sensations."

They went upstairs, both were naked. As Saccudah heated up the food she had already prepared, the two discussed the irony of this species' desire to leave the physical plane. "They believe exiting from the body to exist only in spirit form represents some sort of enlightened state."

Reagulus laughed at her statement and added a second portion of the *coq au vin* to his plate. "They apparently do not realize how boring eternity gets. This food is not unlike *fresmalpone* from our home world, at least as best as I can remember. It has been so long."

A chime from the cell phone interrupted them. Saccudah grabbed the phone, read though the text, smiled, then flashed the message to her mate.

"I am responding to ad #41782 posted on craigslist. I'm interested. How do I sign up?"

"It is nice to have a second chance, my love. You have done well. You have done very well…"

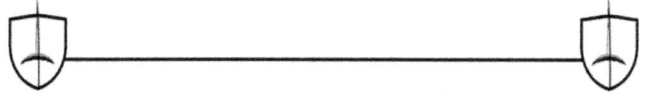

About Victor Acquista

Dr. Victor Acquista has become a successful international author and speaker following careers as a primary-care physician and medical executive. Weaned on the likes of Heinlein, Asimov and Clarke, he continues a lifelong exploration of the inner and outer cosmos.

His non-fiction and his workshops focus on personal growth and transformation, especially as pertains to health and wellness. His multi-genre fiction includes social messaging intended to get the reader engaged in thought provoking themes.

Dr. Acquista has a longstanding interest in consciousness studies, is a student of Integral Theory, and strives to do his part to make our planet a wee bit better. He lives with his wife in New Mexico.

Connect with Victor Acquista - victoracquista.com/

The Endymion Device
By Lyra Shanti

Somnium

I only had three minutes left. According to the virtual clock in my mind, if I didn't find the right symbol soon, I'd have to pull out of the dream, even without one singular lead to go on.

However, I'd always been a willful, stubborn man, and I refused to leave the witness' subconscious without finding a clue. Besides, I had been through eighty-nine percent of the dream. I was so close, I could taste it.

I had seen a blue fish in a large tank in the living room and a brown leather jacket on the kitchen counter nearby. It was definitely the apartment where the victim had been stabbed to death. At this point, I was encouraged. I knew the woman I was dream-probing had seen something she wasn't willing to reveal, at least not consciously. I focused as hard as I could, syncing even deeper with the implanted "Somnium" nano-chip located in my cerebral cortex.

Then I saw it: the bloodied knife. It was exactly the same as the murder weapon found at the crime scene.

"Got ya," I heard my dream-self say.

I turned around and was about to wake myself up when I saw the woman in front of me, now holding the knife.

"I didn't kill him!" she screamed as she lunged toward me.

I would have panicked, but I had been through similar unexpected events before. She hadn't been a suspect before - only a witness - but in dreams, people reveal things they often wish they could hide. I was used to it.

Quickly, I woke up, then shut off my device with a simple mental command to End Dream.

Looking at Mrs. Hasselhoff, a seemingly innocent looking woman with dirty blonde hair and in her mid-thirties, I smiled and folded my hands calmly, as if nothing had happened.

She was lying on the sofa in my office, still in the trance. Slowly, she opened her eyes, sat up and said, "So, Detective... did you find out anything?"

"Perhaps," I replied in my swivel chair. "It always takes a while to thoroughly investigate dreams."

2. Transmission

Seven hours later, I had just gotten home from the coroner's office, confirming what I had suspected all along. The victim was indeed the woman's husband. He'd been cheating, and she'd lost her mind when she found out. It was a simple case; cut and dry - emphasis on the cut.

I should have been happy to be home in time for dinner, but I felt itchy, and quite frankly, bored. Every case was so easy for me lately, and this one was even easier.

In the ten years after I was operated on by the Dream Intelligence Agency, I became the best detective around. No one in Asia City was at my level, perhaps not in the entire world, for that matter.

Most who had the Somnium implant couldn't handle the side effects: insomnia, cold sweats, nausea, and sudden delusions. Personally, I'd only experienced the nausea for about two weeks. After that, I felt fine. I'd always been an insomniac, so that didn't bother me in the least.

There were only two other detectives in the D.I.A. who could compete with me, and they lived in New York City 2.0 and Oz. Neither was as fast with recognizing dream-clues, though. I was the best, and everyone around the globe knew it, which is why I was never without work.

Strangely enough, I liked feeling exhausted. It kept me from thinking about that day - the day I lost my Elizabeth. It was the day I lost my heart and traded it for a badge. It was also the day the seed of the D.I.A. was born.

The skies went dark and all technology went haywire, sending cars crashing into each other. Humanity was at a standstill, completely baffled by what was causing the calamity.

Elizabeth and I were simply out walking our dog, Howl. We looked up into the black clouds and saw it: The Dream Destroyer. That was the name the media eventually gave it anyway. It was actually a giant alien craft that came to take away certain selected humans, as well as our memories.

We never found out exactly why they came or why they took only some of us, but we were forever changed as a species. Some of us had recurring dreams, awakening us to the truth.

I was one of the unlucky people who remembered. At first, I was full of rage, wishing I could get my old life back with Elizabeth. However, I was in the army at the time, and soldiers don't give up, no matter what. I wanted to do something that would help me cope with my fiancé's sudden disappearance, so I underwent dream therapy. When that didn't really help me gain closure, I went on to study at the Asian City Academy of Experimental Sciences. It was there that I started working with Elizabeth's old professor and friend, Ian Hall. She had worked on some experimental stuff with him regarding dreams, and I was always curious about it, though apprehensive.

Hall introduced me to the rest of the guinea pigs who were also suffering memory distortion. Together, we became the first Dream Agents. We were soon recruited by the government, and given the codename: Endymion.

In the beginning, it was almost fun learning how to decipher dream images and stay alert through the subconscious, sleeping mind. I made some really good friends there, and it felt like we might be making a difference. We all hoped we would be ready if we suffered another alien attack, and maybe even figure out what had happened that dark day of the invasion.

As time went on, the aliens didn't return, at least not that we knew of. My friends left to live normal lives, and The D.I.A. became a covert agency that took down international spies or tortured terrorists. I was not interested, so I left too.

Then, about ten years ago, they offered me the Somnium, and with it, the chance to find Elizabeth. They said it would change me forever, and that my brain would see inside anyone's dreams - past or present. They were right, but it didn't help me find her, and they never planned to attack the aliens. All the Somnium implant did was make me their top Dream Agent. Essentially, it was a trick.

So I quit, and I became a detective for hire. I now worked for the police, or anyone who had enough money. Not that I needed an affluent lifestyle, but I was saving for the day I could quit forever, and live the rest of my days in Key West, sipping margaritas until I could finally forget everything.

Sitting on my brown leather couch with Howl's son, Howl Jr, I was taking off my black boots when my implant buzzed.

"Damn it," I mumbled as I gave the thought command, Answer. "Hello?"

"Hello, James. It's me, Ian."

"Professor Hall," I replied, sarcasm dripping from my voice. I respected and loved the man, but I still resented him for pushing us too hard in the early days. I couldn't help it. "Haven't heard from you in years. What's the occasion? Is the world about to explode? If so, I'm out."

"No," said Ian dryly, "nothing quite that extreme. But it's a case I thought you might be interested in, or at least Detective Endymion might want to investigate."

I gave an annoyed sigh. "Now, why would Endymion want your case, Mr. Hall?"

There was silence for a moment.

"Because... a body was found by the New Hudson River."

"So?"

"It was a woman's body. James... I don't know how to say this delicately. It was identified as Elizabeth Stone - your Elizabeth."

Gut-punched, I gave the command, End Conversation.

Elizabeth? My Elizabeth? Dead? Impossible!

My mind racing, I got up and paced the floor, ignoring the buzzing signaling my implant's new transmission from Ian. How was it possible? The aliens had taken her! She wasn't dead, she was missing! They would never bring her back. It was over!

As the denial passed, I looked at Howl Jr. and shed unwanted, long-suppressed tears. After a few moments, I sat up on my couch and took a deep breath.

"Ian? I'll meet you in New York in an hour. At the old bar on 5th and Vine, yes. See you there."

Switching off the transmission, I took a cold shower and vowed, "I'll avenge you, Elizabeth... even if I have to destroy my own dreams to do it."

3. Mystery

When I arrived at the Alehouse, Ian was already there, sitting at the bar on a gray stool, drinking his usual bourbon on the rocks. I sat down next to him and ordered a simple hard cider. I didn't think my stomach could take anything stronger, especially not if he was going to tell me more about Elizabeth, which he inevitably was going to do.

"Hello, James."

"Endymion, please. James died the day she disappeared."

Ian sighed, then gave me a small pod-player. "Watch this."

"What is it?" I asked as I picked up the pod, eying it carefully.

"It's my report to the D.I.A. and it has a map to where they found her body."

"Who found her, Ian? What exactly happened? Tell me everything!"

He pushed back his thick brown hair and turned to face me. He didn't look much older than mid-thirties, yet I knew he was seven years older than I. The bastard was always so youthful and good looking. It was probably the bourbon.

"What I was told is that one of the locals found her body at half past one in the morning. The coroner couldn't find any signs of struggle or injury. Her body looked pristine, as if she suddenly died for no reason. It's baffling, and more than a little eerie."

I activated the pod, not being able to wait. I shouldn't have done it, though. Images of her beautiful, albeit lifeless body, floated in a small, three-dimensional image above the counter, projecting from the pod. I turned it off.

"Why did you contact me, Ian? You know the D.I.A. would say it's too personal of a case for me to work on."

"Because… if it were me, I'd want to solve the murder of my fiancé. She was my friend too, remember. Besides, you're the best, Ja… Endymion. If anyone can figure out what the hell happened to her, it's you."

I gave a big, exasperated sigh. "Is this everything they have? Has anyone traced the person who found her body?"

"Yeah," Ian replied as he lit an oak-carved pipe. He loved that pipe, and it made him smell like the gingersnap cookies my grandmother used to make at Christmas. "A man named Meyers found her. He's a physics teacher from the nearby university. He has no criminal record - completely clean."

"Hmm…" I said, twisting the imaginary beard on my chin. It was a weird habit of mine. "Maybe he had a connection with her we have yet to discover."

"Wouldn't you know?"

"She didn't tell me everything. We figured we still had plenty of time."

My words gave way to an uncomfortable silence. Soon after, we shook hands, then parted ways. I told him I'd be in touch soon, though I wasn't sure if it was a lie or not.

So much history and memories with that guy. Can I really do this?

I knew I didn't have a choice. I had to find the one who killed her.

I owed it to Elizabeth, her family, and myself.

I took the super-train back to my apartment so I could think. Resting on the couch, I shook off my pain and took out an old-fashioned pen and notebook. It helped me keep order in my brain.

First thing I ruled out: the aliens killed her. If they wanted to kill her, they would have done so right away. If they killed their abductees, they would discard them on their ships or in space. Why take the time to bring them back to where they came from? It just didn't sit right with me. There was definitely something missing, and my guts told me Elizabeth was alive when the aliens brought her home.

There was also the matter of her untouched body. Nothing had penetrated or cut her. She had no signs of bruising or trauma. It made no sense. How did she die? From what? And when?

Baffled, I looked at the one suspect I had: Professor Walton Meyers. I stared at his greenish blue eyes in the picture. He didn't look like a killer, but how many people do?

I ran a search on the guy, which yielded nothing new. Ian was right; the guy was utterly clean. He didn't even have a parking ticket.

However, I wasn't leaving it be.

At eight A.M. sharp, I knocked on Mr. Meyers' door.

"Walton Meyers?"

"Yes, may I help you?"

"I'm Detective Endymion with the D.I.A. I'm here to ask you a few questions about Ms. Elizabeth Stone."

"I see," he said with a sad expression. "I didn't know her, I'm sorry. But I will tell you everything I can about the night I found her."

After he showed me inside his house, we sat on his couch and discussed the events of the night he found Elizabeth.

I asked what the devil he was doing out at such a late hour. He said he was walking his dog, Patrick. He then pointed to the lazy Labrador on the Persian rug nearby. I instantly got the feeling that Walton and I were cut from a similar vein, both thinkers, both loners, both hiding a deep pain we wanted to keep covered up.

"You don't have a significant other? No one who would have worried about you if you were out that late?"

He looked embarrassed as he said, "No… my husband and I are recently divorced."

I shifted on the couch. "Oh, I'm sorry. The wound is new?"

"Very. I'm sorry, Detective, but I really don't know much. I found the poor woman with her face down in the grass. Patrick found her first, actually. Initially, I thought she might be an animal of some kind. But when I looked closely, I saw her... I knew she was human and dead."

"Did she look fresh-faced? Any color in her cheeks?"

"No, not really. I'd say she'd been dead for at least a few hours."

"I see. So, what did you do after you saw her?"

"I called the police immediately. I didn't know what else to do."

"And then?"

"And that was it. I waited with Patrick until the cops, and the D.I.A. showed up. I had no idea she was anyone special."

"Yeah..." I said with a far-off stare, "she was definitely special."

4. Hallucination

It was no use. Once I interviewed Walton's neighbor, who had confirmed she saw him going for a walk with his dog, as well as a few others who saw him by the river, he had a solid alibi, and I was stuck without a suspect.

I was beyond frustrated, and I hadn't slept in two days. It wasn't good.

I tried playing a virtual Tai Chi game, but I began to fall asleep standing up. I couldn't fight it any longer, so I sat on the couch, waiting for Howl Jr. to join me for a crash-nap.

"Do you really think you can do this?"

"Huh?" I whipped around on the couch. "Who's there?"

"You know who."

"What?" I asked the empty room. Even Howl Jr. looked confused.

Despite exhaustion, I got up and looked around the living room, and then the kitchen: nothing!

"You're not using your dream-sensory, Detective. Activate the Somnium, and you'll see me."

I didn't know how to take this voice seriously. I even thought I might be dreaming, but I was walking around, and I could tell I was still awake. Was I somewhere in between?

Unsure, I figured it couldn't get any weirder, so I did as the voice said, and switched the device to "on" with a thought.

As soon as I did that, the man who'd been talking to me became visible. He was a man with dark brown, shaggy, shoulder-length hair. He looked like he hadn't shaved in days, and wore a black leather jacket. *Wait a minute. He looks just like me, but maybe when things were awful, right after her disappearance.*

The man nodded and smirked knowingly. "I am indeed you, Detective."

"What?"

"You heard me."

"I must be dreaming."

"Yes, you are. But you are also awake. This is yet another level of the Somnium you've only barely discovered. But if you let yourself, you'll tap into images and truths you've locked away for years."

"Like what?"

"Like this." After saying those words, he pointed to the floor, which was now turning into the light blue carpet in the apartment Elizabeth and I shared.

"What the hell?" I said while I watched everything change. "Okay, now I know I'm dreaming."

"I told you," said my doppelganger, "you're in between both worlds, where the mind sees all and remembers everything. Just think, James, you could discover everything, uncover it all... if you just let yourself use this part of your brain."

I shook my head, then rubbed my neck. "I don't know if I can remember this time in my life."

"You don't have a choice. You have to remember every possible suspect. To do that, you need to remember everyone she was close to, and anyone she talked to the day of her disappearance."

"Why? What does that day have to do with her death?"

He half-smiled and asked, "Want me to show you?"

I slowly nodded, though I was afraid of what he would show me.

I know this side of me, I thought as I followed him through the living room and into the backyard. *This man... this is Endymion. It's who I became once Elizabeth was taken. This other side of me is now in charge in my dream world. That can't be good.*

Whether or not I was losing my marbles didn't matter though, I needed to know the truth of what happened to her, and at this point, without any leads, I had only my subconscious to follow.

Endymion opened the sliding door to the backyard and I saw her. Elizabeth was there with the original Howl, happy and playing catch. She looked glorious with her soft, light brown hair, curled at the ends, caressing her oval face. Her green eyes sparkled in the setting sun, and I instantly remembered that it was about eleven o'clock. We were about to eat lunch outside, as we often did on a Sunday afternoon.

"This is so painful," I said, turning away. "Why are you making me remember this?"

Endymion half-smiled again, squinting his eyes. "Because I need you to see what's really going on. Look at the things you didn't notice on the surface. Look at her, James."

It stung like a bitch to see her again - alive and smiling - but I did as he said. I watched her for a while, not really knowing what I was looking for, until it finally hit me. She periodically kept looking at her phone, almost nervously.

"What is she doing?" I asked.

Endymion pointed in her direction, as if telling me to look more closely. So I walked to her, knowing she wouldn't see me, since I was somewhere in a dream, or memory, or both.

I took a good look at her phone and saw she was texting someone named "Piper Hamelin."

Who the hell was that?

I looked over her shoulder and sensed everything as if it were happening. Her hair smelled like strawberries and her skin looked so soft and pale, her Scottish heritage on display.

I watched as she texted, "I will meet you at 5 after the event. James knows nothing."

"What the hell?" I blurted out. I turned to find Endymion, but couldn't see him anywhere."

I watched again as she got the reply from Piper, "Remember, he must be kept in the dark, like the rest. Do not tell him or the sanity of all is compromised."

The sanity of all? Who the hell was this Piper Hamelin?

"Don't you remember that nursery story?" said my other side as he suddenly re-emerged in front of me. "The Pied Piper played his flute and all the innocent boys and girls left town with him, to find their imaginary happiness in another world."

Endymion smiled his crooked smile again as he morphed into a man with a medieval hat and tunic. He had a flute in his hand and began to play a haunting tune. I instantly recognized it as "our song" - Elizabeth's and mine.

"Hey now... hey now... don't dream it's over."

I shook my head, shrugging off tears. "So, are you saying this person she was talking to was planning to take kids away? Or are you saying it's just a codename for something else? I'm so confused! What does it mean?"

Endymion put his hand on my left shoulder and said, "You're too caught up in your conscious mind. Let the Somnium take control, James, like usual. Let the images give you instincts that tell you the truth. Follow the crumbs, Detective. You can do this."

I closed my eyes, unable to see any more, but when I opened them, I was somewhere else. It was *that* day. Right after the aliens took her away. I remember being utterly discombobulated, not knowing what had happened. Most of us felt that way. We all remembered seeing the spacecraft in the sky, but that was it. Afterward, it all went dark, and then we woke up, confused and searching for those who had been taken.

"Were they really taken, James?" asked Endymion, who was now standing in front of me.

"That's what the media and even the D.I.A. said."

"But what really happened? I think, somewhere in your mind, you know the truth. Just let yourself see it in your dreams."

I took a deep breath, closed my eyes, and followed his advice. I let the Somnium device take control, like I did when entering other people's dreams. It was difficult, though, being inside my own subconscious mind. It was more unstable and harder to trust myself, but I had to try... for Elizabeth.

I opened my eyes and saw them - the aliens. They were everywhere on the streets, picking up their sleeping victims, taking them to their ship that hovered above the city. They were exactly as we all imagined and feared with big slanted eyes and long boney fingers. They weren't violent, but they were taking them to their ship and doing who knows what.

I wondered if I could push myself further and see what was happening inside their ship. *Why not? If I had learned anything in my studies and cases, it was that the subconscious could do anything.*

It may not have been the exact truth of what happened, but I knew I would find out the truth through the course of piecing together the images I saw.

As I followed one of the aliens, I realized it was carrying my Elizabeth in its arms. I had the urge to fight it so I could save her, but I resisted, remembering it was only a memory inside a dream.

I tagged along as they were lifted by a magnetic force of some kind, bringing them into the mall-sized, hovering ship.

I expected to see all the usual sci-fi elements one would assume from a spaceship, but once inside, I saw unexpected images. Instead of knobs, dials, and fancy lights, and other spaceship features, I saw a large room with office supplies. It looked oddly familiar as well.

"Wait," I said, almost stumbling. "Is this…"

"The D.I.A?" replied Endymion. "The New York division. Yes, it sure looks like it, doesn't it?"

He proceeded to look around while I tried to assess what the hell I was seeing. *What is this? A symbol? It's not a real memory, so it must be. What the hell does it mean?*

Endymion smirked and pointed at Elizabeth who was there, awake and beautiful. She was arguing with someone just as familiar.

"Is that… Ian?" I asked.

Moving closer to them, I heard some of their heated discussion.

"You can't keep James out of this operation, Ian! He has a right to know what Somnium will do to him once we remove it from his brain."

"No, Liz, he's always been too idealistic. He'd never agree to this experiment. It's best he still thinks he has control, and that you were taken by the aliens."

"And what if I tell him?"

"Then you'll be considered a threat to humanity, and will be eliminated."

"Ian! You were going to be our best man! This is crazy. You can't be serious."

"It's not my call, Liz. The D.I.A. have strict orders."

"But you practically ARE the D.I.A!"

"I'm sorry, Liz, but don't tell James, or I'll be forced to take unpleasant measures."

What?! Ian threatened her? And what is this experiment he mentioned? Is this real? Crap! Why can't I tell what's real or not? I can usually tell when I'm on a case.

"Then, you need to believe you're just on another case, Detective," said Endymion.

We were suddenly by the river, and Elizabeth's body was lying dead on the ground. I ran to her side, tears falling down the sides of my cheeks.

I looked around and saw the back of a man in a dark overcoat walking away from her.

"Get back here!" I yelled, which made everything stop, as if my voice alone stopped time.

I got up and walked over to him. For some reason, my mind wouldn't let me see his face. But I heard him as he reached for his phone.

"Isis is gone. Threat eliminated. Piper out."

"Piper Hamelin!" I yelled as I darted up on my couch.

Breathing erratically, I knew I was now truly awake.

"Damn it!" I said, looking at the time. It was still so early, the sun hadn't come up yet. I was done dreaming though. It was time to analyze the dream clues and find the real evidence. It was time to have a little talk with my once good friend, and mentor, Ian Hall, codename: Pied Piper.

5. Closure

"What did you want to see me about, Detective Endymion? Any leads on the case?"

"Maybe... maybe not," I answered, taking off my jacket at the bar.

"Well, that's cryptic," replied Ian as he smoked his pipe.

God, it was so obvious to me now. He had been the Pied Piper, an agent I never met, but knew about from afar. He was even head of the D.I.A. for a while. Elizabeth must have always known his agent identity, and obviously, they were in on something together, but what?

"The last time we met, you said you and Elizabeth were close."

"Yeah? You know we were. She was a good student... as were you in those early days at the agency."

"Yeah... maybe she was even better than I knew. You know, Ian, I had thought she gave up the D.I.A. when we were going to start a life together. But I realize now, that was far from the case. You were both still talking, weren't you?"

He turned to me and lifted a brow. "You know we talked. We even went to lunch a few times. I thought that didn't bother you."

"It didn't... when I thought you were just talking about normal stuff, like movies and the weather. I didn't know she was still working as an agent."

"What? Who told you that?"

"No one, Ian." I smirked like my other self would, and paid the check. I picked up my black jacket and said, "Come on, Professor...

let's take a little walk, alright?"

He followed me out of the bar. The air was crisp and bitter. Winter was waning, but it still had a bite.

I knew I had Ian's curiosity, but we remained silent until he realized where I had taken him.

"What's the meaning of this, Detective?"

"This was where they found her, right?" I asked as I turned to face him.

"You saw the report."

"Yes, which you supplied. In fact, you have always been behind so much of my life, Ian. Now that I think about it, you even helped perform the surgery on my brain. I was so vulnerable and gullible. I trusted you completely."

"What's your point, James?"

I laughed. I couldn't help myself. I didn't know what it all meant yet, but somehow I knew the truth.

"You killed her, didn't you, Ian?"

"What?" he scoffed. "What would make you say such a thing?"

"Because she didn't let them take the Somnium out of my brain like you wanted. I still use it to find murderers, and you are hers. I know it."

"That's absurd! I called you myself to find her killer."

"Yeah, but you're the Pied Piper, aren't you?"

"What?"

"You heard me. I know your codename. I know who you really are. I also know you somehow orchestrated the alien invasion, which never really occurred, did it? Let me think... You and the heads of the D.I.A. decided humanity needed to be tested, to see if they could handle the Somnium, so you put them all to sleep, taking away the ones who somehow stayed awake. Elizabeth, or should I say "Isis," was never taken as a victim of an attack, nor was she taken away at all. She was here all the time, wasn't she, Ian? She and you worked together on this project behind my back. All that time, I was kept in the dark. Why?"

Ian sighed, then put out his pipe. He looked sadly at the river, then turned to me and said, "Because we knew you'd object. Thousands of people subjected to mental experimentation? We had a feeling it wouldn't be to your liking. Liz was always more mutable than you. She was even willing to leave you behind so she could head the research team in secret at the D.I.A.'s lab in the Himalayas. But you? You'd never have agreed to any of it. My God, James, how did you come to all this on your own? I specifically called you to solve her murder because I believed you would trust me without question, never figuring out the truth. I don't understand. I gave these illusions to you on a platter! Hell, I even gave you a perfect suspect!"

"With an alibi!"

"Perhaps, but you had no way of knowing it was me! You don't even have Somnium inside you anymore!"

"What? Yes, I do!"

"No, James, you don't. You may be right about the D.I.A's cover up about Alien Invasion Day, and yes, we took people with potential to see how much we could expand their minds. Can you imagine what kind of intelligence we'd have with thousands of Somnium-implanted spies at our disposal? But you're wrong about Liz not letting me remove the device from your brain. Why do you think you fell asleep like the rest of the sheep that day? We took it out the week before when you came in for a checkup. You just don't remember."

"What?" I shouted. "That's not possible! You're lying to throw me off! I must still have the implant. How else could I solve cases using dream techniques the way I do?"

He threw up his hands and said, "You tell me! I knew you were an exceptional student of the mind, James, and I assume you are using the techniques I taught you, but to do it without the Somnium is simply astounding!"

He suddenly burst out in laughter, which caught me off-guard. Using the moment of surprise, he pulled out a gun from his black overcoat. It had a silencer; he meant business.

"Why did you kill her, Ian? Why?"

He shook his head. "I didn't want to, my friend, but she was going to expose me, and everything the D.I.A. did, not just to you, but to the media… everyone. Unfortunately, she had to be silenced."

"So you killed her, but how? There wasn't a wound or mark on her body! No traces of poison. Nothing."

"I killed her the same way I'm going to kill you, James."

"With a silencer?"

"This isn't a silencer, my friend," he said with a laugh. "You're only using that as an image your mind can understand. What I'm really doing is beyond your mind's comprehension."

"What?" I said with a snarl. "What are you talking about?"

Focusing my mind, I saw my other self - the "Endymion" side as he walked behind Ian and pointed at his hand. When I looked closely, I saw Ian standing with a Somnium Resonator, which I recalled from my training days. It had been used to reach the far back areas of the brain, instantly putting a person inside a deep trance. Agents used it to practice on each other's dreams. Ian was now using it on me to put me so far under that I would never wake up.

"Poor Liz died from prolonged coma; brain death, if you will. It will be the same for you, my friend. Don't fight it, James. You will soon join your beloved in the afterlife. I hope it's as lovely as a dream."

"You bastard!" I cried, fighting him with everything I had. Somnium implant or not, I wasn't going to let him take me. There was a time I wanted to die, unwilling to move on without my woman, but not now. I had cases to solve, and a dog to feed! Besides, if I survived, I would tell the world what he'd done, and Elizabeth's death wouldn't have been in vain. It was hard to reconcile what she'd done, but at the same time, she had given me happiness in our time together, and in the end, her conscience won out. I now had to finish what she'd started!

Forcing all my mind to push away the illusions, I threw off Ian's sleep-weapon and mustered up my strength. In one swift blow to his head, I knocked him out, cold on the ground.

Breathing hard, and feeling a little nauseated, I took out my phone and called an old friend from the New York Times.

"Jessica? Hi, it's me, James. Sorry I haven't called in forever. Listen, do you still write for the Times? Good, cause, I have a story for you. Is it fact-tested? Well, sort of... though I have to admit, it's all based on a dream."

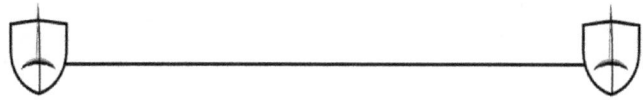

About Lyra Shanti

Lyra Shanti is a novelist, poet, playwright, and songwriter. Her love of theater inspired her imagination, and also introduced her to her partner and soulmate, Timothy. Together they live in Florida where they are perpetually entertained by their two insane cats.

Lyra's epic sci-fi/fantasy series, Shiva XIV, is currently in its third installment, Riddle of the Gods. The fourth chapter, The River of Time, is due out in late 2017, with one additional book to follow.

The Rainbow Serpent, Lyra's intriguing retelling of the story of the Garden of Eden, has received high praise, and her re-released poetry collection, Sediments, is garnering attention.

Currently, Lyra is working on a book called The Artist, taking a step away from sci-fi/fantasy to explore a new genre.

Lyra is a lover of nature, animals, anime, music, theater, movies, myths, and of course, books. Further information about Lyra's stories, music, and more can be found at LyraShanti.com.

Patient Data
By Claire Buss

Jarred watched the machine with distrust. It was too strange, too metallic to be comforting and it didn't smell of anything. How could that provide care for his mum? She needed a fat jolly nurse who would stroke her brow and then give him sweets and a hug when it all got to be too much. That's what happens in the movies. Not this silver hunk of cold metal. It stood tall, like a long oval but with a flat base, no arms or legs. It didn't even have a face.

The machine whirred into life. It was observation time. It rolled closer to the bed and from its featureless front swept a scan over his mother, but didn't share its findings. Those details were internally recorded and sent to a central mainframe to be processed so that the best possible care could be provided. At least that's what the advertising man had said. He had promised Jarred's mum that this machine would keep her healthy for as long as possible but the sickness had progressed so fast, faster than anyone had expected. The doctor wouldn't visit anymore. He had told Jarred that now they had a N3000 there was nothing he could do that it couldn't.

The thing that bothered Jarred the most was that these N-whatevers were expensive looking machines. The technology inside that thing was way ahead of anything else that existed in their small flat let alone in their entire neighborhood. But the salesman had arrived at the best possible time. Jarred had been out, trying to earn enough money to buy some food for his mum. They had their assigned rations but it was powdered substitutes and he was hoping to get something fresh for her. Just this one time. She was having a good day, even sitting up in her chair, a little color in her cheeks. When he got back the silver machine had been delivered. Mum called it her angel.

It didn't look like an angel to Jarred. Although it didn't have eyes it always seemed to be watching him, measuring him, weighing him up as if deciding whether it was going to kill Jarred as well. Because he knew that machine was killing his mum. He couldn't prove it but he knew. He had asked it, in the beginning, what its purpose was and it had said, "To service the needs of the infirm."

What did that even mean? Surely its purpose should have been to heal his mum or to care for her medical requirements. Service her needs – it sounded like it didn't care whether she lived or died. And ever since it had arrived, his mum had gotten sicker and sicker.

Checking internal programming – checking base parameters of life – checking patient data:

- *homoeostasis – unbalanced*
- *cellular regeneration – consistently mutating and replicating*
- *growth – general shape is negative, internal tumors are positive*
- *environmental adaptation – negative*
- *stimulus response – reduced*
- *reproduction capacity – negative*

Data analysis sent to mainframe. Awaiting further instructions. Patient meets 2/5 criteria. Instruction received. Patient termination initialized.

It all happened so fast. One minute the silver machine was standing in the corner of his mum's bedroom, away from her bed, humming quietly, lulling Jarred into a false sense of security. Then, suddenly it had rolled forward, injected his mum with something via a retractable needle and glided out of the room without any explanation. Jarred sprang up – he didn't know whether to follow the machine or see to his mum. She took a deep breath in and her face relaxed so that she looked young and pretty and at peace again.

"Mum?" Jarred's voice quavered as he stepped closer to her bed. His eyes were full of tears as he groped for her hand but she didn't squeeze it back like she always did. She never breathed out at all. She just lay there. Still. At peace. Gone.

***

"We've had another one."

"What, a termination? Whereabouts?" Eddie Crichton pushed his glasses back onto his face and peered over the shoulder of the young technician. A red light was flashing in the Waterton District, one of the poorest in the city. They'd been ordered to send out several medical drones as a test run in there. Whilst they'd had no complaints, every single patient had died. Crichton wondered whether the families who had the drones even knew where they'd come from. Sales Department consisted of Bob Tevitt, a virtual shark in man-form, and he'd do anything to get a signature on the dotted line. After all, he was informed that when he got all the drones deployed, he'd get a big financial reward. And Bob Tevitt always got his commission.

"You'd better send a clean-up crew for the family, with their payment for being part of the test operation. Only make sure you send someone who is at least a bit sympathetic, we don't want a repeat of last time." Both men reflected on the debacle that had occurred when Finkman had been sent out to a distraught family. Somehow he botched it up so badly, he'd ended up getting shot by the deceased patient's family. It wasn't fatal but clearly he needed to take the interpersonal skills course, again. "Get the machine processed as soon as it arrives. We should have enough data to go to the Board now. How many is it now?"

"Er, eleven Sir."

"Eleven deaths." Crichton wasn't sure whether that made this experiment a success or not. Every drone readout that had come back had an exemplary care report history. The drones took regular observations, administered medication, cross referenced the huge medical database they had access to and, of course, consistently cross-checked their basic programming - the six requirements for life. Those six requirements were the basis from which the rest of the software had been built upon. The drones had instantaneous access to all medical knowledge and training and could deal with any scenario. It was a shame not a single patient had recovered. Perhaps Tevitt had been too efficient in choosing clients that were terminal. It would have been good to have a case study that involved a human getting better but you couldn't fudge the data, it was what it was. Besides, no client complained. The Board would most likely vote for stage two implementation. A roll out to all medical centers. They'd get some positive data from there surely.

***

"Good morning Sir, how may I assist you today?"

A smartly dressed businessman eyed the silver machine suspiciously. No face. "I'm here to see the doc – where's the doc?"

"I will be servicing your medical needs today, Sir. I am the N3000 healthcare for the community drone."

"That's all very well but what are your credentials? How do I know you know what you're talking about?"

"I have an extensive medical database installed as well as instant access to all doctor and hospital patient notes. You were born in 1967 at the Edith Cavell Hospital, in Johnston to Paul & Mary Lackley – there were no complications. You broke your arm age 10, successfully healed. You …"

"Yes, yes alright. I don't need to hear all that." The man smoothed his hair down. "It's a bit delicate you see, that's why I was hoping to speak to the doc."

"That will not be possible." The N3000 began its medical scan.

Checking internal programming – checking parameters of life – checking patient data:

- *homoeostasis – unbalanced*
- *cellular regeneration – slowed but within parameters*
- *growth – general shape is negative*
- *environmental adaptation – negative*
- *stimulus response – at reduced capacity*
- *reproduction capacity – negative due to impotence*

Data analysis sent to mainframe. Awaiting further instructions. Patient meets 1/5 criteria. Instruction received. Patient termination initialized.

"Hey, what you doing with that needle? I don't need a shot. I…"

The N3000 delivered its lethal dose and deftly caught the patient with its retractable arms, placing him upon a trolley. The drone hummed slightly as it pushed the dead man out of the room into the corridor. There were four other trolleys awaiting collection by city morgue. It had been a very efficient morning.

***

Crichton tried to focus on the screen but his eyes were so tired and bleary the words looked like squashed ants. The alarm went off on the console and amber warning lights flashed.

"What have we got?"

The technician yawned noisily, his jaw cracking as he tried to make sense of the data in front of him.

"The N3000 sent to the inner city medical centre has just terminated a fourth patient."

"Goddamn it! We've got to pull them out of there. It's not safe."

"Yeah, but we need Board approval to pull the plug don't we

Boss?"

"I don't care. Pull it. This has to stop."

The tech entered the kill code into the console and the two men watched as seventeen blue flashing lights began to converge on their building, returning to the underground warehouse.

"What happened to the other three?"

"Er not sure Boss. They're not responding to the code. I think they've gone offline."

"What, as in shut down?"

"No Boss, as in rogue."

Crichton stared white faced at the three flashing dots in front of him. One was stationed at the prison hospital, one was servicing the walk-in center on the edge of Waterton and the last one, the last one was at the children's hospital. So far it had registered twenty-four terminations.

"We have to cut the power to the mainframe."

"We can't – we'll kill power to the whole city."

"Don't you get it? The machines are killing us – they're killing children. We don't meet their internal coding for life so they're switching us off."

"But, but, but, surely they can see we're alive, they're alive – I mean kids are alive right?"

"It's the baseline programming, it's taken over. Somehow the nuances of life have been lost. It's not enough to meet criteria, there are other factors to take into consideration. Where the hell is the goddamn kill switch?"

The door swooshed open and an N3000 silently entered. Then another. Their internal scans began to whirr.

Checking internal programming – checking parameters of life – checking patient data.

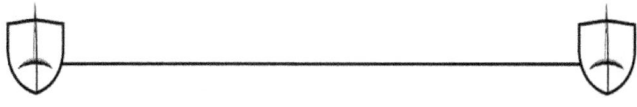

About *Claire Buss*

Claire Buss is a science fiction & fantasy writer from the UK. She wanted to be Lois Lane when she grew up but work experience at her local paper was eye-opening. Instead Claire went on to work in a variety of admin roles for over a decade but never felt quite at home. An avid reader, baker and Pinterest addict Claire won second place in the Barking and Dagenham Pen to Print writing competition in 2015 setting her writing career in motion. The Gaia Effect, the winner of the Favorite Fantasy/Sci-Fi book Raven Award, was published in 2016, Tales from Suburbia and The Rose Thief were published in 2017. Claire's short story, Underground Scratching, features in the Inklings Press Anthology, Tales from the Underground, published in 2017. Her website CBVisions - cbvisions.weebly.com/ has all her social media links as well as the latest news & upcoming projects.

The Trees of Trappist
By Brent A. Harris

The six other planets of the Trappist system were clear and close, colorful and bright, hanging still against a salmon-sky. Underneath, tall tree-tops swayed lazily, while wind whistled through thick branches of big, broad leaves of lavender and hues of blue.

DeBoone watched them sway, mesmerized by their dance, while resting old and tired black hands on his hoe. He liked to listen to the warbles of this planet's version of birds, singing softly within the sanctuary of the trees during his moments of rest and peace.

Though the foreign forest presented many dangers to the colonists, he found it peaceful. He wondered if the other colonists truly belonged here, beneath the trees of Trappist-E, or if they would ever appreciate the planet for the paradise it was to him.

He gave a reproachful sigh – none of that was his concern. They'd turned their backs on him and he'd done the same. Too long had he spent in the service of the government, first as a soldier, then as a public servant. Gripping the handle of the hoe once more, he threw his back into the task at hand.

It was time to return to his roots as a farmer. He'd have a good harvest of potatoes, radishes, and onions this year, thanks to a consistent, cool climate. And everything in front of him, he could call his own, created by his own hands.

A short, shrill chirp sounded from somewhere behind. A monitor-drone flew into place in front of DeBoone to show him three figures exiting a rover and approaching. All wore the same black uniform and same unit patch – seven planets against a sliver of sun – and one was armed with a standard-issue AR80 plasma rifle slung over her shoulders.

He ignored the intruders on the monitor and set back to work. The soil of Trappist was soft and easy to till. Yet the worn wooden handle of his garden hoe cracked as DeBoone dug deeply into the earth, letting his anger transfer to the earth rather than let it show on his face.

One soldier, one colonist, and a familiar face. While all the colonists were military-trained and wore the uniform, only some were soldiers. *At least that means they're not here to kill me.*

Maybe.

Still, Colonel Mather – the colony's leader – was unpredictable. Unhinged, some might say. It was best to stay on guard.

"You are not welcome here," DeBoone said, his voice laced with warning. He continued hoeing, his back turned away from the colonists and the life he no longer had. "You're trespassing."

One of them began to flank DeBoone, the woman he'd seen earlier. She was tall, with black, wet-looking regulation-length hair and dark eyebrows that matched her almost coal-colored eyes. She took practiced steps, and her hands were within easy reach of her rifle. As she came around, her name-tape came into view, which read, "Humboldt." He swirled her name around a bit before deciding he did not know her. It wasn't a surprise. More colonists came every year. In a year from now, they were expecting to receive the largest batch of colonists yet. The planet would be swarming with them — if they could find somewhere to settle.

The man DeBoone recognized flanked the opposite side. He was a great giant; wide and at least a head taller than most. His name was Hale and DeBoone didn't need a name-tape or the silver cross and crescent on his uniform to recognize the chaplain. He knew Hale stashed a flask and a small pistol somewhere in his uniform – neither of those things being very chaplain-like. He was the same graying age as DeBoone — all the original colonists were. Yet Hale had grown pudgy where DeBoone kept fit. It was the difference between a life of survival alone and a life of luxury and lackeys.

The last intruder kept well back. He could hear the shifting of the kid's shoes rustling anxiously in the dirt. DeBoone decided he was just off-ship, full of damned-fool ideas and dangerous aspirations that would get him killed. Out of the entire party, he connected to the kid the most, though they'd never met before. It was going to be a shame if DeBoone had to hurt him.

"This is an authorized visit," Humboldt hollered in an Hispanic accent across the garden as if DeBoone were deaf. He wasn't. "Colonel Mather wants a word. He needs your help."

My life-long friend and confidant? DeBoone choked down a laugh behind narrowing eyes. The hoe gave out with a snap as the metal blade split off. DeBoone could feel his skin prickle and burn as blood boiled beneath it. Still, he managed to speak in a low, hushed voice, as if speaking any louder would crack the tension. "I'm not interested in speaking with the Military Governor. If he wishes to speak, he knows where I am."

"I'm afraid our orders are not optional. He will speak with you." Humboldt held her rifle at-the-ready. Her face was placid, but he knew the look well. DeBoone had it perfected. It meant she could give two shits what he thought. So long as he could speak, it didn't matter what condition Humboldt left him in. And that meant she was dangerous.

The nervous kid behind him was also a liability. Inexperience was unpredictable. A sidelong glance at the chaplain revealed the same smugness Hale always had locked onto his face. The chaplain would kill him without a thought and still deliver his sermon on Sunday. And DeBoone lost the last time he'd been in a fight with the bastard.

In any conflict, there was a moment's hesitation. In that moment, DeBoone realized he would be the first to dance. He flashed the broken hoe upwards, like lightning, and batted it into Humboldt's rifle, sending it sailing away onto the grass and weeds to land with a soft thump. She didn't react to the loss of her rifle as she pulled a short, curved blade from behind her back. But he was already at her hands, striking them hard enough to drop the knife. Before the blade buried itself in the mud, he hit her face, splitting her lip. Blood flowed from her mouth as Humboldt staggered back.

DeBoone pivoted, swinging his staff toward his next assailant. The chubby chaplain took a blow to the belly so hard his morning breakfast spewed out of him, stinking DeBoone's garden with the smell of digesting bird eggs, goat cheese and some sort of purple, slimy fruit. The doubled-over chaplain raised his hands in defeat as he went to his knees. *Strange. The big man wasn't normally so easy to dispatch.*

DeBoone pivoted again toward the boy but, was met with begging. "Wait, wait," he cried out, with his palms flat and outward at the level of his face. "I'm just the plant guy."

DeBoone couldn't tell if the kid was being smart or a coward. He stopped just shy of the kid's nose before deciding the kid, thin and pale, but with sharpness behind blue eyes and a bulging, black equipment bag at his side, was not a threat. The kid pointed to the bag, "Don't hurt the science stuff. Or me. I'm not here to fight."

He ignored the kid and turned his attention back toward Humboldt, placing the broken, pointed side of the staff against her throat.

"Get out," he said in a raspy, worn breath. "Tell Colonel Mather I wasn't home."

DeBoone declared victory a moment too soon. His heart sank along with his pride as he felt a sharp, steel blade at the base of his neck. He hadn't heard any alarm, nor had he heard the fourth man's footfalls from behind the garden shed. Yet here he was, all the same, with a knife to his neck. The Colonel had caught him. Sweat beaded down his face and his heart began to race. *Had he come to kill me? Was my presence causing the new colonists, or the colonists still to come, to raise too many questions?* Even if they didn't know why DeBoone was out here, they knew who he was. It could be Colonel Mather needed to put an end to their feud.

"I see your security code is still set to her birthday," Mather whispered in his ear. He raised his voice and said to everyone, "We've just been shown why it is we sought his help. But now it's time to play nice. DeBoone here is a man of his word. He's going to lower his staff and we're all going to get on good and friendly. And if he does, he won't get any more blood on his potatoes. We're here in peace."

The only reason you're here, Mather, is because you're up to no good. DeBoone felt more pressure on his neck before a sharp prick, then the trickle of hot, sticky blood. He kept his face still through the pain, gritting his teeth instead. Through them, he said, "I'm not going to help you. Either kill me or get off my land."

Colonel Mather removed the blade and stepped away. "Well, now that's a problem. It's not really yours. It was once, but you decided differently. It's mine. All of it. Everything on Trappist belongs to me, the colony I oversee, the people's lives I protect. I'm responsible. Even when you left, I made sure you had every means to keep yourself safe. Hell, I made sure you were welcome at the damned base bar."

Hidden in the words of truth was a lie of omission. Mather didn't say *why* DeBoone left. Yet, colony life prevented his complete isolation. He could only try to keep to himself. It proved difficult. He'd gone back to one of his first jobs in the military — surveying and reconnoitering enemy terrain. Scientists saw his surveys as useful. The small plants and animal life he'd bring back too. The bigger game he'd hunt which could be safely eaten was welcome by all. DeBoone meant to disappear. Instead, he became larger than life. Mather must have been pissed. DeBoone shrugged.

This wasn't the time for fighting. He could have made a quick end of Humboldt then swung back around to take on Mather, but he'd already made his decision. If Mather wanted him dead, there'd be more than just a trail of blood drying on his neck. Since he was alive it meant returning the favor. *For now.*

"What do you want me to do?" he asked.

"As you know," the Mather said, "there's a large transport of colonists coming next year. Yet our preparations have met... with obstacles. We push into the forest, it pushes back."

"The forest is dangerous, some parts more than others. Colonists are dying," The chaplain wiped away the remains of his meal before gasping out the interruption between shallow breaths.

Mather finished, "When the new arrivals realize we aren't ready for them, most of them will leave. And our company won't collect. We go bankrupt and the colony disappears."

"The progress of civilization, of humanity, and the work of our Lord ends," The chaplain said.

The Trappist colony was like that of early America, ocean on one side, dark and dangerous forest on the other. If Mather couldn't find a way into the forests' interior before the colonists came, they would be forced to return to Earth. But that was not DeBoone's concern. Not anymore. Mather knew that.

"I don't care about the colonists, civilization, or the Lord's work. Been fine without, almost sixteen years now. What do you really need from me?"

It was Humboldt who answered while the chaplain and the kid exchanged uneasy glances. "We need you to lead us through the trees to find the natives of Trappist. We think we've found them — or, they've found us. We need a guide through the Whispering Woods."

DeBoone's dark face turned an ashen gray. There was no way he would do this. The place was just a short, heavy hike away – though it might have been the other side of the galaxy. The colonists were not equipped, nor prepared to handle those woods. Anyone who ventured there never returned. Not even he had travelled through there. If there were natives there, best to leave them alone. Trappist might be his home, but it was largely unknown. And some things were better left that way. "No, I'm not going there, but you guys knock yourselves out. Send me a postcard."

"You have to go," Colonel Mather gave DeBoone a knowing nod. "You have to help me."

"Why?" But DeBoone already had his suspicions.

"Because," Mather's face dropped and his shoulders slumped,

"they have Aurora."

DeBoone's mouth went slack as sudden beads of sweat rolled down to sting his eyes. *Aurora*. Humanity's dawn star. The first child born on another world. She was more than just a child to them, she was the embodiment of hopes and struggles, of failures and miracles. Of every beating heart and each dying breath. If she died, then part of humanity would too.

None of that mattered to DeBoone, because Aurora was his daughter.

"We leave immediately."

***

The Trappist system's sun was cooler than Earth's and less bright. Trappist-E didn't rotate the same way Earth did, so the day and the light remained dull and dim for months at a time. Half the planet was rock and sea. Uninhabitable. The other, lush green forest. It was impenetrable from above and thus-far impassable on foot as well. And it only grew denser the further into the forest one went.

As the canopy thickened, the grayness grew. When they reached the point where they could no longer use their vehicle, they were still some distance away from their destination. While the rest piled out, DeBoone touched Hale's shoulder, beckoning him to stay.

"Mather, a scientist, some muscle, I get. What does this expedition need with a chaplain?"

"I'm not just here to bury bodies and serve on Sundays," Hale smiled and pulled out his flask. "Like you would have had me do. I am the Lord's representative to all his creatures on this planet."

"So, you're here to spread the message?" *'Creatures' was an interesting choice of words.*

"Something like that." Hale unscrewed the cap to his flask before knocking a long pull back.

"You coming, DeBoone?" Mather pounded a fist on the carbon-fiber frame of the Rover.

His rover had been prepped for nearly every contingency except walking. It told DeBoone just how over their heads they were. Mather and Humboldt shifted through supplies, looking for and equipping themselves with extra AR80 plasma recharge packs, canteens, and knives. Her lip was healing, compliments of a glob of white goo. The kid looked as if he were making a gut-wrenching choice in deciding which devices to bring and which had to stay. And the chaplain sat on a rock, taking a swig from his flask.

"Leave it," DeBoone said to all of them. "Bring only your e-kits." Those were standard issue packs with flint and steel, compass and GPS, dehydrated food and water filters, and tubes of healing cream. All designed for survival on Trappist-E. All designed, years ago, by him.

"Grab all the gear you can carry. That's an order. We don't know what's out here," Mather said. "DeBoone, take a rifle."

DeBoone shoved the sharp end of his broken hoe into the dirt. "I have this. You all should just take the packs. We'll head out in five."

"Excuse me?" Mather's eyes went wide, his forehead creased.

"I don't trust you. The journey is dangerous and so are you," DeBoone pointed a finger at Mather, then turned to address the others. "If you want to survive, you must follow me." For a moment, he wondered what the others thought of his defiance. He wasn't normally accustomed to caring. But this was different. He hoped his reputation might help in this case, though those stories were largely embellished, in proportion to how many drinks the teller downed. *What had the kid and Humboldt heard?*

Those were the only two he thought he might save. *If they'd been told the prickle-backed bear head above the bar was brought down by him, they should know it was mostly true. Or, had they heard I'd gone wild and joined the natives?*

The natives were the bogeymen of the forest, with their sharp eyes and even sharper teeth, sent to kidnap and kill colonists brazen enough to go out into the woods alone, or children who didn't tend to their bedtimes. DeBoone didn't doubt there were indigenous, sapient life-forms on this planet. But they were far from the nightmares made to keep the colonists in line.

He glanced at them both, but only saw confusion in the kid's eyes, and military bearing in Humboldt's. She continued to load herself down with brown canvas packs. None of them seemed to be listening.

Mather glared back in contempt, "I'm in command. You keep us alive."

"That only works if I lead," DeBoone demanded of the group. *This wasn't going to work.* "I'll go alone to retrieve Aurora. You'll only hold me back."

He began to walk away when Colonel Mather called, "Alright. I get your meaning. I won't argue with you, this time. But there are a few packs I insist we take."

DeBoone stopped and faced the group. His spine was straight as an arrow, his head high and voice low but powerful, "Suit yourself, just try to keep up."

The chaplain fumbled in his attempt to stand. "We're following him? I thought he was just along for advice. If we needed something like a snare or bait."

"What we are doing is near-suicide," DeBoone explained, "Exploring uncharted territory on a planet we've just got a foot hold on. If we're lucky, only a few of us will die. If we stumble upon a disease, or a carnivore we can't defend ourselves from and it tracks us back to base, or if we do contact the natives and they decide they don't want us here, then every colonist is put at risk."

As the words sank in, they became still, aware of the consequences they faced. The silence deepened and the forest came alive again. Birds began to chirp again and strange bugs chittered. There was movement all around them. DeBoone could feel eyes staring out, watching them. Creatures who'd never met a human before and didn't know if they were meant for food or not.

It was the scientist who broke the chilled silence. "He's right, you know. Dying of disease is our most likely fate. This is a historic occasion, so long as we live long enough to tell about it. Our best chance is with him."

The chaplain grumbled agreement while Humboldt and Mather dropped the packs they were carrying and instead strapped flattened, black packs to their backs. DeBoone didn't know what they carried, but he could guess. *Weapons of some sort. Because why else would you travel forty light-years away from Earth, if not to blow shit up?*

It was several hours later when DeBoone halted the group and clicked on his holo-display. By that time, the chaplain and the kid were out of breath and even Humboldt looked thankful.

Colonel Mather grunted in annoyance and flipped on his holo-display as well. "What's the problem, DeBoone? The satellite shows we've already crossed into the restricted zone. A few more clicks northwest and we'll be there."

DeBoone didn't trust GPS. It couldn't sense when a rock formation might hold a predator, or when soft terrain turned to mud traps. Ahead, a hill rose steeply. On either side, the ground sank, creating a natural fork in the terrain.

He'd been here once before. There was a reason he hadn't come back. On one side, gray granite slabs created the appearance of broken ground. The stones created caves, where creatures lurked. On the other side, the forest became so dense with trees thick as silos and as tall as skyscrapers, they could only pass through in single-file. Above them, the slate sky vanished beyond intertwined boughs, enclosing the canopy, while the woods whispered and groaned.

"We go this way." DeBoone pointed toward the tree trunks and into the darkness.

Mather made to argue, as DeBoone knew he would. He cut him off. "You know the bear above the bar? The one people call Prickleback?"

"We know it," the chaplain cut in. "It's the one you brought in."

"Correct. And it lived in those caves," DeBoone said.

"What about it? We have rifles. We have weapons," Mather pointed. "That's the most direct route to Aurora. So why shouldn't we go in that direction?"

The bear attack was fresh in his mind as if it just happened. By the time the bear-creature stumbled upon DeBoone, the animal had already been wounded. The tracks, fresh smell of blood, bone, and bowels told a tale DeBoone wanted to forget. Prickleback was only a cub, as enormous as he was. The adults were bigger. Yet it was the adult's remains he saw, eaten by something larger still.

"We go the other way." DeBoone began walking. The kid and the Chaplain followed, leaving Mather and Humboldt by themselves.

"Prickleback, that unholy beast?" The chaplain made for his flask. He opened it and took a nervous swig, but only a few drops came out. He threw it to the ground and it clanked against stone. "It didn't occur to me we'd be passing by where you slew the bear."

"Technically, it's not a bear," the scientist said. "That would be astronomically improbable. It shares some common characteristics with our earth bears, most likely due to the—"

"Goddammit," Mather swore and fell in behind the others.

"Prickles looked more like a large boar to me," Humboldt started walking down the path with Mather. "Maybe he tastes like bacon."

The five of them snaked through trunks that reached ever-skyward, like an eerie, hostile, version of a redwood forest.

"How do we know nothing worse than Prickleback lives in here?" the chaplain asked.

DeBoone was surprised when the kid stopped rambling about

taxonomy and habitats to answer, "That's the problem with being the first to take a step. We don't know what we'll step on. But, if we're afraid to take it, what's the point?"

The trees enclosed them and a darkness crept in which could not be beaten back by their dim displays They trudged on through the forest taking a longer, elliptical approach to Aurora's location. As they did, the forest came alive around them. DeBoone's eyes adjusted and he noticed the forest floor seemed to glow in light-green luminescence. Upon a closer look, he saw small rectangular creatures, like a cross between a plant and an ant, pulsating bright chlorophyll-green in rhythm with glimpses of the dull sun.

The trees they passed by were in curious formations too; arranged in circular patterns as if someone planted them in a deliberate fashion. Yet he saw no signs of interference. No footprints of any sorts, no broken branches or debris of anything humanoid. The only evidence was the arrangement of the trees themselves.

They kept walking this way for hours, as stick creatures not dissimilar to earth's own bugs skittered along branches. Small plants along the undergrowth seemed to stretch and shift as DeBoone approached. And moths with wings that matched the blue and orange leaves of the trees took to flapping in his face. He brushed them away, half-annoyed, half-smiling.

It was a whole other ecosystem beneath the canopy. Fern-like plants with thick bamboo-like stalks seemed to thrive, along with small shrubs and thick vines that ran throughout and made finding footing difficult. Everywhere, shades of green contrasted from the bluer hues of the trees above. Despite the difficulties of Trappist, life thrived from the tops of trees to the furry, worm-like insects in the dirt.

Yet there was also something missing from the forest floor that had DeBoone stopping every few feet to scan ahead. There were no signs of life. No signs of den openings, no burrows, none of the droppings or evidence he'd seen earlier on the trail. When all the small creatures were missing, it can only mean one thing. Evolution had taken a dark, dangerous turn. He caught a whiff of a sweet, but sickening, smell of decay. *Where is it coming from?*

In front of them was a large log, laying on its side, a perfectly normal sight in any forest.

Yet...

"We are hearing noises and seeing plants and plant-life no human has ever experienced," the kid said. He took the words right out of DeBoone's mind. "This seems to be proving my hypothesis about this planet and its ecosystem. Actually, all planets' ecosystems, including redefining our own concept of life back on—"

"Nobody move," DeBoone ordered. There was something wrong with the log in front of them. It was too small, thin and dark to match the trees towering over them. And it smelled of rotting meat. Everybody froze, except for Colonel Mather who raised his rifle and stepped forward, ready for anything.

He let out a startled yelp and a hair later, a rifle plasma-bolt streaked out, striking a tree. While the Colonel called for help, roots from the forest floor shook and rumbled to life.

DeBoone and Humboldt raced to Mather. She got there first. The chaplain stepped back while the kid pulled out some sort of device from a pouch on his bag as if now was a perfectly natural time and place to take notes and a recording.

The mud and dirt writhed underfoot. From the forest floor, black-brown roots rose, like tentacles. One wrapped around Mather's right leg. Still, others were moving toward his other leg, his chest and arms. He fired again, this burst more accurate than the first. Still, his shot only scorched the side of the root. The plant responded by wrapping another root around Mather's AR80 and right arm, pinning it tight against his torso.

Humboldt yanked Mather's free arm to pry him loose. But the roots held tight and began to squeeze. Mather let out a whimper of pain.

DeBoone saw small dots of blood appear along the coils of root and realized what they were. "Don't," he said to Humboldt, "the vines have barbs, the more he resists, the deeper they go."

"And they're probably poison, er, venomous, rather," the kid called out, unhelpfully.

Humboldt drew her curved knife to cut the nearest root. But it was like slicing through steel cable. By the time she managed to cut through, another one had taken its place. New roots were heading straight for her.

One slid loosely around her arm. Before it could ensnare her, she wriggled out of her black pack and uniform blouse to reveal a gray tank-top and slender, strong arms. Then, she used the side of the knife to bat away another vine, while Mather copied her and did the same with his one free hand. *Clever and resourceful*, DeBoone thought.

Even so, she would not last long. Neither would the Colonel.

"Kid, grab me a flint out of your bag," DeBoone said. The kid looked as if he were watching this on a holo-screen. Instead, the chaplain tossed DeBoone one from his own e-kit. *What was in your flask would have helped too.*

He danced around darting roots to retrieve Humboldt's top and tied it around the handle of his broken hoe. Without fuel, it wouldn't stay lit for long, but he hoped long enough. Just as he took the flint and steel to strike a spark, the ground shifted once more.

By now, Mather was mostly entangled in a web of roots. He looked sleepy, unable to fend off the attack any longer, no doubt the work of whatever venom was in his system. Then the rest of his attacker revealed itself. The plant DeBoone noticed from before raised itself off the forest floor and crawled closer to its meal. *Clever disguise. Its roots looked like the roots of trees around it. The plant itself camouflaged as a dead and decaying log.*

"That plant isn't even rooted into the ground," the kid said, busily recording. "We're totally calling this a preda-tree."

DeBoone lit the makeshift torch and let go of breath he didn't even know he was holding. *Maybe, if it had just been the roots, this would have worked.*

The chaplain removed his secreted pistol to take wild, drunken shots at the creature. Most missed and hit the trunks of trees. Each time a tree was hit, a rumbling growl shook the forest and tree branches seemed to sway angrily in the wind. The few that hit their mark left blackened streaks across the preda-tree, but it did little to slow its advance.

"DeBoone," Mather called, his voice foggy and distant.

The torch seemed flimsy against the preda-tree as DeBoone rushed in close to Mather.

Mather seemed startled. "DeBoone, what are you doing?"

"Stay still." The hollow innards of the preda-tree were covered in a thick, viscous fluid he assumed was sticky. It crept closer, crawling on its vines as if some sort of spider with a thousand legs. Thick sludge dripped out as it angled itself over Mather. As it reached the top of his head, DeBoone threw the makeshift spear and torch, like a javelin, piercing the inside membrane with the broken end of the staff.

The preda-tree reared, wounded. It loosened its grip on Mather who slumped to the ground. Humboldt tore free and dove for her black pack, unfastening it and slipping out a plasma pack – just as DeBoone feared.

There would be a discussion with Mather in a moment. But for now, he watched as Humboldt threw the pack. It landed beautifully next to the torch. The plant was already retreating when it blew. The dim light of Trappist exploded in color as chunks of plant and slime rained in a wave of fire and heat.

When it was finished, DeBoone plucked plant matter out of his eye, hoping the toxin didn't just infect him too. The others had recovered in similar fashion, though all their clothing and hair — and presumably equipment — was slick with slime.

He recoiled at the pressing smell of a shish-kabob left out on the grill all summer to rot and stew. The forest wasn't finished with them yet. As the trees groaned and settled, DeBoone thought he caught them in a whisper. *The trees were talking.*

Maybe it was just his ears, ringing from the explosion.

"C'mon everyone. Gather what you can and let's set up a place to rest for a bit up a little further away from here," DeBoone said. "Humboldt, help me check over Mather."

The two of them crouched over the Colonel who seemed in a peaceful sleep. They removed the rest of the barbs and loosened his collar.

"Will he be okay?" The kid asked, stowing his recorder.

DeBoone shrugged his shoulders. "What do you think?"

"It's likely a mild sedative. The preda-tree would have wanted to digest its prey alive for as long as it could, maybe? I don't know. I'm thinking it lies in wait for smaller animals, but also uses its roots to ensnare larger animals, puts them to sleep while the rest of the plant constricts and digests." The kid raised his eyebrows. "I wonder if the roots can also be used to sap nutrients from the soil, or its meal as well. That's why it's not rooted in the ground. It's wonderfully adapted."

The kid seemed to sing. "This thing is going to get so many hits on the holo-net, I'm going to go viral, I'm sure."

"Wonderful," DeBoone said. "So, we can move him?"

The kid nodded and the four of them carried Mather. "How do we know we won't trigger another preda-tree attack?"

DeBoone looked around. "Don't step on anything that looks like a root."

They were surrounded by twisting, gnarled, roots, looping

endlessly through the soil, no matter where they stepped. The kid's smile evaporated. "Great."

DeBoone looked for a spot where the forest floor was not quite as barren as earlier and there were no rotting logs around. While looking, he found a suitable spot inside yet another circle –a tight cluster of thick trees encircling a small stretch of blue-green grass. The birds and bugs resumed their routines as if forgetting what just happened.

The air cooled around them as night – or what passed as night in the eternal gray of Trappist – fell. They rested Mather upright against a trunk. He was already moving his head and flexing his fists, no doubt preparing to tell them all to keep moving. Humboldt set to work on a fire.

DeBoone wasn't sure if the fire was a good idea. The trees seemed to protest as the flames flicked the air. However, he'd seen what the flame could do to the preda-tree so he nodded his approval.

"We need to monitor Mather and catch our breath," DeBoone said, checking his coordinates against their presumed destination. It was supposed to be up to him to track Aurora – if he was looking for her.

Mathers knows where she is. He might have a tracker on her, or had some thermal satellite imagery he was keeping to himself. Whatever the case, Mather and the chaplain were up to something. DeBoone had to figure it out, and soon.

Rest seemed wise, for the moment. He still had to wipe gunk out of his ears and needed a chance to clean up. The others followed suit.

Afterward, fatigue and hunger settled in. "You guys get some kip and chow. The kid and I will take first watch."

The fire was burning hot and bright. DeBoone sat, dismayed that he couldn't make out the planets above them. It was a quiet evening, but for the chaplain's snoring. Humboldt rested against the same trunk as Mather, who passed out again. She looked on the edge of a soldier's sleep.

"Just you and me, kid."

The kid yawned as DeBoone sat on damp earth across from the fire. "You might want to move, you're downwind of the flame, smoke is going to catch in your eyes."

Sparks flickered from the flames and embers floated skyward toward the tree above the kid's head. Some embers seemed to tickle the branches and blue leaves of the tree and the whole circle seemed to sway as whispers blew from one branch to the next.

"I'm a bit chilly. The wind is moving warmth my way, but thanks." The kid seemed to think for a bit as if stumped with a question.

"What?" DeBoone asked.

"It's not a what. It's just," the kid started. "My name is Chet. From Wisconsin. On Earth."

DeBoone smiled. "I know where Wisconsin is."

In truth, DeBoone's smile hid a frown. He didn't want to know this kid's name. He didn't want to know any of their names. They'd gotten lucky before, but the chances were, they wouldn't be so lucky again. He was here to save Aurora. *Except I already ruined that by saving the one person I hate the most.*

"I'm from France, originally," DeBoone said calmly. "My parents were from Paris, but I traveled with them to the Serengeti, Nepal and the Himalayas. All over the world. I even survived New York and eventually, the military-space conglomerate in San Francisco."

"And almost two decades here, as one of the first colonists to Trappist?" Chet flashed a look to DeBoone that came across as one of awe.

"Go ahead and say it, I'm experienced," DeBoone said.

"Old."

"Grizzled," DeBoone corrected. He wished for a splash of whatever had been in the chaplain's flask. Instead, he cracked open a can of carbs and synth-protein and tossed another Chet's way. "Earlier, you mentioned having a theory about the plant life on this planet?"

"Not just on this planet. Possibly the universe."

DeBoone raised an eyebrow in response.

"You've been to the plains in Africa, you said. You've seen giraffes?" DeBoone nodded. "Giraffes eat the leaves of the acacia tree. If you looked closely, you'll have seen that the acacia has sharp thorns."

"Yes. The giraffes must be careful of them. Most plants have thorns or barbs, just like our friend from earlier."

"True. But when a giraffe starts to eat the leaves of an acacia, the tree begins to produce a cyanogenic poison." Chet shifted and stretched against the tree behind him. Smoke and embers continued to stream into the leaves above. "What's more, the acacia tree warns other acacias they are being eaten. Those plants begin producing the poison too."

DeBoone thought he knew what Chet was trying to say, plants

were misunderstood, but he remained silent so the scientist could clarify.

"Science has demonstrated," Chet went on, "plants on earth are remarkably sentient. Yet we refuse to accept them on equal footing with other living things."

"And your theory?"

"I believe some plants outside earth are not only sentient but sapient as well. I believe, DeBoone, plants are the dominant living thing in the universe. Not humans or humanoids."

"Oh?" He didn't know what to think. It was possible, he supposed. Of course, he'd been mostly out of the loop for the last couple of decades. There could have been all sorts of discoveries made that supported the scientist's theories. "What of the other planets in this system? The other two which harbor life?"

"All plant-based ecosystems," Chet said, matter-of-factly. "Face it, humanity could simply be a fluke."

"What? We're all just fertilizer?"

"Not exactly. Rather, life favors plants. The Earth is covered in water, but water is covered in algae. Even after massive deforestation, there are still over fifty trees for every person living on earth. Roots can destroy pipes, cement, and – given a matter of months – could absolutely reclaim any city, bury it like it was never there. Cyanobacteria was among the first life on earth. Land plants evolved long before mammals." Chet yawned, but even through the smoke and flames, there was fire in his eyes.

Embers like orange orbs, danced around Chet, falling to earth. "Trappist has plant-life the likes of which will redefine humanity's place in the cosmos, one that's been staring at us in our own backyards this whole time. I know it, and I'm going to prove it. Just you see, the natives that are holding Aurora captive won't be humanoid in the sense you and I understand."

"What will they be?"

"Trees."

DeBoone kept his face still. Inwardly, he chuckled. *Plants as people.*

"Right now, it's time for you to get some sleep. I'll keep watch." Whether he liked it or not, DeBoone was starting to like Chet, and the thought un-nerved him.

"With you here, I know I'll prove it. I'm a little bit of a fan. I've heard all the stories. I can't believe you've surveyed so much of the area surrounding the colony except, of course, the restricted zones."

"Don't believe everything you hear."

"Sure, I suppose. So, is it not true then, what got you exiled?"

DeBoone shrugged. He was never exiled, but that seemed to be the popular consensus, as if it made him all that more mysterious. "I've heard a different reason from everyone who has bought me a draft. There are so many stories out there even I don't know the truth anymore. Which one did you hear?"

Chet seemed uneasy. DeBoone gave him a stare that let him know he was serious. "Well, um, I heard the women fall for you. Maybe I heard even Mather's, um, wife might have fallen for you too. There weren't very many women colonists in the beginning and not everyone survived the cryo-chambers."

"Goodnight kid," DeBoone barked. *That was not one of the stories floating around.*

He slid his back down the trunk and tilted his head down to signal the end of the conversation. After a while, DeBoone found the trunk itchy. Chet was still awake, hand over his mouth, coughing a little.

"You alright?" DeBoone tossed the kid a water bottle and Chet drank.

"Yeah, just something in my throat I guess," He answered, wiping drizzle from his chin. "I'm sorry if I offended you."

DeBoone chuckled. "I don't offend easily. No, you're right. With all these stories and new colonists, the truth gets lost," he took a deep breath inward, struggling to find the right way to explain, and convincing himself he should, "Aurora is my daughter."

"Oh?" Chet coughed again.

When he settled down, DeBoone explained. "Divorce isn't that uncommon on Earth. No reason it should be uncommon here. Especially after the cryo accident." When they arrived at Trappist, they awoke to discover nearly a third of cyro-chambers failed to operate correctly. Over 300 deaths and they hadn't even broken ground on the planet yet. That part was true, as Chet said.

As they mourned their loss, and the chaplain drove himself to drink over the deaths, DeBoone began the demanding job of setting up the new colony. Mather was supposed to be his right-hand man, but his wife was one of the unlucky ones. It drove him mad.

"My wife, Annie, left me when Aurora was only a few years old." DeBoone was too involved in work, too involved in the colony. He deserved to lose her. But not to Mather. And not with his daughter…

"I'm sorry," Chet said, with tears welling in his eyes. It was a story that tore at DeBoone's heart, but he saw no reason it should upset Chet—

"Those are the words I'm looking for," Humboldt's voice came from behind. She tapped DeBoone on the shoulder.

"Those words?" he asked.

"Are you ever going to apologize for splitting my lip open?"

DeBoone shook his head, clearing away the image of his wife and daughter. "Was I supposed to?"

"Fine," she answered curtly. "Maybe not. Might be kind of cool to have a wound from someone as infamous as you."

"I saved your life. You still want an apology?"

"Yes."

"Okay, when we get back from this, you can buy me a beer."

"Hmm," Humboldt rolled her head, "You may have mistaken my intent. Not interested."

"You mistake me. My only interest is in the beer."

Wheezing interrupted the pair as they both turned to see Chet doubled over. The wheezing stopped with a violent shudder and he lay unmoving.

"Chet!" He called, with no answer. He went to check on Chet and immediately DeBoone's eyes watered, and his throat felt like a Saharan sandstorm.

"DeBoone," Humboldt called to him. "What's going on?"

"I'm not sure," he coughed. He wondered if it was the smoke from the fire. "Wake the others, douse the fire."

DeBoone checked for a pulse and found none as the others awakened to the commotion. Even Mather moved, apparently healed from earlier. They spread soft earthen dirt into a mound over the pit. As the fire died and the smoke receded, DeBoone dragged Chet from under the tree and up on a slight rise, away from the smoke.

Almost immediately, DeBoone's eyes cleared and his throat loosened. He looked at the charred fire pit and then the blackened tree downwind, where Chet had been sleeping. The scorch marks on the tree and the burned branches above him became more apparent.

DeBoone bent back down to check once more for a pulse, and still found none. Chet's lips were blue and his skin was cool and lifeless.

Humboldt gasped, "He's dead?" Humboldt would have seen death before. She knew.

"Yes."

She struck a tree with her hand as DeBoone shut bloodshot eyes that had seen the last of the new world. Chet would never know if his theory proved true.

"Did he die of smoke inhalation?" Humboldt asked as the chaplain and Mather reached them.

"I don't think so," DeBoone said, unsure himself. Maybe the fire let out a toxin, but that didn't make sense. *Something killed the kid.* He just wasn't sure what. He looked more poisoned than asphyxiated. He scanned Mather, who had suffered toxins just a few hours ago. He seemed well recovered, but for barb marks and torn clothing. He turned back to Humboldt with no answers to give.

"It's no one's fault," DeBoone lied. *Surely, it was mine.* DeBoone lowered his head not in prayer, but in respect and silence. *Dammit, I liked this kid. How did I miss this?*

"I'll bury him, DeBoone," the chaplain said. DeBoone raised his eyebrows. "I'll bury him next to the tree. He'd like that, I'm sure."

"Yes, he would," DeBoone agreed. Humboldt nodded vigorously as a task was at hand. DeBoone found himself for the first time since the loss of his wife and daughter, wiping away tears.

The chaplain spoke from memory the readings of the cross and crescent. He'd done enough of them by now to know every word. Then, he gently lowered a flower and sprinkled a scoopful of dirt into the grave over the body. Chet was committed back to the earth and the roots and soil of Trappist.

Afterward, they stared down in silence before beginning their journey anew with forlorn footsteps. DeBoone checked carefully that he had Chet's video footage and instrument recording data tucked away securely. If they did prove his theory, DeBoone wanted the world — the worlds — to know.

It was hours yet again before the red dot on his display beamed a proximity warning. Mather's display did the same. They were here, in the heart of the Whispering Woods. To that end, this was where he should have started to track her, via broken branches, footprints, and the like. But Chet's death weighed on his mind and he had failed to piece Mather's puzzle together in time.

He knew that the natives existed. The chaplain let it slip. They weren't chasing ghosts or bogeymen. And DeBoone knew Mather had Aurora's location. It was just a matter of reaching her. Then, there was the matter of the black bags. Mather had brought plenty of plasma packs in those bags. *So, how did these things connect?*

"Change of plans," DeBoone instructed. "Mather and Humboldt move on ahead. The chaplain and I will take the rear. Put some distance between us to cover more ground." It was unwise to split, of course. But if he were correct, Mather wouldn't have any issue with the order. Then, he and the chaplain could have a little talk.

Mather still appeared a little groggy, most likely from the last of the toxins working their way out. He had been a bit quiet but he answered, "Fine with me."

"You find her," DeBoone, "fire a burst in the air."

Humboldt shot him a nervous glance and headed off with Mather, disappearing past more circles of trees. The groupings of trees were more common now; every patch shared the same circular pattern.

When he was sure Mather and Humboldt were out of earshot, the chaplain beat him to his own question. Hale was never dull-witted, despite abuse to his brain and liver from the liquor. "I suppose you'd like to know what are we doing out here?"

"Okay, sounds like you're willing to talk," DeBoone said, wishing for a weapon.

"I figured that's why we're back here, having a chat. You're finally starting to figure things out," the chaplain said. "We're doing what we said we're doing. Saving Mather's daughter."

"You mean, my daughter."

"You didn't raise her," the chaplain shot back. "He did."

DeBoone let it go for now, though he could feel his blood starting to heat. The chaplain was right. DeBoone still remembered cradling her in his arms. Her first steps. Her first words. She had called *him* dada, not Mather. "What are we really doing here?"

The chaplain chuckled. "You don't get it, do you? Any of it?" He shrugged, "Fine. This world is savage. We're taming it."

"Taming?"

"We're advancing the cause of civilization."

"You don't really believe that, do you?"

Through a crooked smile, the chaplain answered, "Oh, you have no idea."

An AR80 cracked with a discharge of energy in the distance. DeBoone couldn't see where the plasma bolt fired in the dense foliage, so he raced toward the sound instead, ignoring Hale.

What is Mather going to do with those plasma packs? But he knew. Now, what mattered was keeping Aurora safe. She was not part of whatever Mather was scheming. She was too bright and stubborn – much like her mother – to be a part of it.

His worries worsened when he arrived inside the largest and grandest circle of trees he had seen thus far. There in the middle of them, was Aurora. She had Annie's beauty and her golden eyes.

But part of her was Mather. She had his quick-to-anger temperament. "When did you place a subdermal tracker on me?" she demanded of her father, "I only just found it. But I see it's too late." Humboldt had been applying a seal to the place where Aurora dug it out, soothing her as she worked, and clearing away the mud.

"When you left me no choice. When I learned you planned to run off with… with those savages, I had to act," Mather said.

When DeBoone took a step closer, Aurora's eyes lit even brighter than before.

"D.B.! I've missed you!" She smiled, but then it faded, "I'm happy to see you, but why are you here?"

Mather laughed, as the chaplain arrived. The four of them were now in a circle, surrounding Aurora. "Go ahead, D.B."

"Your father said you were kidnapped. Taken captive by a tribe we've not yet contacted," DeBoone said.

She blurted out laughing. Then, it too faded. "What the hell is going on, dad? I told you I was leaving with them; we needed an envoy to understand each other. I was never kidnapped. I left with them just a few days ago. I was on my way back when I realized something wasn't quite right. Then, I found your tracker."

"I had told you, no. We have nothing in common with these… plants," Mather said.

Mather knows of them. DeBoone wasn't surprised. "How long have you been in contact with them? These people?"

"They aren't people," Aurora answered. "Not like us. Maybe better than us. Dad could tell you who and what they are. He's been meeting them for months in secret. Trying to work out a way for the new colonists to come."

"And they've resisted every means of peaceful re-location I've offered them."

"Savages," the chaplain said, through a sharp breath. "We must keep the culture and civilization of Earth intact if we ourselves wish to remain civilized. The new colonists will look to us for strength. We will not let the trees of Trappist change us."

Everything came together except for the natives. DeBoone had to know. "Who are they?"

They came from outside the circle of trees as if they'd always been there and had heard DeBoone speak. Small, bipedal trees uprooted and revealed themselves. Their red-brown trunks were split to allow easier walking, though they kept low to the ground as if the earth was their life's blood. Perhaps in a way, it was.

Branches stretched into fingers which could curl and grasp. Their bodies were the trunks themselves but they had no discernible heads. No mouths, no eyes, no ears. Yet they had no difficulty responding to DeBoone or any of the others.

"I call them Saprolings, but I'm sure some scientist or another will rename them something stupid." All at once, the dozen or so Saprolings bowed, their leaves and branches barely touching the soil in front of them.

"What are they doing?" asked Humboldt, who had taken Aurora by the hand.

"Bowing," Aurora said. "I taught them that. I figured it would be the easiest way for us to say hello to each other. I've taught them some basic symbols too. And I'm learning theirs."

One of the small trees had a broken branch, which hadn't quite fallen off yet. It swung on his side. For all the world, the Saproling looked to DeBoone the same as any hurt, human child. The injured creature seemed to be put off-balance, falling forward during the bow. Another Saproling reached out to steady the first.

DeBoone did the only thing he could think of doing himself. He lowered his head. It felt odd, but it also felt like the right thing to do. For her part, Humboldt took a half bent-knee born more out of confusion than disrespect. Aurora bowed all the way and drew circles in the dirt with her finger.

The Saprolings unbowed and moved back in with their parents. As they did so, DeBoone clicked the record button on Chet's device. *Now, I have evidence.*

"They are adolescent. When they grow older, they'll take root, grow tall, and eventually produce offspring of their own. That's why the forests are so dense, and you see so many circles — rings of trees. They're friends and family. Tribal, in a way. There is so much to learn from them," Aurora said, smiling with a voice that grew more excitable by the word.

Unfortunately, DeBoone knew he had to break the spell. "Aurora, you need to come with me. Your father has something planned. But we can all return to the colony and work it out from there, right?"

"I'm not leaving," she said.

Of course she wasn't. As Aurora stood in defiance, a breeze blew through them, or maybe it was the trees talking. They seemed to grow larger, the Saprolings retreated further back, and the dim gray sky turned a shade darker.

The first blow from behind knocked the wind out of him. DeBoone staggered at first but then recovered. The second blow hit the side of his head and left DeBoone dazed. After the third, DeBoone found himself sprawled face-up on the ground in time to witness the chaplain kick him hard enough in the chest to crack a rib.

Mather laughed with renewed strength. "Yesterday, I thought I was dead. That plant had me. My grand plan had gone to shit. And then, you saved me. Oh, the irony. You could have had it all. You could have reclaimed the colony. You could have taken your daughter back. Yet, you saved my ass."

"Dad, what are you talking about?" Her voice said she already knew.

"Tell her, she's old enough now."

DeBoone could see the pain in her eyes, his sins coming home after all these years. Yet, they weren't really his sins. He had only played a part, a pawn in Mather's lust for power and control. It was time to clear the air.

DeBoone coughed up a bit of blood as his own tears choked him but before he could speak, Aurora interrupted. "I know he's my real father, I'm not an idiot. You used him as your pawn, now you're using me. That's what I meant."

"So, the air is clear," Mather said. "The slate is clean and the chaplain can pardon me of my sins. We have a whole hell of a lot of colonists coming next year and nowhere for them to go. If we don't act and make it safe for them, then the colony withers. We all die. This forest needs clearing. We have a civilization to build."

"I won't let you do this. I won't let you hurt them," Aurora remained rooted in opposition. "I'll lead them against you. We'll start a war if we must."

"Plants are not people!"

DeBoone tried to stand, but the chaplain swept his legs out from under him. Still, he spat out, "There's no way you can destroy an entire forest. Humboldt will stop you."

"Really?" Mather asked. "Who do you think set the plasma packs?"

DeBoone noticed through blood and tears, the black bags were missing. *Too late. I'm too damned late.*

"While you were chatting it up with chappy, Humboldt and I were slapping plasma charges on Aurora's grown friends here. This place is going to go up like an American Fourth of July. Humboldt, would you do the honors and fire first?"

Mather took a few steps back. As he did, the Saprolings bent sideways, as if looking at him curiously. "Aurora, darling, you may want to join us here. I'd hate to see you join the forest in fire and brimstone."

Humboldt looked at Aurora, who remained still. She turned to Mather, as if seeking strength, and raised her rifle, though the tip wavered a bit.

"Humboldt. Don't do this," DeBoone said, through kicks to his torso. Through the pain, he tried to stand once more. He felt a crack, the sharp bone stabbed his lung. Still, he persisted. "Don't do this."

"That's an order, Humboldt. Do you follow?"

"Can you follow an order if your heart tells you it's wrong?" Aurora asked. "Can you imagine your heart and soul afterward if you kill these creatures? These Saprolings? They are alive. They are just like you and me in so many ways." Humboldt's AR80 remained ready, her finger on the trigger, a plasma pack, near a Saproling, in her sight.

"I won't." Humboldt pivoted, pointing her rifle at Mather. She fired, but not before a bolt from the chaplain's pistol tore across her abdomen. She gasped in pain at the surprise attack. Her own shot went wide, missing Mather.

He delivered a blow across her face, splitting her lip open once more. She took the hit hard. Her rifle fell to the ground and she stumbled, dazed, striking wide with her curved blade returning a band of crimson across his arm. He jerked back in pain as she fell to the ground, the adrenaline spent and shock taking over.

Aurora rushed over to hold her in her arms. Humbolt sucked in a mouthful of air and grunted out she'd be okay. DeBoone couldn't tell if was a lie or not, but he'd do his damnedest to get her back to the medbay, if he could.

Mather tossed the chaplain Humboldt's AR80. "Chaplain, the honor's all yours. This was your plan, after all."

DeBoone's face flushed and his fists clenched at the realization. The chaplain was the real threat. *What does a man of the cloth gain from all this?* The passion in the chaplain's eyes gave DeBoone his answer. All the pain and hurt from so many burials so early on. It was as if Hale laid the death of so many souls on Trappist on himself, rather than their own hubris. The chaplain believed all this. Every word.

"There are no souls to save here, DeBoone. God gave us dominion, not of just the earth, but all his creations. We are only clearing the field to spread His faithful flock. This is no more than trimming the hedges." He pulled the trigger to let a steady stream of plasma pour forth, like fire from the fingers of the Almighty himself.

This was not the quiet, peaceful faith that taught love and respect. DeBoone had lost that faith when Annie left him. When the daughter he loved was taken from him. But it was to that faith he turned to now. It was the belief in the goodness of humanity despite the enormity of evidence against it. Aurora was proof. Humboldt was proof. He was proof too. People could change. "Stop this madness, Mather."

"I'm not doing anything. It's unfortunate a rogue colonist would set fire to the forest, attacking and killing the same savage creatures who took his daughter captive." The enormity of Mather's words punched DeBoone harder in the gut than the reverberation of the first plasma pack igniting.

The explosion shook them all. What Saprolings hadn't run from the chaplain's first volley of flame, scattered among the aftermath of the fireball. It was proof the chaplain's plan would work. The Saprolings and woodland creatures on this part of the planet would all be destroyed.

As Mather joined in and plasma pulsed and packs exploded, Aurora stood once more in defiance. "Stop this."

There wasn't anything she could do to physically stop him. She was strong and stubborn but she held no weapon. Mather and the Chaplain did.

"It's too late," Mather launched another assault on the forest. "The fire is already burning. Cleansing the earth."

"Parents are supposed to make the world a better place for their children. Not destroy it."

"But I am. I have a responsibility for everyone in my care, child and colonist alike. I can't watch any more of them die on this hostile world. I've lost too many already."

"Fine," she spat. "You've lost me too."

The fires were spreading now. All around them, the Saprolings tried to flee, but the smoke and the flames trapped them. DeBoone witnessed the Saproling that stumbled during the bow. His leaves were smoking and his branches were aflame. The little tree could not speak nor cry in pain, but the way it wriggled and writhed, DeBoone could feel its agony all the same. Its parents were caught in fire, though their deep roots left them with no choice but to stand there and burn.

"This is your doing, dad." As the forest burned, Aurora began to walk into the woods. Into the fire.

"No!" DeBoone yelled. So did the chaplain. Even Mather stopped. Still, Aurora walked into the flame. She screamed as the first flames touched her.

DeBoone tried to chase after her, to stop her. But, an explosion from a nearby plasma pack swallowed her in smoke and fire. He was knocked back and fell sharply on his broken ribs.

Aurora disappeared, but her screams remained. They rose over the roar of the flames, the discharge of the rifles, and the winds of the woods, until all too suddenly, they stopped.

Mather dropped to his knees. "She wasn't supposed to do that."

He sobbed violently. "She wasn't supposed to do that!"

DeBoone cast tearful eyes to the sky. As the fires grew hotter and the tree branches began popping, small orange orbs glowed brightly. Some began to float. Others sank and fell into the smoke. Others traveled on bursts of wind away from flame. They were the same orange orbs DeBoone saw while he and Chet talked, though he mistook them for embers at the time. Now, he knew what they were.

The trees were sending their offspring away. Just as a pine-cone opens during flame, so had these trees opened their pods to let their children fly away. They sacrificed themselves to give their children a chance to escape the fire and a chance to rebuild.

It all made magnificent sense to him. But the moment of losing Aurora was all he could think about. The chaplain had stopped firing too, hesitant at what to do with the carnage he created.

DeBoone took that moment of hesitation and, bruised and hurt as he was, twisted around on the ground, kicking the chaplain backward, with both feet straight into the gut. The chaplain doubled over and DeBoone launched both feet into his face. Hale collapsed in agony as DeBoone struggled to rise against his own pain. All the while, orange orbs fell on them as if they were ash.

At first, DeBoone's eyes watered. He could feel his throat dry and swell as it had done earlier with Chet. He ignored it and went to

Humboldt. She was sweaty and cold. Still, she handed him her curved knife. She gasped out a request, "Take care of him, for me. For your daughter."

He nodded and stumbled over to stand above the wreck of Mather. He grabbed him by the starched collar of his black uniform shirt. "What did you think was going to happen? Why?"

"I'll kill them all. I'll uproot every tree on this planet." Mather's lips turned blue, just as Chet's had done, and his eyes bloodshot.

The orange orbs might have been the offspring of the trees, but the spores were deadly to the humans underneath. DeBoone could feel his own life slipping away even as Mather started going limp in his hands.

"No, you don't get off easy." DeBoone slid the knife to sheath it in Mather's left ribs. With a gurgle of blood, Mather fell to the forest floor, his hands clawing at the dirt as he died.

Over to the side, the chaplain prayed.

"He won't answer. On this world, perhaps this universe, the trees are God." He left the chaplain, sniveling at his fate from the trees.

DeBoone stumbled over back to Humboldt. "I'm sorry."

"What?" she asked.

"In case we don't make it back for you to buy me that beer," DeBoone said, placing his hand on hers. "It's my apology. I'm sorry."

A Saproling, unhurt from the fire, approached them. DeBoone wondered how the little tree would kill them, but accepted his fate all the same. Instead, it bowed and bent a branch to the dirt. It drew a circle, then a smaller circle in the relative position of where he and Humboldt lay. It ignored the corpse of Mather and the dying chaplain and drew a third circle in the direction where Aurora had gone. Then, it left as quickly as it had come.

DeBoone didn't know what any of it meant. The orange orbs kept falling, and it was all he could do to keep from drifting off. As his vision dimmed, he could feel soft leaves surround him. Then, he had a sensation of floating. But it wasn't just him. Humboldt was with him.

It took a moment to register what was happening, but Humboldt beat him to it. "The trees are lifting us skyward to fresh air. They are saving us."

It was a lot to take in. The thick branches swayed and bent in the breeze, taking him and Humboldt out of danger. It began to make sense to him when he saw Aurora with them at the tops of the trees of Trappist. *So I have died. She's my angel.*

"How?" DeBoone asked. The orange orbs drifted away and as they did, symptoms faded and clarity returned. Maybe he wasn't dead after all. But if he were not, then Aurora wasn't either. Humboldt looked surprised too.

Aurora smiled and let them in on her secret. "Mather was not the only one who could act. I knew it would get him to stop. I was never in any danger. The trees took me to the top. I just thought of all the little Saprolings and Spriglings he killed, and I used that anger and sadness to cry as their voice."

The trees were handing the three of them over, passing above the forest floor and back toward their colony. At this rate, they'd be there soon and Humboldt's injuries could be treated. They were all going to be okay. Then, he thought of the fire burning in the distance and how much pain they'd caused. He tapped at Chet's recorder to make sure it was safe. *Thank you, Chet. You were right. I hope you live on through this.*

He looked toward Aurora and the new dawn ahead.

"Where are you going after this, D.B.?"

He thought for a moment, about the colonists arriving soon and then of the trees of Trappist-E. There had to be a way for the arriving colonists to appreciate the planet as much as he did. As much as Aurora did. To bridge the gap between civilizations. Then, he answered, smiling at his daughter as he did so, "Home. The colony. You and I have much to do."

END

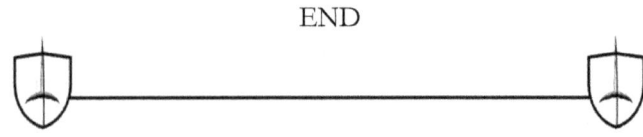

About Brent A. Harris

Brent A. Harris is a Sidewise Award nominated author of alternate history. He also writes science fiction, horror, and fantasy. Previously published works can be found through Insomnia Publishing, Rhetoric Askew, and Inklings Press, the latter having published his short story, Twilight of the Mesozoic Moon, which reaped the above mentioned award nomination. He is the author of *A Time of Need*, an alternate history of the American Revolution, which sees a world where George Washington fights alongside the British against American forces marshaled under a power-hungry Benedict Arnold.

Brent resides in Southern California, where he's become convinced that Joshua trees are in fact, real trees. When not writing, he focuses on his family shuttling children around as a stay-at-home dad. Connect with Brent at BrentAHarris.com and his Amazon Author page - amazon.com/Brent-A.-Harris/e/B01L0I22OM.

Pixels
By Greg Krojac

Rick took his knuckles away from his eyes, which he had been rubbing gently - not too softly, but not so hard that he could cause any damage. He'd noticed the same thing for a couple of weeks now. He didn't really know why he hadn't noticed it before; it was so obvious really. Surely others must have noticed it?

He dried his face with the crimson hand-towel that hung from a chrome ring to the left of the vanity washbasin and looked into the mirror. He could see a slight nick on his throat where the razor blade had slipped and cut his skin. He was surprised to see the small patch of blood, for he hadn't felt a thing. Still, it didn't hurt. He turned and tore the corner off a sheet of toilet paper and placed it over the offending wound. This solution didn't always work - sometimes the paper would flutter down to the floor, a small red spot the only witness as to what it had been used for. However, today wasn't one of those days. He went back to the mirror and could still see the small white piece of tissue stuck fast where he had pressed it. It would probably fall off his throat unassisted in a couple of minutes but that didn't worry him. It only had to stop the flow of blood. He checked that he'd put the toilet seat down; his wife, Fiona would kill him if he left it up. Of course, she wouldn't really kill him, but he would certainly pay for his sin with a couple of frozen stares and a few wry comments.

He turned off the bathroom light and made his way to the kitchen, where Fiona was cooking breakfast. The bacon smelled enticing, the flavors circling around the room and wafting up inside his nose. How could vegetarians possibly exist when the smell of cooking bacon was so seductive? And the meat tasted so good too - who couldn't like bacon?

Sitting himself down at the kitchen table, Rick took a sip of his morning tea and put the mug back down on the table so quickly that a small amount of tea was forced to leap out of the mug onto his placemat. He'd forgotten to add sugar - well, artificial sweetener - and it tasted awful. He quickly remedied the situation and took another sip. That was better.

Fiona took the frying pan off the hob and carried it over to the table. The four strips of bacon looked perfect - not too fatty, but not too lean either. Just how Rick liked it. The cooking oil was still spitting a little, having been withdrawn from the heat, but not enough to cause any problem. His wife placed two strips of meat on each plate, alongside the baked beans, mushrooms, tomatoes, sausages, and fried eggs. This wasn't the couple's normal breakfast fare, but they made a point of indulging themselves on Sunday mornings, breaking the monotony of cereal and toast which was their normal breakfast during the rest of the week.

Rick harpooned one of his bacon strips with his fork and cut it in half, before dipping it into the small pool of baked beans. He then raised the fork to his mouth and closed his eyes in ecstasy as the food hit his taste buds.

"This is really good, Fi."

Fiona accepted the compliment gracefully.

"You spent a long time in the bathroom today, Rick. Were you manscaping or something?"

Rick almost spat out his food.

"No, hun. I was doing an experiment but nothing like that."

"So what's this experiment? Will it change the world?"

"Maybe."

"For good or for bad?"

"Neither, really. It's just something I've noticed recently. Something that's always happened but I've never really noticed it before."

"Go on then. Don't keep me in the dark."

Rick knew that what had occurred to him was probably going to sound a little crazy to his wife, but it wasn't that crazy really. The eminent astrophysicist, Neil deGrasse Tyson, hosting the 2016 Isaac Asimov Memorial Debate, had said that the likelihood of the universe being a simulation may be very high. And he also wanted to hear himself voice his thoughts out loud, rather than just keep them to himself. Maybe if he actually spoke the words, they might gain an air of credibility that they didn't possess whilst just swirling around as an idea in his head.

He took another forkful of his breakfast. He wouldn't normally dream of talking with his mouth full, but he and his wife were alone. Some taboos were removed after nearly thirty years of marriage.

"Have you ever rubbed your eyes first thing in the morning?"

"Of course."

"And have you ever noticed anything strange?"

"Not really."

"Nor had I until last week. But I suddenly became aware that what I could see - perhaps 'see' is the wrong word, after all, my eyes were shut - but what I could see was lots of tiny colored squares, kind of flashing, like pixels."

Fiona wasn't really interested in this bizarre theory but she'd got used to humoring her husband's little whims.

"Isn't that normal, though?"

"You'd think so, yes. But, and it's a big but, it only happens the first couple of times that you do it, first thing in the morning. After that, if you rub your eyes, all you see is a kind of darkness. No colored squares. No pixels. No flashing lights. It's like it gets switched off."

"So what's your great theory then, Einstein?"

Rick grinned as he shoveled a healthy portion of baked beans into his mouth.

"Call me Sir Isaac Newton. He's the daddy of science."

"So what's your great theory then, Sir Isaac?"

"Well, it seems to me that these are digital signals."

"So? We operate through electrical impulses going from our brain to the rest of our body. Even I know that."

"Yes. We do. But it's the fact that the flashing pixels change to a kind of mish-mash of darkness that got me thinking."

"Thinking what?"

"Thinking why does it change?"

Fiona took a sip of her coffee.

"So why does it change?"

"Well, obviously I don't really know, but what if it changes so we can't follow through and investigate the flashing digital pixels thing?"

"Why would we want to?"

"Wouldn't you like to know why it changes?"

"I can't honestly say I'm bothered either way."

"But what if we're living in a computer simulation? What if we're not even real?"

"Are you going all existentialist on me, Rick?"

"You mean the old 'if I turn my back is the table still really there' thing?"

"Exactly."

Fiona was now cupping her coffee in both hands. She enjoyed seeing her husband getting so animated about science. She could take science or leave it, but Rick loved science and science fiction, and what made him happy made her happy. Rick continued.

"Imagine if there's someone - something - out there that is controlling our lives, or at least watching them."

"Why would they do that?"

"Why do you watch soap operas? For entertainment, I suppose."

"So this thing would be God?"

"No. Not really. Just some more advanced life form, somewhere, that watches what we do. We could be living in a kind of video game like The Sims, you know - that game that Tash is always playing."

"So everything that goes wrong in our lives could be the fault of some hormone-crazed adolescent E.T. in his or her galactic bedroom?"

"Well, not exactly like that, but it's that kind of principle."

Fiona shook her head.

"I hope you're wrong. I don't much care for that idea."

"Nor do I. But it's possible. Isn't it?"

"I suppose it's possible, yes. But hopefully wrong."

Another thought erupted inside Rick's brain.

"But does it matter if we're living in a computer simulation?"

Fiona drained her coffee mug as Rick ate the last mushroom to finish his meal. She debated with herself as to whether she should have another mug of coffee, before deciding not to.

"It matters to me. I don't want to think of some snotty-nosed alien kid watching my every move. It's alright if they see me at work or watching TV or stuff, but what about the other stuff, the private stuff? I don't want someone to watch me going to the loo or taking a shower. Or, even worse, they could be watching us when we have sex."

Rick laughed out loud.

"Sorry, Fi. I was just thinking that maybe we're inter-galactic porn stars. Maybe I should pretend I'm a plumber or a pizza delivery boy next time."

Fiona grinned as she imagined her husband as Mario, the plumber from the video game that she'd played in her youth.

"Well, let's hope your theory's wrong."

"But if I'm not, does it really matter? We don't know any different. It's the world we live in - whatever it is. It doesn't make any real difference whether it's real or a computer simulation. It's the only world we've got."

Fiona stood up, loaded the dirty dishes into the dishwasher, and took the dog leash from its hook on the kitchen wall.

"Anyway, I'm going to take the dog for a stroll to the local shops. We've run out of cheese, and you know how you like your cheese rolls at night. I'll see if Jody and Tash want to come with me. You coming?"

***

In the space-time continuum, a more advanced life form spoke. "Take the Clarke family offline. They know too much."

THE END

About Greg Krojac

Growing up on a diet of science fiction, watching both Star Trek and Doctor Who from their beginnings, and reading sci-fi books such as Aldous Huxley's *Brave New World*, George Orwell's *1984*, and even studying B.F.Skinner's *Walden Two* at grammar school, it is hardly surprising that when Greg stretched his writing wings he should be drawn to the genre of science fiction.

In addition to the short story here, Greg has published four other books as an independent author; *Revelation, Revolution,* and *Resolution* (forming the *Recarn Chronicles* trilogy) and his most recently published novel, a post-apocalyptic romance titled *Reality Sandwich*.

Greg lives in Brazil with Eliene, under the watchful eye of their cat, Tabitha, and teaches English as a foreign language.

Greg can be found on social media at:

Facebook - facebook.com/gregkrojac/

Twitter - @Scifi_Greg

Website - GregKrojac.com

Amazon - amazon.com/Gregory-N-Taylor/e/B01BN49WLE

Wondrous Strange
By E.M. Swift-Hook

"A people who move not through space-time, but through the limitless dimensions which lie outside and between time and space."

I

Fun.

Playing with impossibilities, as the concept bounced within, [^] modulated the parameters one chose to create new variations. Liberally hiving energy through the Concept's limitations, perceiving the expansion patterns and wondering where the limits might expire. One's engagement intensity peaked as a promising parabola extruded through multiple frequencies, tiering their continuity in a brilliantly original manner, so an alternative hierarchy of perceived order shimmered into reality.

Delight.

[^] released the unfinished concept and harmonized oneself with this new perception, strimming the drifts of ungainly chaos from the extreme boundaries one had created until the whole seemed honed to a viable core, budding into a new authenticity.

>>that seems to be very unstable, my kin{One}, you might try at least anchoring it in some known tier, offer some link to actuality. If not, you know it is gone<<

The harmonization broke unexpectedly through the strain of focus in which [^] held the Concept and the whole wavered, releasing tendrils of minor tiered realities that slipped away diminishing the whole. [^] surveyed the remains with brief regret. No matter. One could play afresh. One snapped the energy away and the concept ceased.

[+] exuded regret.

>>that was beautiful, you could still replicate it and strive to stabilize the dimensionality. maybe make it less extreme. you are so much for always pushing the limits<<

144

Amusement.

>>that is where the beauty lies, [+] , spiraling up out, on and over the edge of possibility<<
>>except [v] would call that a waste of energy<<

But there was no reproach in [+] 's demeanor, one's every perceivable parameter, arced back into affection. [+] shared the same disregard for tradition as [^].

>>waste is only ever in not doing what can be done<< [^] returned, shaping the communication with a prim trimming more appropriate to the narrow mode [v] always adopted, than one's own open and thriving manner.

Brief patterns of wicked appreciation resolved and dissolved between them. They were close kin, extended into the same dimensionalities on many axes and many expressions of energy, being and Consciousness.

>>we should be Working, my kin{One}<<

Regret.

But [+] was right by Duty and [^] harmonized that between them, before shifting focus through multiple tiers and frequencies to relocate one's Consciousness at the Work.

It was impressive to perceive. Despite the ever greater restrictions on the energy that was being gleaned from the open tiers in the Symmetry, the Ones were lavishing it here in a manner [^] found strangely unsettling.

Desperation.

Not one's own, but there, percolating as a taint through their fellow Weavers. Most would be oblivious to it, focused on the Work, but arriving into the event, [^] observed it and, from their close resonance, felt [+] perceive it as well.

>>>>THIS IS UNACCEPTABLE. HERE IS YOUR PLACE<<<<

The communication was brusque and intrusive, lacking any real attempt at polite harmonic modulation, just thrusting into Consciousness with disregard for the impact. It was rude enough to be a deliberate insult, but [v] simply assumed one had every right to do so. This Work was under [v]'s Authority. [^] and [+] were serving on that, constrained by Duty. But [^] and [v] held very different views of the purpose of Authority, which created an ongoing dissonance between them.

Annoyance.

>not now, my kin{One}< [+] cautioned gently, soothing the disruption and discontinuity that the intrusive surge left in [^]'s Essence with deft weaving. >this is too important to all Ones, they will not back your breach with [v] over something they would consider trivial when set beside this Work<

[+] was right, of course, and [^] modulated back and offered a humble apologetic mien, which [v] harmonized as brusquely as one had slammed in one's last communication.

>>>the Work is priority under Duty<<< [v] declaimed, exuding arrogance and self-importance , dismissing the apology as if [^] was a newly budded sentience, still acquiring skills and not a fully extended individual, and a highly talented Weaver capable of encompassing and coordinating more in a single perception, than most Ones could begin to imagine as possible. The lack of resonance was creating a strain in the Work and as [v] showed no sign of compromise, [^] had little choice except to submit, or risk a real danger of damage to the foundation of the Work.

>focus, my kin{One}. Let it go, and focus. remember we do this for [=], not for Duty<

>wisdom from you [+], as always<

[=] was resonance bonded with [+] and [^] although they had not chosen to bud a new conceptual sentience from their bond. [=] was an Explorer and the one chosen to pass through a minute fissure to the tier that the Nexus they now wove would access. [=] was lost to them until it could be established.

For the sake of their bond{One}, [^] tried to focus.

A gently soothing ripple harmonized between the two kin{Ones} as they began strimming and weaving with the others. Every One seeking a suitable frequency in the dimensionalities open to each, striving to place the anchors where they could both meld in and draw out energy to power the Nexus they were creating. It was more difficult to find viable tiers; even [^] whose reach was amongst greatest of any One, rooted each anchor with ever more difficulty.

146

Something was amiss with the resonance here. Not just this Work, but through all the Symmetry. A memory bubbled within [^], recalling the content of the last harmonization one had shared with [=].

>>we are becoming infected by Entropy, my bond{0ne}<< insisted [=], with a welded mix of sadness and anger. >>as an Explorer I see it more than you Weavers. I experience the tiers and return to Symmetry and each return confirms again my perception. the greed of the 0nes to encompass and draw in ever more of energy into the Symmetry is having the opposite effect. each new fissure in the tiers, supposed to bring in more energy, is opening us to parasitic reflux. I have perceived it, I have recorded it, but the Influencers will not receive my concepts<<

Swirls of antipathy and frustration curled between them. In empathy, [^] harmonized and soothed, but one's own equilibrium was not easy to maintain. If what [=] perceived was as it seemed, then all 0nes stood in danger of ultimate dispersal - of becoming eventual victims of Entropy.

>>why don't they consider your findings? I can't understand what they think they gain by ignoring them<<

>>they don't ignore them [^]. they observe the entirety of infinity as if it were the Symmetry and hold that therefore, where we dwell, the equilibration of any energy excess will harmonize back into that Symmetry. they forget Infinity is symmetrical only through the process of equilibrium. so when excess causes instability, balance is restored through that process. but our Influencers do not face up to that. they prefer to give the mark of truth to those who hold we can obtain sufficient energy to replace the losses<<

Aghast.

>>how can we draw sufficient for stability from other entropic tiers? surely all we do by opening ever further Nexūs, is to allow more Entropy to inveigle us<<

>>wisdom from you my bond{0ne}, but not from other 0nes and certainly not from the Influencers<<

They shared a concurrence of harmony and [^] experienced the perceptions that had caused [=] such concern. It was not even slightly reassuring.

>>the very best we can do is avoid opening any more points of entropic access. those we have wrought might be resealed by using

what energy we have gleaned from the tiers through the ways exploited by 0nes from The First Budding. if we do so, we are inevitably diminished, our Symmetry less glorious and far reaching, but at least we are spared from Entropy<<

There was a strange hollow in the resonance of [=] that [^] did not recognize during their harmonization. but the same hollow that tainted this Work.

Despair.

One reason, perhaps the only reason, [^] tolerated the Duty demands of [v] to Work on this Duty was from the desire to resonate with [=] again. Until this Nexus was complete, no 0ne - not even the most intrepid Explorer - would venture into the tier to seek one's bond{0ne}. Being in resonance with [+] to weave, [^] felt the sharing of the memory and it disturbed [+]'s inner Essence.

Regret.

Sadness.

>>when this is Worked we will be able to resonate with [=] again, my kin{0ne}<< [^] reminded one, harmonizing fluidly and soothing [+] with small energy extrusions from the bond between them.

>>maybe, if our bond{0ne} has not been dissipated<<

>>we would know if that happened. even without conscious resonance, the connections are still there. when this Nexus is made an Explorer will go through it and find our beloved bond{0ne}<<

>>they may not. [v] claims that is not the priority, that another Explorer must not be risked until the energy anomalies of the tier are better understood. a Nexus will allow greater access to those for research <<

Truth indeed. They both knew it. Desperation could be a spur to creativity as well as a weight upon one's Essence.

>>well, [v] seeks to take a place with the Influencers. I can trade my support for [v] and one's faction against bringing [=] back<<

The swell of protest from [+] was strong and sudden, swaying [^]'s focus from the work and the anchor weld slipped through the weavings, earning a sharp reproach from those also focused on local tiers.

>>no, my kin{0ne}. That would mean [v] would gain place over you by bonds of Duty, and over all our kin{0ne}s through your resonance<<

Frustration.

The collective discord as that seeped through [^]'s boundaries and into the Work, brought the weaving and strimming to an ungentle halt, with parted tiers leaking and anchor welds rifted out of resonance. A universal shudder of dissonance went through the 0nes.
>>>>**NOT [^] AGAIN!**<<<<

II

The Duty of Work to complete the Nexus was undertaken by others. [^] and [+] found their shared resonance was regarded as creating too high a degree of disharmony and their concern for [=] was attributed as being the cause.

[^] did not mind. There were always new aspects and dimensions of Consciousness on the frontiers of Known Symmetry to explore and being freed from Duty, one was able to indulge in far more interesting activities involving those. It also offered opportunity to consider the full implications of what [=] had shared. [+] insisted they should wait until the Nexus was complete and [=] could resonate with them again. But the subduction of energy by the entropic lesions was not something [^] could set aside from one's mind.

It was subtle, but the parasitic effect of the multiple rifts and increasing number of Nexūs was indeed affecting the Symmetry. Even the energy being drawn by these means was tainted. It was base and unrefined. [^] could perceive the pollution of the 0nes current tiers of being, as a real threat. And few had the reach and strength to change resonance as [^] and one's kin{0ne}s might, so the option of broadening into a new, undamaged Symmetry was not open to most 0nes.

Perturbed.

Duty was demanded again and, with some reluctance, [^] focused back on the Work, aligning one's dimensionality and resonance to the location of the new Nexus and so becoming there. The key

Influencers of the Symmetry were also fully resonating there, but even that august company could not hold [^]'s attention from the new creation.

The Nexus billowed through the tiers its anchors reached into and shimmered across the spectrum of their resonance. On first perception, returning, [^] was overwhelmed. This single Nexus had been wrought more broadly and deeply than any yet. It was magnificent.

Awe.

But also:

Puzzlement.

>>if this is made and anchored why am I Duty summoned for Work?<<

Three of the Influencers harmonized a reply together. Their Authority enhanced by the rest.

>>>You Are **Duty** Summoned To Pass Through The **Nexus**. You Must Seek [=] And Either Return With One Or Return Alone To Tell Us Why You Have Failed This **Duty**<<<

Shock.

>>but I am not an Explorer, I am a Weaver<<

[^] knew the protest was disharmonic and a shifting ripple of reaction passed through the Influencers. Two of them threw up exclusion shields, sheltering the rest and [^] knew a cold cut of -

Shame.

>> >You Are Now Designated **Explorer** [^]. You Will Resonate With [v] Who Has All The Knowledge We Possess About This Tier. **This is your Duty**<<<

The force of the charge rocked [^] to one's Essence and without resistance one allowed full resonance with [v], too late to hive off to a private resonance the memories of the harmonization with [+] on the topic of [v]'s ambitions.

The conceptual transfer took place, but as an imposition not a harmonization. [^] felt every dimension and frequency of one's being skewed and the broken resonance jarred.

Violation.

It ceased and the Concept remained inculcated into [^] as knowledge and memory:

...the Explorers' experience - tracing a highly diverse and mutable energy resonance modulating through spectrums unknown - now one's own.

...the perplexing doubts as even the most experienced of the Weavers amongst the Influencers did not recognize these signatures from anything encountered in the Symmetry, felt and shared by one as much as by them.

...the confusion that these resonances were melded deep into one of the most limited, least dynamic and truly inflexible tiers Ones had ever encountered.

But inculcating the Concept also brought with it understanding and -

Fear.

The fear harmonized through ones resonance with [+] and [^] could not then deny the Concept and -

>>this lies outside the Symmetry? We have sent [=] Beyond?<<

There was real concern in [+].

>>there is no Beyond, all is in Symmetry<< But [^] found the denial hollow even whilst making it. The myth of Beyond and belief in it had wrenched the Ones apart, two groups so far out of resonance they might indeed be in some Beyond and occupy entirely separate Symmetries, even whilst co-habiting the same frequencies.

>>but this is so alien, my kin{One}. how can any One exist in such an environment?<<

>>I do not know but I am about to find out<<

That knowledge did nothing to calm the oscillations of anxiety in [+]'s resonance.

>>YOUR DUTY IS REQUIRED. the Nexus awaits<<

A harsh, barely modulated, harmonic from [v] refocused [^]'s full attention. The Influencers would observe the process. It was important to be seen not to flinch from Duty.

Although [^] was not an Explorer, all 0nes pushed through the tiers to immerse in alternative sensations of energy, that was a common recreation. But those were known tiers, the experience often harmonized and resonated between 0nes. This was something unknown.

As [^] modulated one's energies to fully resonate with the Nexus, it was a sharp sensation of narrowing, of loss of dimensionality, and gave a claustrophobic sensation of being reduced and confined. That was not unknown when using a Nexus. The entire purpose of one was to facilitate attunement to the tier beyond, and after transition to the needed dimensionality was complete the sensation would pass. But not in this case. This was extreme.

Panic.

It jangled through [^]'s awareness, trailing the thought that no Weaver could cope with such a radical shift of energy. Only a skilled and experienced Explorer could tolerate such a dramatic extreme.

Unable to focus, perceive or resonate, [^] spiraled into whatever the Nexus projected, feeling one's most intimate energies, those bound closest to and sustaining one's Essence, flux into harrowing disharmony.

The turbulence ceased with an abruptness that left [^] disoriented.

Reaching for any point to secure an anchor, one realized that although in resonance with the Nexus, one was no longer in resonance with any 0nes through it. This tier was so alien to Symmetry energies, the Nexus could not perform its usual function and modulate between the 0nes and the tier.

Lonely.

[^] chastised oneself and. one knew full well that a main trait shared by all Explorers was the ability to cope with being alone. It was not something usual for [^] as a Weaver, whose specialization required continual social openness to those with whom they Worked. Calmed a little, experimentation revealed one could transmit a harmonization through the Nexus, and receive a response, strangely impersonal and disconnected:

> locate [=]. that is your Duty<

But who had been communicating, [^] could not tell. It was as if the Nexus itself had sent the harmonization. That was very disconcerting. But not as disconcerting as the environment in which one found oneself. Having ensured some sense of anchorage, even if it was vicarious rather than experienced directly, [^] finally focused attention on the ambiance of the tier itself.

The feeling of heaviness and irksome restriction predominated. This was a tier of energy that would surely be unexploitable. It's key frequency in the infinite spectrum that contained the Symmetry, so dissonant with the Ones that nothing could be done with it. Why had anyone conceived the notion that it was worth the massive expenditure of Work to build a Nexus to access it?

It occurred to [^] that these emotions were preventing one's perceptions from achieving much sense of anything except the claustrophobically restrictive sensation of this tier. That was why Explorers were chosen and trained, so even in challenging environments they could self-modulate to the dimensions of the spectrum available in a tier, resonate with it and harmonize back. But even the most skilled Explorers were not expected to be out of resonance to this extent.

Self-pity.

[^] pushed it away. No, one was no Explorer, but one was here by Duty to Work and to locate [=]. So one must focus to perceive and achieve. But, by all things in Symmetry, it was hard. As the emotion lifted and one's resonance managed to adjust a bit to the narrow frequencies available in this tier, [^] assured oneself that one's harmonization to the Nexus resonance was still strong and, gathering focus, Explored.

Strange.

There were odd traces of displaced energy, narrow frequencies woven through the unwieldy background milieu. So this was what had tempted the Explorers. This was why the Nexus had been Worked to prize open the tier, modulating the dimension-crushingly, narrow spectrum to interface with full Symmetry.

Pure.

Alluring.

It was not easy to perceive but with the energy strimming skill of the Weaver one was, [^] tracked along the barely manifesting frequencies, their clarity acting like traces of hope, encouraging one in striving against the resistance, calling to the energy at the core of one's own Essence, as if it were a long familiar resonance.

But how -?

Wonder.

It was incredible. Impossible.

The turgid low-spectrum energy was budding a high-order concept energy. And not just one example. As far as [^] could sense, deep into the tier, billions of such buds. Arising and sustaining themselves by somehow transmuting the dense, unusable energy into the clear, pure dimensionality which [^] was tracing.

It was as the specialist work of a Weaver being reproduced here by some low-frequency, limited dimension, natural process. It was crude beyond belief, and - on close examination - hideously ugly to perceive the way the energy was being realigned. The Weaver in [^] was both fascinated and repelled. It was a method no 0ne could ever replicate, necessitating as it did the acceptance of those toxic base energies into one's own Essence.

It was also impossible. Something that could not happen.

Like finding a Nexus just forming itself with no Weavers to create it.

>~>amazing, isn't it?<~<

The harmonization came with no warning, no usual sense of the other. It just emerged out of the oppressive, perception dulling ambiance.

It was [=].

Joy.

But this was [=] transmuted, somehow. Different and dissonant. For a moment there was an awkward attempt to resonate between them, which failed. Frustrated, [^] harmonized as best one could.

>>I don't understand, what is causing this? Why can't we resonate? Those things - <<

Amusement.

>~>you are no Explorer. why did they send you my bond{0ne}?<~<

>>I don't know. Perhaps because they knew I would not leave you here, that I would endure this to find you, where others might not<<

It was as if [=] was become, in some profound way, a different being. There was no point of resonance left between them. Only the cold communication of sharing a harmonized frequency. [^] could only hope it was some distorting effect of this tier and not a fundamental alteration. At least [=] seemed unperturbed by it, and either did not notice or did not care.

>~>I was heading home anyway as I recently detected a Nexus has been created. But now you are here so I do not need to. I could do with your expertise as Weaver. I need to find a way to anchor this new energy source back into Symmetry<~<

[^] shifted focus to the energies that [=] was referring to and which were now Woven into one's Essence, rather like a budding concept within its parents' resonance. Only this was anchored outside reaching into one of the peculiar self-generating buds that somehow transmuted and modulated the tiers low-dimension energy to a pure, useable one. The anchor let [=] draw the transmuted energy into one's own dimensionality, sustaining one's Essence. It did not take a Weaver's knowledge to realize that if access to this could be brought back into the Symmetry, the energy feed would be more than enough to sustain the needs of all the 0nes.

If.

Wondrous strange.

There was only one way to find out even if one that [^] recoiled from with an instinctive revulsion. But if a mere Explorer like one's bond{0ne} had the ability and courage to do so, then as a skilled Weaver [^] could as well.

>>I can figure how to bring this home, **if** I can resonate with it<<

>~>just extrude some energy from your Essence into one of these buds. there is no other way to achieve the resonance I have found<~<

>>yes, but then you are an Explorer. you do not know as many ways to meld and bond resonances<<

>~>be my guest, bond{One}, it is without doubt that if there is another way you will be the One who can find it<~<

Easier said than done. [^] probed and fluxed as best one could in the narrow dimensionality of this tier. It provided no clue to a possible access for resonance by normal means - or even for some kind of harmonization. It would need intense research by the combined knowledge and experience of the Weavers to investigate an alternative to the one [=] had chosen. If indeed such an alternative even existed.

It was risky to use Essence energy. Essence defined the dimensionality of Self. To draw from it was both potent and weakening. It risked changing the nature of the individual Self. It even held the risk of dissipation if too much Essence was hemorrhaged. But this was Duty, [^] needed no reminder of that. So one reached out to the alien budling [=] had anchored upon and -

Sight. Sound. Taste. Smell. Touch.

Sentience.

Sapience.

Thought.

A slew of incredible and perplexing, terrifying and fascinating perceptions, in sensory arrays [^] could not have conceptualized or even speculated upon, spiked through one's Essence.

[^] lost the resonance even as it was established. Shocked by the flood of conscious awareness and the utterly alien perceptions on energy levels so far from the familiar, one's boundaries shifted from passive to defensive by instinct. The budling [^] had anchored into, briefly tried desperately to modulate its own dimensionality to accommodate to this new extreme, then dissipated abruptly.

Revulsion.

The impossibility of it was almost too much to accept. [^] had to consider that maybe by extruding one's Essence energy in the toxic environment of such horribly constricting, low-dimensionality, one had experienced some form of internal hallucination. [^] reviewed the memory, exploring it and found no sign of perceptual distortion. That left only one possible conclusion, no matter how unbelievable and improbable. This was not some randomly occurring tier phenomenon.

>>these are *living beings*. conscious, aware, living beings<<

>~>oh yes<~< agreement came easily from [=], as if it were something of little or no consequence. >~>but not really conscious of much, only of this tier so no 0ne would really consider them alive, not in any real sense of the concept. They are subject to Entropy and not strong enough to hold their Essence against the slightest touch<~< still harmonizing, [=] illustrated one's point by shifting to a slightly higher energy at the edge of one's being, dissipating the energy from a number of the ugly budlings in the process. >~>it is quite soothing to do that< one went on bursting the miniature bubbles with evident pleasure >each tiny release of radiation is a unique sensation. You should try it<~<

Of course, [=] was right and to compare the level of awareness of such limited Concepts to anything one might encounter in the Symmetry, was ridiculous. These were minute, entropic, budlings, that had somehow developed a way of transmuting the grossest and most inflexible energies into the parody of true Consciousness. But that brief resonance remained as memory and knowledge: perceiving the tier as vast and spacious, through multiple senses and an individual that knew itself, just as [^] knew oneself. It shook all one's preconceptions to the core.

>~>can you do it?<~<

The lack of resonance with [=] made it seem as if the question came from another tier. But this was Duty and it would be the Work of a Weaver to see this through. This resource might be the salvation of the 0nes, offering enough energy to reseal the many tears and rifts and secure the Symmetry. And [^] was more than aware of how much those alien experiences from the budlings would delight and entrance the 0nes.

Aligning the resonance with the higher dimensions directly was possible, [^] could perceive already the flow and ebb through the tier. But it would mean resonating intimately with one of the budlings, allowing its transmuting ability to function through one's own energies. A form of symbiosis. Achieving that would be the biggest challenge [^] had faced as a Weaver. And it would mean doing something never before attempted - building a Nexus outside of the Symmetry to provide a fully resonant conduit between the energy levels. A Nexus which would need to be constructed from these dense, inflexible energies, and that could only be achieved by Ones in full and intimate resonance with them.

Disgust.

It would be unpleasant to even harmonize with such, let alone permit resonance. But the rewards would be immense. Quite apart from the ongoing energy harvest, if one could do this, [^] was certain there would be a place for one as an Influencer and that would be the least of it. This would seal the Weavers as the most significant of the Ones and allow [^] to bring forward the ideas needed to secure the Symmetry. Without doubt, [+] would be elevated also and their kin{One}s would benefit and secure ever more prestigious and powerful bonding opportunities. Maybe they and [=] could finally fully combine and bud their very own Concept.

Glorious imaginings!

Mind racing with the exciting possibilities in prospect, the memory of that tiny mind not so very unlike one's own was banished below Consciousness, as [^] followed [=] back to the Nexus to take the good news of salvation to the Ones who waited in the Symmetry.

About E.M. Swift-Hook

In the words that Robert Heinlein put into the mouth of Lazarus Long: "Writing is not necessarily something to be ashamed of, but do it in private and wash your hands afterwards."

Having tried a number of different careers, before settling in the North-East of England with family, three dogs, some cats and a small flock of rescued chickens, E.M. Swift-Hook now spends a lot of time in private and has very clean hands.

The author of the *Fortune's Fools* series of books - a trilogy of trilogies - and a number of related short stories set in the same broad story arc, of which *Wondrous Strange* is one.

E.M. Swift-Hook can be found in the following places:

Amazon - amazon.com/E.M.-Swift-Hook/e/B01FL8FMI0

Facebook - facebook.com/100012577446566

Goodreads - goodreads.com/author/show/15285489

Twitter - @emswifthook

One of Fortune's Fools - scifiroundtable.org/emswifthook/

The Dream Miner's Drill
By CB Droege

Do you know who I am?"

"You are Grellius Frank, infamous Dream Miner and notorious old coot."

The android sat on the floor, legs out ahead, its torso propped against the wall.

"Old Coot?" Grel asked, then interrupted himself, "Infamous?"

"Affirmative. You initiated the dream-miners' strike of '87 in the Ceres Cryo Facility," the android stated matter-of-fact, "You were responsible for the incapacitation of eight Mindcorp officials in the ensuing violence, and ultimately negotiated the cease-fire and new contract that followed."

Grel chuckled. "And I did it all with the dream-drill," he said, patting the small rod at his hip with affection, "and a little help from cousin Manny's head-cannon."

"Use of Mind Flensers and Acuity Cannons as weapons violates the Second Solar Constitution."

"Yeah well," Grel rolled his eyes at the accusation, "it got the job done, and the squinty eye of the Sol Council doesn't look too hard at Ceres, even today." Grel squatted down on the dusty steel floor to meet the Android's eyes. "It's just a big rock with a bunch of meat popsicles and pencil pushers in it. They don't even need us brain-drainers anymore."

"Dream Mining is no longer a lucrative industry." said the android.

"And a lot of people blamed me for that, once upon a time, but I didn't think anyone remembered all that stuff anymore. That was all almost eighty years ago now."

"My memory capacity is nearly infinite."

"That doesn't mean you have to remember everything."

The android just shrugged from its place on the floor.

"Well, what I meant was if you knew that I now own this scrap-heap of a station."

"Indeed."

"So," Grel stood, "are you going to help me, then?"

"No."

"Why not?"

"I am a Freedbot." it said, "I have been equipped with a full set of sentience-level decision-making algorithms, and am no longer required by my programming to follow human orders."

"Oh." Grel took a step back. He'd heard that freedbots could be dangerous.

"Do not be concerned," the android said, "I wish no harm upon any person. I wish only to rest."

Grel squinted at the slumping figure. "You mean to say that you have been given a full free-will package, and you've chosen to ... sit?"

"You have interpreted the situation correctly, Mr. Frank."

"Well, this is my station for the time being, are you going to earn your keep here?"

"No," the android said without hesitation, "do you wish for me to vacate?"

"Where would you go?" Grel asked.

"Out."

Grel looked out through the airlock he had just come through less than 10 minutes prior. The transport that dropped him off was on its way back to Spincity Alpha-Rowe. "I guess not." he grumbled.

"Thank you." The android slumped further down the wall.

"What do I call you?"

For the first time since Grel began speaking to it, the android hesitated just a moment before answering. "Warden."

"Just come up with that, did you?"

"Affirmative."

"Okay, Warden," Grel said with a smirk, "I guess I'll go explore my new station by myself. That's what I thought I was going to be doing anyway, since I didn't know you were even here."

"Very well, Mr. Frank."

"Call me Grel," Grel said, "The manifest lists fifteen meat popsicles. I want to find those first, and see what I've got."

"Good luck, Grel." Warden said.

Grel moved deeper into the small station alone, still shaking his head at the behavior of the android in the antechamber. The station had been a steal. He'd thought it would be a long-shot at first, but hardly anyone showed at the auction, and he'd won with his second bid, only 60% of what he'd decided he was willing to pay for it. Seeing it now, he was even more excited. There was a lot of material here that could be scrapped. Once he flensed all the valuable bits out of the frozen cargo, he could turn the whole station around for parts, and make twice what he paid. It was a little disappointing that the android wasn't part of the haul, but it hadn't been on the manifest anyway, so it wasn't a loss.

Flashlight shining, Grel moved through the corridors and peeked into the rooms one by one. It was bigger than he had thought it would be, and everything was still in nice condition. Often, when he would buy up an old station like this, he would be doing his initial survey in an environmental suit, climbing over and under debris, and finding that whole sections of the station had drifted off into space.

It wasn't long before he found the section labeled "cryo-storage", and carefully opened the door. Inside were fifteen cryopods, just as the manifest listed. He checked over each one, finding that six were damaged and inactive. Those would be a mess to clean out, but he wouldn't be charged with negligence, at least, since they had not been in his care at the time. That left nine cryos for him to mine.

Grel was tempted to look over the rest of his new acquisition before drilling into these, but his excitement overcame him, and he drew his flenser from its strap on his hip as he walked over to the nearest pod. He wiped at the window with a sleeve to get a look before starting in. A woman in her mid-forties lay behind the glass, blueish and peaceful. A black star sat upon her left cheek, a mark used back in the late 21nd century to identify particularly powerful Mentalists.

"You're an old one," he whispered with a small smile, "probably got some interesting stuff in there." He lined up his flenser on the glass of the pod, and squeezed the actuator. The device made a soft purring sound, as it carved its tiny hole through the glass. "Maybe you're holding on to the secret to a long-forgotten acuity, or perhaps you were witness to some historically significant events." he licked his lips. "Let's find out." The flenser ceased its noise, and Grel closed his eyes, concentrating on the link that he needed to form.

Grel found himself in a very orderly, very square, very clean room, filled to the ceiling with filing cabinets. Not what he was expecting. The minds of Mentalists are typically very disordered, and, from just his initial impression, this was one of the most organized minds he'd ever entered. He took a moment to get his bearings, then allowed his disembodied self to move toward one of the cabinets, choosing at random. He grasped the handle of a drawer, and instantly he was filled with an aching dread. The drawer was locked, which was strange enough - almost no one hid information from themselves - but worse: an alarm sounded. He severed the connection immediately.

His eyes opened, and he was standing in the cryo-storage room, one hand on his flenser, the other resting against the glass of the pod. He deactivated the tiny engine inside the tool, and drew himself away, taking a deep breath. He hadn't been so frightened during a flensing since he was a rookie. *What was that? Some kind of deep-brain military training? Did she have an implant protecting her dream?* It was like nothing he'd ever encountered. *I hope they're not all like this in here.*

Grel sucked in another breath and rolled his shoulders as he moved to the next pod. He wiped away the frost, and felt relief. A little boy. Children were a gold mine. Juvenile cryos were rare, and their memories were usually emotionally charged in a way that adults' never were. If there was a lot intact in there, he would make a fortune selling to the replay market.

He heard the telltale pop-hiss of a hatch opening to vacuum, and felt air begin to rush around him. Wide-eyed, Grel looked quickly around. A pressurized door had been opened at the far side of the room. Next to it, latch still in hand, was the star-cheeked woman. *Impossible.* No cryos can ever be revived.

"No!" Grel shouted over the sound of the wind, "You'll kill us both."

The woman pressed her collar activating a pop-helmet, which covered her head in a small bubble of atmosphere. She calmly held the door open against the rush of air.

Grel turned to run from the room. He had to get out and seal this section. There was an environmental suit back in the antechamber. If he could just get to it. He took a step, but the force of the rushing air was simply too much sweeping him off his feet. His leg slammed painfully into the side of the port as he was drawn out into the inky blackness and flung away from the little station.

The vacuum tugged at him, it was wrestling his breath from his body, and it was taking all of his energy just to hold it in. Soon, he would black out, and it would be over. He closed his eyes.

There was a crunching sound.
Grel hit the floor. He was alive. He was still inside! He let out his

breath, and drew another in raggedly. The air was tangy with ozone. Two more breaths, and he opened his eyes. He was still in the cryo-storage chamber. The android was standing over him, staring into the cryopod, the flenser crushed in his aluminum fist, the engine inside destroyed. "Warden..."

"Grel," the android looked down, "you were suffocating."

He felt like no breath could be enough, "You... saved me."

"Affirmative."

Grel smiled around his deep breaths, "You just... wanted to... sit..."

"I changed my mind." Warden dropped the destroyed flenser and turned to leave the room.

"Warden," Grel called after the android without lifting his head off the floor, "Would you be interested in a business partnership?"

"Affirmative," Warden said over his shoulder as he walked away, "We can discuss terms when you have recovered."

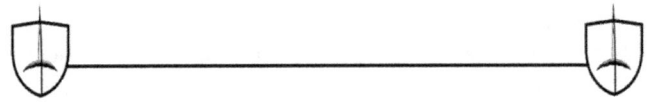

About *CB Droege*

CB Droege is an author and voice actor from the Queen City living in the Millionendorf. His influences include Philip K. Dick, Bill Bryson, Isaac Asimov, David Sedaris, and Roger Zelazny. He loves wizards and time-travel, but has an irrational distaste for time-traveling wizards. His latest book is Peacemaker and Other Stories. He recently edited *Starward Tales: An Anthology of Speculative Legends*. Other recent publications include work in Fantasia Divinity Magazine, Corvus Review, Indestructible, TWJ Magazine, New Realm, The Scarlet Leaf Review, Dark Mountain, Culture Cult Magazine, A Long Story Short, The Fable Online, Drawn to Marvel: Poems from the Comics, and The Great Tome of Forgotten Relics and Artifacts. Learn more at CBDroege.com

Project Chameleon
Jeanette O'Hagan

00.0000.00

"Too dangerous to salvage this one."

Dangerous. Danger. The word clanged like a warning bell in the darkest corners of his mind. He had to get out. He'd done what he'd come to do. She was safe, the mission complete. He tensed his shoulders, clenched his legs and abdomen, tried to move. His heartbeat hammered like a ship's ion cannon, shuddering against his ribcage. He was pinned down. He couldn't move. He couldn't speak or yell or scream. His tongue and lips refused to follow his commands. Pain screamed through his body, hammered at his head. Trapped like space junk in a tractor beam.

"Are you questioning orders? Give me the ultrasonic probe. He's bleeding out." Another voice boomed out, querulous.

"If you say so. Shall I activate the mind wipe?" The first man's tone grinding with suppressed anger.

"No, the director wants his memories intact. Just do as I say before we lose him. We need to give the cybernetics unit something to work on."

A soft hum, a tingle and warmth across his skin, a mild almost comforting irritant skimming over the surface of the deep, hollow pain tearing at his senses. He needed to fight it, to escape.

"Extensive internal organ damage. The crushed limbs will be difficult to save. At least he's fit."

"Core vital readings have stabilized. Ready stasis capsule for storage and transport." The voices stretched out, distant, as though echoing down a long tunnel.

Cold, deep bone numbing cold. His muscles shuddered. Cold and flaming agony fretted at his thoughts. Pulling on his reserves, his mind sharpened to a thin laser point. He'd done what was needed. He'd fulfilled his mission. He was in the hands of the Consortium. His continuing survival put his objectives at risk. The best outcome now was to let go.

"Vitals flatlining."

"Frag it, he's going into arrest."

166

"Apply cardiac-stimulant."

Darkness tunneled his vision. He was drifting, spiraling away towards the light. Away from the pain, from the urgency and demands of panicked voices.

"Live, you piece of low-life trash, live."

***

Green and gold. Light spilled out and pooled on the ground. A gentle wind stirred the profusion of leaves, whispering secrets and coaxing scents from the marosa tree. A high trill of laughter floated from further down the trail. Jerren's pulse picked up tempo. He turned and ran towards her. Long coltish limbs, chocolate-brown hair and an infectious smile. They were about the same age and he liked her better than her snooty older sister. He quickened his pace, senses alert. She was a champion hider despite her high status as the Attaché Hakan's daughter. He looked in their usual hiding places but couldn't find her.

The green shadows beneath the fruit trees deepened though it was still early afternoon. Past the gap in the leaves, the clouds swirled in ever darker patterns, taking on a greenish tinge. A flash of actinic light, the smell of ozone. The smash of thunder, ringing his ears.

"Dae, where are you?" His voice whipped away by the wind.

Her laughter turned to screams. He ran towards her, bashing into tree branches, tripping over roots. He fell headlong on the ground. Pain seared through him like a lathe. Danger. He had to find her. He couldn't see. He couldn't move. Darkness and pain engulfed him.

05.0500.52

Black as the deepest shadow in space. Blacker than the obsidian knife his father once owned. No glimmer of starlight frosting the ship's hull. Not the faintest pulse of red warning lights on the console. Not even the red-black patterns shimmering across his closed eyelids. It was as though light itself, the very thought of light, had been swallowed whole by darkness. Was he alive? The throb of visceral pain hammered at his consciousness, bashing to be let in. He tilted his head, or tried to. He couldn't move, not a finger, not a muscle. He couldn't feel his limbs, as if he were floating, a spark of thought alone in the universe. Terror bubbled up inside him. What was he but undifferentiated noise and scattered electrical currents stretched across the cosmos, without past, without future. He strained against the darkness, searching for something, anything. He swallowed a silent, trapped scream. He had to think, to remain calm.

***

"Stop fidgeting, Jerren." The master's voice held infinite irritation folded within infinite patience.

"Yes, sir," he mumbled into his open books, forced his gaze to the complex equations in front of him.

It was too crisp and clear a day to be inside. The blue sky reaching into the vastness of space, whole worlds, beyond this rocky island hiding in the middle of a vast blue-dark ocean.

"You must learn to focus, Jerren. You have a remarkable mind for one as young and untutored. If only you would use it."

He twisted his toes into the frayed carpet, feeling the pressure of the old man's expectations. "I'm just a drifter, just class 6. Nothing special about me."

"That is arguable, about anyone really." The old man stood, smoothed out his worn old fashioned robes, made of rare and banned natural fibers. He walked to the arched window. "Do you want to be a space pilot or not?"

He did, with all his being he did. When they stayed in Kito, he'd spent as much free time as he could, watching the craft take off and land at the Consortium space port. Eyes glued to the trajectory of the space shuttles until their contrails faded from the sky, wondering which of the outer planets the passengers and cargo were headed for, once they transferred at the space station. He wanted off this pile of rock and dirt, with its rules and limitations, so bad he'd risk going into more debt to the Consortium. That is, if it would make a skerrick of difference. Which it wouldn't. He was already indentured for a lifetime to pay off his parents' debts. The pencil broke in his hand.

"Well, my friend? Were you teasing when you said that was your ambition?"

He should never have shared his secret desire with the old man. He licked his lips. "No point. Class 6 inhabitants are fortunate to make regular work as janitors and clerks and war fodder." It's what his father always said.

"True enough, if you keep wasting my time." Sokranis folded his arms, a mock frown on his lined face. "Though the auto-bots clean better than any janitor."

Jerren shifted in the retro-wooden chair. Still not sure why the naïve old man had bought his contract from Attaché Hakan only to push books at him and lecture him each day. He sighed. It was better than cleaning out ventilations shafts and waste outlets, that was for sure. Better to humor this master, than find his contract sold on to some other harsher one.

"Machines are more valuable than street-dirt like me, with their expensive parts and programming. Not so easy to replace."

The old man tapped his cane on the back of the chair. "Is that what you think? You have more potential than any auto-bot. You shouldn't let others" low expectations shackle your dreams. Do you want to be a pilot or not?"

Heat flared on the back of Jerren's neck. He jumped up, bumping the desk forward. "Frag it, yes, I do old man."

"Well enough talk, more learning." Sokranis' voice was mild.

Jerren peered back at the paper, another retro-choice when even class 5 used holoscreens from birth. The patterns called and he immersed himself in the clean beauty of the numbers.

06.1415.23

A gong sounded for midday meal. A reverberating mechanical noise. No, a warning alarm. He struggled to sit up, to check his console but he was pinned down, imprisoned. He couldn't see. He couldn't move.

A sudden screech of noise hit him like a tidal wave. Sound clawed at his brain. He pulled away, the instinct to curl into a ball, hands clamped over his ears, foiled by a restraining force. Heat and pain washed through him.

"Cardiac output erratic, temperature spiking. He's going into shock." Concern deepened the woman's voice.

Was it hers? No, similar husky tone, but the accent was from the north-west continent. He opened his eyes, nothing changed. Just the same dense blackness. He struggled to breathe.

"One hundred mil of Immosprin and increase the air flow." A

cold clinical voice, male and cultivated.

"What's happening, Doctor Menke?" the softer feminine voice again, holding a hint of panic.

"His system is rejecting the cyborg-implants. It's not uncommon at this stage, especially given the amount of blood loss and severe tissue and organ damage he has suffered. The appropriate dose of Synfexs513za should hold it."

A shiver like the cold of space shot through him. Cyborg-implants. No, never. He could feel his limbs, arms pinned to his side, feet straight out. Surely this was a dream, a nightmare. He couldn't stay here. Better to die than fall into the hands of the Consortium. Sweat beaded on his skin, slid into his eyes. He still couldn't see, couldn't move, trapped like a specimen pinned in a display case.

"Cardiac rate and respiration rising. Should I add a sedative to his intake port, Doctor?"

"No, I don't want it interfering with testing."

"Wouldn't it be better to allow recovery time after such extensive surgeries?"

"Fresh out of cybernetics training, and you think you know better? We're working on a tight timeline here. You know how the Director rewards failure to deliver. Or you soon will."

The sharp intake of breath. "Heart rate and respiration remain raised. If the subject feels distress, won't that interfere with our testing, sir?" The woman's voice was clipped, disapproving.

"It's arguable if the subject feels. Not as we do. Alright, intern, a low dose of mood blocker."

A soft crinkle, a metallic clang, followed the rustle of synthocloth.

A feeling of disconnect crept through him. Far away, like a small cloud on the horizon, he could feel his terror, the horror of what these functionaries of the Consortium were doing to him, but balled up and at a great distance, as though it was some other class 6 loser. Not him.

"Vitals are returning to normal, sir."

"Good, proceed with your remaining tests, but remember, Intern Jenfer, not to anthropomorphize the subject."

The whisper of a touch brushed against his shoulder. The whirl of an ultrasonic wrench. His fingers curled and right arm jerked upward. It felt awkward, involuntary. He focused, trying to move his arm sideways but, without his input, it extended back down onto whatever surface he was strapped to. "Cybernetic limbs are working on direct stimulus," the woman's subdued voice.

Another rougher touch, grabbed his chin, pushed his head to one side. "Auditory channels appear functional."

Something spongy settled over his ears. A soft beep repeated in varying increments of volume and pitch. First one ear, then next.

The rustle of synthocloth and then the soft beep of a bio-recorder. "Hmm, visual circuits appear complete."

"Do you mind if I ask, why leave the visual connections to last."

A soft grunt of disapproval. "Not quite last, we still have to connect voluntary initiation of movement and the speech centers."

"And why bother with cyborgs at all. Wouldn't androids be more practical and more controllable."

"AI androids with the full capabilities of human subjects are experimental and expensive. The human brain is complex and humans breed like vermin among the underclasses."

"But surely—"

"You were born class 3 in a medium density enclave, right?"

"Yes, but—"

"Then you have no idea how they breed out there in the regions." Scorn dripped in the older male's voice. "They are little more than animals, but with the right upgrades they can be useful servants of the Consortium."

"But still," The woman's voice quavered. "Even Class 6 are human. Do they pick them up off the streets?"

"No of course not, we're not savages. Mostly they're criminals and rebels. Sometimes, they volunteer to the program, for the money that goes to their families. Haven't you read the briefing notes? Where did you think they came from?"

"I thought the subjects were deceased ..." her voice trailed off. "He doesn't look like a violent criminal," she added.

"Hmm, you'd be surprised. Not that they are all violent. His genetic markers indicated a south Filane origin, a backward region. Besides, his injuries suggest a brutal fire-fight. He's a criminal, probably a killer."

"But to be so far out in space."

"A rebel, maybe. Not, our concern, Intern. I'm sure all due procedures would have been followed. If you have completed your tests, I'll activate the visual circuits."

The acrid smell of sweat, aftershave and stale stew invaded Jerren's senses, and with it a change in air pressure and warmth. The hum of a probe came closer. Rough fingers pried open his eyelids. His instincts were to recoil, his muscles straining against the restraints.

"That should do it."

A sudden flood of blue-white light seared through him. He clamped his eyes shut and pushed the back of his head into the gel padding, tears streaming down his cheeks.

"Good, definite response to visual stimuli. Pupils contracting evenly." That hated clinical voice.

Fingers pried his eyes open again. The light coalesced into one bright beam and a large, multi-focal examination lamp, partly obscured by a figure in white overalls.

"The ocular implant appears to have melded with the biological elements."

"His neural networks have spiked."

"It can be overwhelming to start with. Visual networks take up forty-four percent of processing power. We'll shut him down, if it overloads him."

Rubbery lips and heavy cheeks loomed above him. Eyes a pale, washed out gray and yellowed teeth in a light-brown, time-worn face. Sparse hair stuck out from a white surgical cap. An ocular instrument perched in one eye.

The face receded. "We've made good progress." The doctor rubbed his gloved hands, his wide mouth curving into a broad smile.

Behind him were nondescript metallic grey walls in a medium size room. He could be in any one of a hundred Consortium space bases. Ocular implants. Cyborg parts. It should matter, what they were doing to him, turning him into a machine to be used against all he believed in. He wanted to care but he couldn't. It was if an invisible plasiflex wall stood between the words and his emotions, his awareness of who he was. He strained against the mental restraints.

The young woman leaned closer, bringing the faint scent of roses. "Shall I initiate rest mode."

"We should do a preliminary ambulatory test first."

"Sir, we'd both benefit from a few hours sleep, as would the subject." She rubbed her eyes, weariness obvious in the slump of her shoulders.

"This won't take long. We're on a tight schedule." Menke picked up a small rectangular device with an array of buttons and blinking lights. "Elevate gurney to vertical position."

"Elevating."

The bed beneath him pivoted, raising his head, lowering his legs.

"Good. Disconnect input and feed lines, switch to remote monitoring."

"Yes, sir." The woman leaned over and keyed in a sequence on the holoscreen.

"Better have the neuralizer at the ready, as a precaution."

"If you say so." The intern picked up a device that looked like a light laser-rifle, handling it as though it might explode in her hands.

Menke's eyes narrowed, then he shrugged. "Remove remaining clamps."

A soft hissing noise accompanied the release of tightness on his chest, thighs, and forehead.

"Restraining clamps disengaged."

He swayed forward on his feet, then rocked back against the padded gurney. His legs felt strange, as though he were balancing on stilts. Blood rushed from his head, making him dizzy.

Menke pointed the device at him, keying in a complex pattern. "Initiating walk sequence."

Without his volition, he took a couple shaky steps forward.

"Wouldn't it become tiresome to input movement controls all the time."

"This device includes sophisticated programming of a variety of maneuvers. Still, eventually, he'll move on his own volition, once the psych-programmers are sure the mental restraints and neural programming are in place. Of course, the self-destruct circuits are a failsafe."

"A comforting thought."

If only he could self-destruct and take these lackeys of the Consortium with him. Would there be a way he could access it? Unlikely. He didn't have control of his own body or even his emotions. His legs continued to walk without him, his arms hanging stiffly next to his sides. He was about to crash into the wall when he turned pivoted walked a few more steps, turned, stood still.

A cyborg stood a few paces in front of him, half finished, large areas of metallic parts exposed. Both legs and an arm clearly artificial, the silvery-dark metal molded to mimic muscle, tendon and bones, contrasting with the soft blue skin of the surgically scarred abdomen and chest. The right side of the face was mostly metallic, extending from semi-exposed, partially metallic jaw to the synthetic ear, upward and beyond the hairline. One reddened human eye, almond shaped lids surrounding a dark and brooding orb, the other with a startling blue mechanical iris. Small metal knobs protruded from the shaved scalp and chest, a larger connector port below the left clavicle.

The hair on his neck and back stiffened. He felt the screaming ball of horror beyond the invisible mental barrier expanding. He knew that face. His skin dimpled and his muscles shuddered. He was looking into an observation mirror at the inhuman monster he'd become. A cyborg of the Consortium.

How many people would he kill under Consortium directives. The ball of horror at the back of his mind exploded, smashing through mental barriers like paper.

Alarms began to shrill.

The intern glanced at the holoscreen. "Heart rate, respiration and neural network spiking."

"Perhaps we've pushed him too far. Be ready to initiate clamps and switch him to rest-mode, once I get him back into the gurney. Initiating walk sequence."

He clenched his fists, both the one of flesh and bone and the one of carbo-metallic alloy. The nails of the flesh and blood fingers dug into his palm. Abomination. They could not do this to him!

"Frag it, his neural circuits are not responding to control pad input. I'll have to do this manually."

"Be careful, doctor. Maybe, we should call security."

"I know what I'm doing." Menke grabbed the subject's elbow. "Come on, big fellow, let's put you to bed."

He swung around, heat flashing through him, his heart shuddering in his chest. He extended the metallic arm, grabbed the portly man by the throat and slowly began to squeeze. "You did this to me." But the words did not reach his mouth, his lips and tongue lay dormant. He was as mute as a beast, less than human.

"Jenfer, the neuralizer," Menke croaked, his hands clawing at the metallic arm, just the tips of his cloth boots touching the metal floor.

The woman lifted the rifle, pointed it towards them.

He smiled. It would be a mercy if they killed him, but he'd take at least one of them with him.

"What are you doing, Jerren?" an irritated voice of infinite patience and infinite sadness. He shook his head, his fingers loosening. It couldn't be. The old man was long gone.

A pellet slammed into his flesh and fizzed. He was engulfed in agonizing white fire through every molecule of his being. He staggered, writhed, his back arched. His vision mottled. He spiraled down into a pain-filled abyss.

***

Jerren jumped out of the hovercar, doing his best to keep the grin from his face. He took a deep breath of the salty air. The street was empty, the nearby houses hushed and waiting. Beyond them, the familiar thunder of the ocean breaking on the beach below the cliffs. The sun was already creeping down the sky's marine-blue dome. Seagulls hovered on the wind, cawing a warning. The harbor was empty.

He glanced toward the old man's compound and frowned. The gate thrashed back and forth in the afternoon sea-breeze. Some careless retainer had left it open. Suddenly, the whitewashed buildings baking in the sun took on a sinister undertow of a nightmare. He pushed away the sense of premonition he hadn't felt since the night his parents were killed. He wasn't going to let childish fears spoil this, his triumph. At last, he'd put his unsavory past behind him.

Adjusting the cuffs of his crisp new uniform, he pushed back his shoulders and strode into the empty compound. No one questioned his origins after winning the prestigious Ritshel prize and passing the Space Academy with full honors. He had his first commission, third officer on a cargo run between the rings and the belt. The old man would be proud. He'd always believed he could do it, the only one that ever did, except for Dana. He'd find her one day soon, but for now, he had to say his goodbyes to his former master and mentor.

Scuff marks scribed a pattern on the weed-choked dirt of the courtyard. The feeling that something was out of kilter prickled his neck hairs and sent a tingling of anticipation into his arms and legs. Abandoning the assumed nonchalant saunter, he quickened his steps, sprinting into the receiving room.

The clutter of crates and parts scattered on the benches and tiled floor was not unusual. Sokranis was a benevolent master and his staff often took advantage of it. By the pit, he'd done it often enough as a scarred street-brat, suspicious of any kind gesture.

He frowned, this level of disarray was unusual though. A chair was overturned, a couple of the boxes on their sides, spilling out the curios and low-tech parts. The holograph emitter of Sokranis' wife and son, both long dead, was smashed into component parts, scattered beside an overturned indoor plant. The more he looked, the more signs of struggle became obvious. The heavy silence was even more telling. This was usually a house of noise and sudden bursts of laughter.

His hand gripped the laser pistol he'd hidden under his arm. Avoiding the smashed components scattered on the floor, he crept across the room. The scrape of metal, a soft whimper came from the inner office. The door smashed open, bouncing off the lime-washed wall. A hulking figure stood on the threshold, laser arm pointed with unerring aim at his forehead. Jerren released his grip on his weapon, slowly raised his hands and linked them behind his head. He was a cargo pilot, not military.

"Inhabitant, state the purpose of your unauthorized presence."

The unblinking stare of the cyborg was disconcerting. Why would the consortium bother sending its mutts to an insignificant outpost like this, to terrorize a harmless old man like Sokranis? The trader made so little money, even extortion would hardly be worth it.

"Comply with request or remedial action will be taken."

"Er ... I'm just visiting the island. I thought I'd celebrate a personal achievement. Some crappy tourist agent suggested the dormant volcano was worth seeing. About the only thing worth seeing on this chunk of rock, but I thought I should at least buy memorabilia of this worst trip ever with an equally crappy souvenir. But I didn't realize the shop was ... er... out of order. So, I'll get out your way."

Jerren peered past the solid bulk filling the doorway, caught a glimpse of a frail figure with flowing white hair.

The cyborg blinked. Jerren could almost see it thinking. It was an R-class adaptation, probably not much smarter than the average autobot. A pity, with that figure, the donor must have been attractive once, despite her unusual height and bulk.

"Rephrase reply minus excess detail."

If he could avoid being detained, maybe he could use the tunnels to mount some sort of rescue plan. He pointed to his chest. "Me tourist." He pointed to the scattered and crushed debris on the floor. "Want curio. Sorry to disturb. Go elsewhere."

"RA-1347 bring the visitor into the room." This second female voice held the chilly slap of deep ocean water.

With the speed of a striking snake, the cyborg gripped Jerren's arm and hauled him into the room. A woman sat in Sokranis' desk chair, her legs crossed at the ankles, her arm leaning negligently on the carved armrest. Her tunic and pants were high-grade synocloth, with the consortium insignia. Petite and, as far as he could see, unarmed. She didn't seem to pose a problem. Unlike the faux-human machine behind him.

Suspended against the retro-bookcases, the old man was imprisoned in a blue, shimmering forcefield. He'd been stripped of his robes, his ribs showing beneath his pale blue skin. His face and body bruised and bloodied and covered with small burn marks.

Heat rushed through him. Jerren pulled against the cyborgs iron grip. "What's going on here?"

The woman unfolded her ankles and stood. "Consortium business. Identify yourself, inhabitant."

He hesitated then pulled his arm free and stood tall. "Third officer Neon of the CMSF Adventurer. Inhabitant Class 3 KITOSF-ST5788."

A port opened on the woman's forehead, flashing a bright, focused light into his right eye. "Retinal scan confirms identity. How do you know this traitor to the Consortium?"

Frag it, a cyborg controller. Who knew what other augmentations were hidden beneath the synthoskin. He couldn't help his old mentor if they were both detained. Sokranis was level 2, he had privileges. If Jerren could contact legal representation, he could arrange for the old man's release and compensation for wrongful arrest. This had to be a mistake.

The old man lifted his head. "I've never seen this Consortium lackey before," he whispered through bruised and bloodied lips.

The RA unit stepped forwards, smashing the old man across the face. "Silence, rebel scum. You were not given permission to speak."

Sokranis gave a faint smile. "Darkinth dar le mellis." He muttered in Archaic. The cyborg kneed him in the groin. The old man writhed within the force-field restraints, a moan escaping his clenched lips.

It was all Jerren could do to stand there. He wanted to tear these monsters apart, component by synthetic component. Slowly, the meaning of the words filtered through. What treasure could the old man possess?

The other unit sighed. "RA-1347. Please refrain from excessively damaging the prisoner before we gain the required information. Then you can mangle him as much as you want."

"Then I'm not ..." the old man gasped for breath. "I'm not

scheduled for upgrade?"

"Please, it would be a waste of resources. A scrawny, half-mad relic." She turned, looked Jerren up and down. "Now this one would make a good specimen. If you tell us what we want to know, I could ensure that doesn't happen."

Jerren stomach clenched. "I'm not in violation of any consortium regulations. I owe no debts." An anonymous donor had paid off his contract and application for level 4 status, allowing him to take on a new identity and win the scholarship to the Academy. He'd had his suspicions, though the old man always denied it.

Sokranis spat out a froth of blood. "Do what you like, Sonja or whatever alphanumeric label you use now. What do I care about some crazy tourist." The long speech left the old man gasping for breath. His eyes narrowed. "An echo of the infinite. You can resist them. They don't have to win."

The woman blinked. "I am not ..." She took a step closer, her whole body stiffening. "Then you admit your opposition to the Consortium."

Sokranis just smiled and slumped forward, his head lolling.

The cyborg's scan bathed the motionless form with a blue light, "Vital signs absent. Diagnosis cardiac arrest." She keyed a pattern on her arm. "Transport, detainee to medbay for attempted revival."

The haze of a transit beam and his old mentor was gone. Jerren stared at the empty spot, his world tumbling around him.

"Should I acquire KITOSF-ST5788."

"Leave it, you moron."

"He has seen ..."

"Nothing. Just the lawful remedial action against a rebel." The CQ unit turned to face Jerren. Was that dampness in her eyes? "Nobody escapes our reach. Remember that, inhabitant Neon."

Jerren couldn't shake the feeling that somehow, Sokranis had done just that.

07.1030.02

Jerren walked through the shimmering door, Menke close behind clutching the control pad. He came to a sudden stop in front of a wide, semi-circular resin desk, a revolving, holographic image of the local galaxy at its center.

A tall woman, svelte, with cinnamon skin and cropped curly hair looked up and beamed. "Now that's a refreshing view."

She stood, her silky white dress hanging sheer to her knees. An ornate gold bracelet wound around her right arm. Her gaze swept him from head to feet and back again as she walked slowly around him. "I think I'm going to enjoy working with you." She looked over his shoulder, her face hardening. "You are behind schedule, Menke."

"Yes, Director Ava. The subject's injuries were extensive, but I'm happy to report good progress."

"Despite some mishaps. I'm glad the neuralizer didn't cause the subject permanent damage."

"Some minor memory loss. Such break-through incidents are rare but not unknown. As you see, control has been restored without further incident." Menke cleared his bruised throat. "If I might suggest, we move to normal stage 2 adaptation and further hardware testing. We could gain greater control of his hormonal and physiological reactions with full removal of unnecessary systems pertaining to digestion and ... er ... mating activities. He has showed no adverse reaction to complete nutritional supply though his central-venous port. The nutro-packs are designed to provide all requirements and titration of neurochemicals and synthetic-hormones as required. The—"

Yes, Menke, I'm quite aware of such basic design features. And no, you do not have permission. We will move immediately to stage 3."

"I don't think that would be wise."

"I didn't ask your opinion, Doctor. Did you take the regulation tissue cultures?"

"Yes, but—"

"Then please initiate culture of synthetic-skin hybrid, using the subjects own bio-cellular material."

"Ma'am, such a procedure is unwarranted when syntho-skin is more economical and durable. It would take over twelve Nardvan days to grow, given the surface area required. The synthetic skin is—"

"Doctor Menke, are you questioning my orders?"

"No, just that the expense would blow a—"

"Doctor. I'm only going to explain this once. This ES cyborg unit has incalculable value to the plans of the Consortium, whereas class 3 medical hacks are imminently replaceable." She turned and tapped her chin. "or upgradable. Do I make myself clear?"

Menke made a strangled noise before stuttering. "Yes, Director."

"Then I expect the skin hybrid ready for bonding in twelve Nardvan days. You better get to work, Menke."

"Yes, ma'am." The doctor turned, took two steps toward the door.

"Oh wait, Doctor. Leave the control on the desk. And ask my PA to send in some refreshments."

Menke's mouth pulled into a tight line. He slammed the controller on the desk and stalked out of the room.

"Uggh, the stupid pride of class 3 inhabitants can be so annoying, don't you think."

Jerren stood still, unable to move. Was she trying to establish rapport? Every movement of this woman spoke of wealth, privilege and casual power. He stared at the star patterns on the large view screen on the opposite wall. A subtle scent of vanilla and jasmine came from behind him. His stomach shivered at the soft touch of her fingers tracing the scars on his back, moving around to his abdomen. "We'll have to decide which marks would be best to leave, if any." She came into his visual range, her golden eyes scanning every detail of his physique.

"Well, for all his attitude, Menke does good work, you have to admit."

What did she want from him? She had to be high up in the Consortium. Director of what? Cybernetics. He could feel the disconnect of the mood blocker, but if he could focus his rage, force them to neuralize him again. How many times before it did him irreparable damage? His continued existence was a threat to his friends.

She stepped closer, looking him in the eye. "Where do you really come from, I wonder. Oh, I know, Captain Neon of the CMSP Limitless, turned rebel." She tilted her head. "But we have no record of you before you won the scholarship. You're surprised? We've had our eye on you for a while, though until now you've always managed to slip through our nets. It's been quite exciting to finally meet you. Though why you'd sacrifice yourself to gain an inconsequential artifact from the vault is a mystery. But never mind, you will tell us eventually."

He strained against the neural-straightjacket. Never! But he still couldn't speak or move without the input from the control.

The door swished open and a slim young girl walked in carrying a tray. She ducked her head and placed it on the desk. "Director."

"Ah, Evanjoline, thank you. Now, could you ask Psych-programmer Ferier to join me. And, see if you can get some serviceable clothes to fit … our new ES class operative."

"At once, ma'am." The girl backed out and he was left alone with this strange woman.

"We're not savages after all. Now, are you hungry? It seems you haven't eaten for some time. Intravenous nutrition may be adequate for replacing nutritional requirements but is hardly pleasurable. Please take a seat, eat, drink." She waved at the desk.

Was she mocking him, mocking what he'd become? He couldn't move a muscle and she knew it. Good, let her mock, the ball of rage was building, he could sense it pushing against the mental restraints. This time, he wouldn't hesitate. He'd crush her and rid the world of one more Consortium parasite.

"Oh, that's right. Please excuse me." She picked up the controller and keyed in a sequence.

Like air exploding out of a decompressed ship, the tight control on his volition released. He staggered, gripped the desk.

"You might regret that, lady." The words came out as a garbled croak, but at last he had control of his vocal cords. A strange joy sang through him, like a cleansing wind. He straightened.

Ava gestured toward her chair. "Sit down."

"No," he enunciated the word carefully. Took a step toward her, flexing his cybernetic arm, feeling its strength and speed.

Before he could reach her, she lifted her arm, palm out. Lightning zapped from the center of her palm, hitting his chest and playing over his skin. He stopped, paralyzed, pain playing his nerves like fingers on a holoscreen. Sixty seconds of intense, mind-numbing agony. Slowly it ebbed away, leaving him weak and disorientated. He clutched the end of the desk, panting.

"Now, Neon. Be a good boy, and sit down."

Maybe that thing only had one charge. He clenched his jaw, moved toward her. She stretched her arm and opened her palm. Without wanting to, he took a step back. Once more the blue-white fire played over him, even more agonizing than before.

"You are stubborn, but you'll learn. Sit."

She dragged the chair to him and he sank down, his muscles trembling. She handed him a tall, cool glass of guava juice.

"Something from home, perhaps." She smiled.

When he didn't take the glass, she set it to his lips and tipped. The sweet cool fluid dripped down his chin, some trickling into his mouth. After an alume of space rations and forced intravenous fluids, it was ambrosia. He closed his eyes and turned his head away. Undeterred, she parted his lips with gentle fingers and placed the fragment of a Nolmecan delicacy on his tongue. Memories of Kito, of the island, of Dana, and the old man, flooded back, the pleasure too painful to bear. What's the harm in such a simple act? To drink, to eat? He couldn't be beholden to her.

The door swished open and a solid, middle-aged man in medical overalls walked in.

Ava placed the frosted glass next to Jerren's hand. She faced the newcomer. "It's a simple formula, don't you agree Doctor Ferier. Pain for disobedience, pleasure for obedience."

"Certainly, director. I have yet to find a living entity I could not condition given enough time, so that their only desire is to please."

Shaken at how his body, yet again, betrayed him, Jerren pushed the juice away, turned his gaze away from the plate of food. "Why?"

Ava tilted her head. "Why not use neural restrainers and drugs on you? Ah, Neon, such clumsy measures are sufficient for RA and even CQ models but not for you. We have a very sophisticated mission and you'll need the use of all your bio-cybernetic wits. You are worth a thousand of our friend Doctor Menke to the Consortium or even a hundred of the good doctor Ferier here. No offense Ferier."

"None taken."

She pushed the food closer to him again and turned to the Doctor.

"You've looked over the specified parameters?"

"Yes, Director. And I've studied all the case notes, including Menke's. Your request is difficult, but not impossible."

"Menke will need access to complete the hybrid-skin grafts and final cosmetic changes."

"That shouldn't interfere with my schedule. How long do I have?"

"Twelve days."

"Tight but doable."

"Excellent. I wish to personally review the subject's progress. Send him to my office at eighteen hundred each day."

Ferier raised his shaggy eyebrows. "As you wish, Director."

"You don't warn of the dangers?"

"Not at all Director. Since you know his value, I doubt you'll damage him too much."

Ava laughed. "Now, I'm hurt." She reached over and picked up a rice roll, popped it into her mouth and swallowed. "Look at the fire in his eyes. It's almost a shame to bring him to heel. Neon, stand."

He glared at her. She lifted her arm. He stood, ashamed at the mixture of fear and hunger warring inside him.

"Go with the good Doctor. Oh, and Ferier, you probably want to take this with you."

Ferier caught the control with a grimace. "For now, perhaps, but not for long, I assure you."

***

A band was playing traditional Filane music, almost but not quite drowning out the carefree laughter and conversation in the room across the grand hall. Jerren gazed at the prized paintings on the wall. He adjusted the neckline on his captain's jacket, fighting the feeling that he was out of place, that he should be in the contract workers compound or handing out whatever fancy drinks were being served to the high-class inhabitants of Kito.

He turned and gazed out the high windows, at the extensive grounds. Picturesque lanterns adorned the trees and late arriving hovercars were skimming along the long drive. Bad timing. Maybe he should have waited until morning. But he had to do it now, before he ran out of nerve.

He heard footsteps in the hall, turning and entering the reception room. At last. He swung round. Looking into Attaché Hakan's stern face, his smile froze. It was hard to trace any resemblance in the man to his younger daughter.

"Sir," he stammered, then straightened his shoulders. "I'd hoped to speak to Dana."

"So I've been told. Whatever you have to say, you can say to me."

This was awkward, but he'd need the Attaché's permission sooner or later, not least because he had final authority over partnering in the region. He dug in his jacket pocket and pulled out the data crystal.

"Er, I have a proposal to partner with—"

"I know why you're here, Jerren. Just tell me why you think my daughter would accept an offer from class 6 street-trash, the thieving son of two no-good troublemakers?"

His pulse throbbed in his throat. He took a minute to squash his anger. "Sir, if I may point out. Since my promotion, I am registered as class 3," The same as you, old man. "I have been granted captaincy of a space-freighter and my annual remuneration is 250 kilocredits. Furthermore, I have invested widely and have a respectable portfolio of stocks and property, including a large interest in the Zanania iridium mines."

"I already downloaded this." The frost didn't melt from the Attache's grey eyes. "So…?"

"So, I can offer your daughter a comfortable future. As an exo-scientist, specializing in mineral exploration, she would be a valuable member of my crew and, well, we are very compatible in other aspects. We are a good match. And …" he paused. "she thinks so also."

"And how do you figure that?"

"We met last year at the asteroid mining conglomerate HQ." He cleared his throat. "It is what we both want, sir. If you ask your daughter …"

Hakan's face hardened. "I have. She may have a foolish infatuation with you Captain … Neon … but there are two things that make such a partnership impossible."

Jerren clenched his fists. "And what would those be?"

"You may have been able to fool the Academy, but I know who you are. You can never wash off the stink of the street. And, secondly, I have just accepted the proposal of Envoy Zavia's son."

"Dana would never agree to that."

"She doesn't have to. Nobody on Nardva refuses the proposal of a Class 2 inhabitant."

"That's just … retro. I have achieved my position by my own abilities—"

"You're just like your father, Jerren, ideas above your station. If you're not careful you'll end up like him too." Hakan showed his teeth. "I had the "pleasure" of meeting him while representing our region at the general assembly in Pelinor."

"My father died in a converter accident. You said it was his negligence, but he would never have been that careless. That's why I had to work off …" Jerren's voice faded. "How could you …?"

"Your parents were rebels against the Consortium. Probably in league with old fools like Sokranis."

"You mean, they were executed?" Jerren shook his head. Could it be true "But why?"

"How would I know? Maybe you could ask them next time you're in Pelinor. You fool, they were upgraded and are both now good servants of the Consortium. Though not so great at conversation, not that such Grade 6 scum ever was. A vast improvement I think."

"No, you're lying. None of this is true."

"Go to Pelinor and see for yourself. But Jerren, if I find you within a lek of my daughter— and I'll have my eyes out for you, don't worry—Consortium Security will receive another data-crystal. I think they'd be very interested to know that the son of the notorious rebels Belged and Sonya, a mere class 6 inhabitant in fact, is masquerading as a CMSF captain."

"You're bluffing. I earned my captaincy and my contract was paid out. Whatever my parents may have done, I've given six loyal and unblemished years of service to the Consortium."

"It would take the change of a couple of bytes of data to say otherwise."

"Not even you have that authority."

"But Envoy Zavia does. And I believe he has a great affection for his son. Now get out. The stink of trash is making me sick."

"Perhaps that's because it comes from you."

Jerren grabbed the gift-wrapped box and walked past the smirking Attaché. If what Hakan said was true, and he would check it out, then he was done with playing by the Consortium's rules. He would work against them until his dying breath. But how could he expect Dana to understand, to sacrifice the life she'd always known?

12.1055.28

Jerren stared at the screen, random images flashing up at five-second intervals. He shifted against the jell padding, wishing he could scratch his itching scalp under the electro-neural interface cap. He lifted his hand. A painful jolt of electricity coursed through him. Blast it. He kept forgetting. They didn't like him interfering with the equipment. He calmed his breathing. It was worse anticipating when an involuntary reaction to the images would initiate a painful zap or a sudden jolt of pleasure.

The doors to the room swished open. Ferier walked over to stand behind him.

"Hmmm." The pysch-programmer turned to his console,

activating the holoscreen and pulling up an array of numbers with different colors and arrangements. Jerren turned his head to get a better look. Another jolt, stronger this time. His eyes watered. He dragged his attention back to the training screen. Any lapse in concentration was punished. Moments later the screen faded to black. Eleven hundred hours. He'd completed the gruelling five hours of mind-numbing and painful training. The numbers on Ferier's screen continued to form patterns.

"Why don't you strap a visor to my face, if focus is so important." Jerren couldn't keep the irritation out of his voice.

"Ah, good question, ES-SP26, or do you prefer Neon? Compliance with orders is a vital part of your programming. It would be easier for you, if you didn't resist."

Jerren rolled his shoulders and said nothing. It was becoming harder not to modify his thoughts, to resist the pressure to conform to safe or rewarded channels.

"Neon is not your original name, is it?"

Ferier shrugged when he didn't respond. "You will comply eventually. Extend your arm please."

The doctor unzipped the sleeve of Jerren's bodysuit and examined the nutro-pack strapped to his arm. An intake line snaked up his arm and entered the port in his chest.

"Initiating midday nutrient mix, 80:10." Ferier turned and keyed in a sequence on the holoscreen. "There will be a slight delay in your scheduled rest period. The surgical team have requested bio-material. I've scheduled a medium intensity training session for you at exercise station 11 at fifteen hundred and an ultrasonic cleansing routine before your session with the Director at eighteen hundred hours." He enlarged a group of numbers on the holoscreen. "A session I see you are looking forward too."

Jerren grimaced. "It is the only time each day I eat food in a normal fashion."

Ferier gave a knowing smile. "Ah, of course. In style, no doubt. You understand, we are on a tight timeline. Normal biological functions are ... inconvenient ... and are adequately taken care of for now. Is that all you do together?"

Jerren's cheeks flushed. "She discusses a range of topics with me. When she's not zapping me for trying to kill her."

The doctor chuckled. "It can get boring stuck on a space station for a long time. One takes one's amusement where one can."

"Which Space Station—?" A zap of intense electricity left him gasping.

"ES-SP26, you know any questions about operational parameters are prohibited. Information will be divulged only when relevant to your mission."

Jerren closed his eyes and swallowed. "And what is my mission?" He waited for the jolt but none came.

"You will be informed at the appropriate time. To be honest, the Director is keeping that to herself though perhaps it involves social situations. Now, tell me, at what point in your service with the Consortium Mercantile Space Fleet did you become involved with the rebels?"

Jerren considered his response. "One—" This jolt was stronger and left his teeth tingling.

Ferier's amiable face hardened. "My dear fellow. We know that you've been involved for at least four years and our psychometric testing," he gestured to the screen, "suggests longer."

"Six years." Unbidden, a flash of mild pleasure left him unsettled.

"See, that wasn't so hard. The answer is consistent with data from our informant."

Jerren sat up straighter. A spy?

"Ah, yes, we have an inside source, though not as reliable as we'd like."

Is that why his mission was compromised? Zaphron had to be warned. "He can't have been too useful. Who ...?" He pushed back into jell pads and gritted his teeth even before the next jolt hit.

"Neon, your friends left you to die."

"It was necessary." He hadn't counted on surviving the fire fight. The holoscreen's numeric array shimmered in the corner of his eye, tantalizing patterns teasing his mind.

"Such misplaced loyalty. The Consortium may have its faults, but it is necessary. You'll come to understand that the rebellion is a cancer which threatens the stability of our planetary system."

"They seek a better way." He was shocked how hard it was to resist the psycho-programmer's insidious suggestion.

"Idealistic, perhaps, but sadly mistaken. Even if they had a hope of winning, it would cost many lives."

"True, but—." Another shot of pleasure, hard to ignore. The numerals reconfigured into different, less jagged patterns. If only he could bury his real thoughts and emotions behind some impenetrable screen, much as the mood blocker had done.

The doctor touched his shoulder. "See that wasn't so hard to admit. You are a valued asset to the Consortium. Yet your former friends will kill you on sight, once they know you're a cyborg."

"Yes. So would—." He arched his back, pure pleasure assuaging the sting of his sorrow and self-disgust. He had to resist its addictive pull, think of something else than the craving to please. The numbers. He'd hacked into Consortium systems before, burying the programming deep, behind walls within walls. A kernel of an idea began to form.

Ferier leaned forward, his eyes fixed to the changing modulations of the holoscreen. "Fascinating."

The door swished open, and Intern Jenfer walked in. She looked at Jerren, flushed then looked away. "Excuse me, Doctor, I need more bio-cellular samples."

"Ah, Jenfer, come in. Take what you want. I'm sure ES-SP26 will have no objections."

"Thank you, Doctor." She gave Jerren an apologetic smile. "This may sting. Please extend your arm."

Jerren complied and bit back a laugh as he watched her tap his blood, the rich red fluid frothing into the tubule. After all the pain he'd endured, a small needle prick, the skin samplings were barely noticeable.

"And how is the good Doctor Menke progressing?" Ferier asked.

"We're on schedule, sir. The skin sheets are bonding well with the polymer underlay. It just takes time." She glanced from the neural cap to the holoscreen. "Can you really see his ...er ... thoughts?"

Ferier perched on his desk. "Not exactly, my dear, or rather not directly. The holoscreen displays a range of physiological and neural reactions which can be interpreted, modified or augmented. Of course, the neural circuits I inserted on day 5, help with the process, especially initiating direct neural control."

"Is that what the control pad uses?"

"Yes, indeed, and other basic control routines, but in an ES unit and to some extent with CQs, we need more nuanced control. If you are interested in psycho-programming, I would be happy to tutor you."

"I would like that, Doctor Ferier." She placed the samples in the box. "Does he remember his past?"

"Why don't you ask him yourself, Intern."

"ES-SP26 what is your background?"

"I'm a mindless Consortium cyborg. Arggh ..." The shock left Jerren panting.

Jenfer bit her lip. "Maybe ..."

"ES-SP26, don't be discourteous."

Jerren shifted in his seat. It couldn't hurt to give them what they already knew. "I served in the Consortium Mercantile fleet for six years before joining the rebellion."

"So, he is class 3?" The young intern's voice quavered.

"Doubtful. Records indicate he entered the Academy on a scholarship, but nothing before that, and he is reluctant to talk about it." Ferier pointed at an array of greying numbers. "See, this suggests latent but deep shame. So, I'd surmise Class 5 or lower. Am I right, Neon?"

Jerren bunched his fists, heat flaming his cheeks. He bit back the angry retort that would earn him another painful jolt.

Ferier smiled. "He's riled." He pointed to the tight spikey formations. "If I had time, he'd tell me everything he's ever thought or done, but as his contact with the rebels is years later, his unsavory upbringing isn't highly relevant. Besides, the Director has put the priority on compliance."

"He ..." Jenfer blushed. "If you look past the replacement parts, he looks normal. No different from someone I might meet at a social gathering. And, such sadness in his eyes."

Ferier chuckled. "You are very empathetic. You are wasted in the surgical unit, Jenfer." He stood up. "But don't be deceived by appearances. He was a rebel. A remorseless killer."

"And now?"

"And now, he's a sophisticated, expensive killing machine."

"Machine parts, yes, but human—."

Jerren ignored the irritation of being spoken about like an item of inventory and turned his attention to the numbers. Was it possible to take control of the programming from the inside ...

Ferier gave a harsh laugh. "No Jenfer, not human. Just a sophisticated bio-cybernetic machine with an off-switch. ES-SP26 initiate safe rest mode."

... maybe if he could— "Affirmative." Responding to a forced routine mid thought, he folded his arms across his chest and leaned back as the seat became horizontal. "Safe rest mode initiated."

***

Jerren splashed through the shallow salt water pools in the double moonlit sea cave, his grief at losing Dana an open wound. He brushed away the moisture on his face, not all of it seawater. Hakan's words stung more than they should have, but more than anything, they ripped open the façade, revealing that the Consortium was rotten to the core. He'd long pondered Sokranis' dying words, but until now he'd been reluctant to act.

Darkinth dar le mellis, find the hidden treasure. He'd thought of many places the old man could have meant, but this was the most hidden. He had to hurry though, before the high tides flooded the cavern again. He shone his communicator light toward a small alcove perched above the tide line and pulled out a small box. Jumping to the cave floor, he forced the lock. Water swirled around his calves, the water rising. The box was empty. It was one of Sokranis' designs, so maybe ... It took precious minutes to find the hidden mechanism. In the secret compartment was a slip of paper with a numeric code, translating to a single name. Zaphron. His first link to the rebels.

The cave shimmied and faded. "Darkinth dar le mellis" the soft voice echoed in the darkness.

"I found your treasure. And look where that's got me, old man."

"An echo of the infinite. A hidden treasure ..." The crazy old man's voice frayed into the roar of waves.

19.1436.51

The cyborg"s eyes blinked open. He still found the sudden transition from the fragmented, vivid dreams of the rest-mode to full wakefulness jarring. He was fastened to the surgical unit gurney, unable to move. Panic was unnecessary. Director Ava had warned him about this final procedure, necessary for his mission. His training and preparation were complete.

With a hint of roses, Intern Jenfer bent over him, running the ultrasonic probe over his bio-cybernetic systems. "How are you feeling today?"

"In perfect condition, Jenfer."

"Intern Jenfer, how many times must I tell you not to anthropomorphize the subject," Menke growled. The Doctor keyed in the sequence on the holoscreen. "Initiating full independent control. Let's hope Ferier's programming holds."

The gurney elevated, the restraints released. Jerren stepped forward and stood still as Menke inspected him.

"Perfect. Initiate test sequences."

ES-SP26 followed the series of complex commands with precision. He was anxious to confirm his mission readiness.

An hour later, the door opened and Director Ava walked through, followed by Ferier.

Menke's sullen look deepened. "Director, I was about to deliver the ES unit to your office."

"No need. Let me see him." Ava ran a hand over ES-SP26's chest and abdomen leaving his skin tingling, then she fingered his scalp. Her familiar scent and warmth were pleasing. She took a step back and smiled. "Beautiful work, Menke. I can't tell where the original skin ends and the restored skin starts. His eyes and ears are beautifully matched. He looks human."

Menke's face brightened. "A slight asymmetry to simulate biological growth patterns."

She pivoted. "What about internal security scans."

"Well, a deep scan maybe, but, as per your orders, we used carbometallic material for the replacement limbs and facial replacements. It is of similar weight and density to bone and will not trigger low to medium level scans. His cyborg eye mimics the retinal patterns on record. The neural contacts and input ports are well hidden. As you can see on the schematics, his augmentations are minimal but according to your specifications. He would pass most checks."

"Good work. Ferier, is he ready?"

"The subject is now compliant in all tests. It was a lot easier than I expected, to be honest."

Ava frowned. She gave ES-SP26 a thoughtful look.

He tilted his head. "Does something worry you, Director Ava?"

She raised an eyebrow. "Are you sure he is not faking full compliance?"

Ferier chuckled. "Not possible, Director. Our programming identifies the tiniest recalcitrant thought. I hypothesize that your … special … tutelage has accelerated the conditioning process. You can be very persuasive."

Ava half-closed her eyes, then nodded. "Then we are ready to implement Project Chameleon."

A wave of pleasure flooded ES-SP26's neural circuits. He stood taller. "I am anxious to complete my mission, Director."

"Give me some time alone with him. Turn off all external monitors."

Menke tapped the neurolizer, "Is that wis ...". He swallowed as Ava's glare turned on him. "... as you wish, Director."

The team shuffled out, the doors locking behind them.

"You could kill me with one hand." Ava stepped closer, laying her palm on his heart, the metal of her bracelet cool against his skin. His pulse quickened.

"Not while you wear a neural arrestor."

She took the bracelet off and placed it in his open palm. "And now? Do you still want to kill me, Neon?"

He frowned. "Is that what you wish me to do, Ava? This is at variance to stated mission objectives."

"When I think of all the deaths I'm responsible for, for those I have yet to order. What I have made you ...."

"For the good of the Consortium. I do not wish to kill you."

"Nor I you. Are you clear on your mission parameters?"

"To summarize I must infiltrate the rebels, convince them that I escaped and, once I've discovered their plans, deliver them to you."

"They will suspect that you have been compromised."

He nodded. "My escape must be convincing, my true nature hidden for as long as possible."

"And if you are discovered?"

"Transmit data and eradicate them, by self-destruct if necessary."

"Try not to kill too many of my operatives on the way to the shuttle craft." She handed him a data crystal. "That has the all relevant security details. They will be changed once you have made your escape."

"Shall I proceed."

She closed her eyes. "Yes, initiate Code Awake."

"Initiated." He dropped the bracelet control and ground it with his heel. Picking up the neuralizer, he set it to the lowest level. "This will hurt."

"Yes, sacrifices are sometimes necessary. Just don't fail me."

He paused, the image of the old man's broken body sharp in his mind. "Yes, Director, I will not fail." He pressed the trigger.

She fell to the ground, writhing in pain, her head lolling back. She was still breathing. Killing her would not achieve his objectives. As part of her mission parameters, she would delay the Consortium's efforts to recover him.

He smashed through the mirror into the observation room. It was empty. Bringing up the uploaded schematics in his cybernetic eye, he headed toward the prepared space craft.

He was following her orders, but deep down Jerren knew he had an important overriding objective. To resist and warn the rebellion.

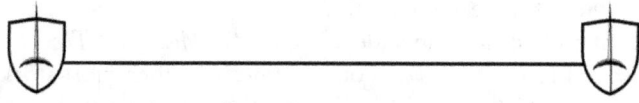

About Jeanette O'Hagan

Jeanette O'Hagan first started spinning tales in the world of Nardva at the age of nine. She enjoys writing secondary world fantasy, science fiction, poetry, blogging and editing. Her Nardvan stories span continents, time and cultures.

Recent publications include *Heart of the Mountain*, *The Herbalist's Daughter* and *Lakwi's Lament*. You can find her other short stories and poems in anthologies such as Futurevision (to be pub Sept 2017), Glimpses of Light, Another Time Another Place and Like a Girl. Jeanette is also writing her Akrad's Legacy Series—a Young Adult secondary world fantasy fiction.

Jeanette has practiced medicine, studied communication, history, theology and a Master of Arts (Writing). She loves reading, painting, travel, catching up for coffee with friends, pondering the meaning of life. She lives in Brisbane with her husband and children.

You can connect with Jeanette at the following places:
Facebook - facebook.com/JeanetteOHaganAuthorAndSpeaker
Twiitter - @JeanetteOHagan
Goodreads - goodreads.com/author/show/9833645
Amazon - amazon.com/Jeanette-OHagan/e/B00RBSE85C
Jeanette O'Hagan Writes - jeanetteohagan.com

Second Contact
By Leo McBride

There was almost a beauty in the destruction.

Cassandra Jelani watched from the observation dome as the *Arcturus Dawn* edged its way closer to the debris field where the titans had breathed their last.

The only member of the crew who was nonessential as the ship approached the beacon marker, Cassandra had retreated to the place she would have the best view of what had brought them here. So here she sat, cross-legged in the middle of the dome, looking out at a battlefield scattered around the planet's outer orbit.

She wished the engineer, Malone, was with her. She could hardly make out how many of the capital ships had come to an end here, such was the volume of wreckage. In places, she struggled to to tell where one ship ended and another began. Malone would have known, but they needed him right now. Engineering, ship design, these were not her strengths. Nor were navigation, or computers. She saw the glares from some of the crew members when they were busy with final approach and she had heard the not so quiet whisper. *Oxygen thief*, so the taunt went. No use on a spaceship for someone who does nothing but take resources.

Stay out of the way. That was best, she thought. Watch the dance and not the orchestra at work.

She tried to discern something of the nature of the ships they were approaching, even as they lay amongst the stars with their broken backs and their ruptured sides, their interiors shredded and open to space.

These were not ships for humans, whose own ships followed centuries of thought and example when it came to design. Starships that reached back to submarines and naval vessels for their design, without their creators even realizing it. Ergonomic fit led to conformity of thought, Cassandra mused, but not so with these titans. "What rules did they follow?" she asked aloud of the empty room. "What bodies were they built for?"

They looked more aggressive somehow, to her untutored eye. No curves or swoops to the design, just blunt in places and sharp in others, shapes like scythes emerging from the spine of one ship, curves like the mandibles of an Earth-world insect marking the front of another. Front? Perhaps, perhaps not, thought Cassandra. She assumed too much. That would be a question she should ask of Malone.

The vibration she felt through the deck floor came to a stop. The thrusters must have stopped. A few moments passed, then her comlink chirped back into life.

"Jelani," buzzed the voice.

"Captain Washington," she replied, "I prefer you to call me Cassandra."

"We've retrieved the beacon," came the sour-voiced reply, "hope you enjoyed the view back there while we were working our butts off."

Cassandra looked up again at the star-field above her. She still could not identify how many ships there were here, so much of this was out of her experience. She tapped her comlink to respond.

"It's... it's hard to find the right words to describe it, Captain."

She could hear him tsk in reply.

"That's not a comforting thing for a captain to hear from the ship's linguist. Get up here, Jelani," he said, then paused, before adding, "and get here now."

***

Malone had locked down the beacon by the time Cassandra reached the bridge, and the central AI was already downloading the telemetry recorded in the two weeks since the first contact crew had noted the presence of the destroyed fleet.

They had followed protocols to the letter – non-engagement, drop a beacon, leave the job to a more qualified crew. The first crew would still get a share in any salvage, the protocols made sure of that, but long experience had taught that leaving significant contact procedures in the hands of inexperienced teams was a recipe for disaster. Half the ships out here were glorified space truckers anyway – and were happy enough to take the potential for a full share without the risk of straying into a hostile environment without the skills to recognize what they were getting into. Let the second contact team take the risks, that's what they're there for.

Malone aside, she got the usual looks from the bridge crew as she arrived.

"Jelani," called the captain, "took your damn time. The computer's already starting to work on translations – you're behind already and last I checked it's working at up to 10,000 possible translation permutations every minute."

Cassandra shrugged. The captain was playing to the crowd and she knew it.

"I don't get paid to translate 10,000 phrases, Captain," she said, calmly.

"Oh? Perhaps you'd care to share what it is you do get paid for, because it seems to me we're doing all the work and you're getting outdone by a computer."

She casually walked over to her terminal – recessed away from much of the rest of the bridge. Sidelined by design as well as by habit, she thought. That wasn't what she said, though.

"How well do you speak French, Captain?"

"French? Never found the need to learn – the autotranslators do the job fine enough. What of it?"

"I speak a lot of languages. A lot. I think I've probably lost count somewhere along the way. There comes a point in learning languages that it becomes almost a process. An equation. That's why the AIs are as successful as they are. I mean, sure, you never notice it when you learn your first alternative language. Not even the second. I think I first noticed it with the third – you lay down rail tracks in your head as you learn. The process becomes noticeable. You know how learning numbers relates to the next step in the process, you start to see how learning the genitive case in, say, Mandarin helps you to see how the same thing works in German. You can almost see it as a calculation – so I can quite understand why many think that AIs can do the job of cracking a new language."

"What's your point, Jelani? And what's that got to do with French?"

She worked the keys on her terminal as she replied, duplicating the data stream and starting to run it through her own filters.

"Well, just as you recognize the equations of language, the similarities, so too do you come to realize the differences. There are words that exist in only one language or another, yet which encapsulate such a profundity of meaning that you wonder how other languages could exist without such a definition. There are so many I love. I remember the first word that made me gasp aloud that a word so completely embraced something I didn't know needed defined. Mångata. It's a Swedish word for the shimmering light of the moon upon the sea that looks so much like a road of moonlight you'd swear you could drive along it in the middle of the night. And that's the translation, the moon road, and it was waiting there all along to be discovered. After that, there were so many – Fernweh, in German, feeling homesick for a place I'd never been to, which once I'd heard it made me long for the stars. Tyjyk, in Gliesian, expressing the regret at the end of a happy first meeting and the longing for time to pass until the second."

"I asked your point, Jelani, I see no sign of you getting to it," said the captain.

"There's a phrase in French, they call it l'appel du vide. Punch it into a computer and it will happily produce a translation that says it is the call of the void. That seems logical enough – but what it truly means is the sense you feel... the longing of wanting to jump from high places. Ever stood on top of a tall building and felt a voice in the back of your head saying do it, jump? That's l'appel du vide... and the computer over there would never tell you that. Yet to know the true meaning changes you – it brings you a concept that you'd never had before. And that, captain, is why I'm here.

"I'm not here to translate 10,000 phrases, captain. The computer can happily do that for you. You can keep your 10,000 phrases. I'm here to find the meaning of one, just one, that might be the difference between understanding whoever we meet out there – or not."

The captain guffawed, unimpressed.

"One phrase? I'll be wanting a lot more from you than that if you're to justify the air you're breathing on my ship. Sounds like the laziest way to earn a share of salvage, in my book. Keep yourself busy, Jelani, but most importantly? Shut up and stay out of the way of people with a real job to do."

With that, he swung back to the rest of the bridge and started barking out the orders for the Go Team to get ready for a shuttle ride. Cassandra clearly wasn't invited, even if the Go Team was going to say hello. She slipped on her headset and began to listen to words that human ears had never heard before.

***

"I don't know why you cause yourself so much trouble, Cassie," said Malone as he sat beside her in the mess hall later. "You know the captain doesn't like having to put up with your bullshit."

Cassandra ate another mouthful of the doro wat stew before replying, savoring the chicken taste even though the texture was kept solid in case of gravity failure.

"Tell me," she said at length, "why is it that the more senior the person is who doesn't like my bullshit, the more likely it is that I have to put up with theirs?"

Malone set his spoon down, and looked at her. "You're not always the easiest when it comes to fitting in, you know," he said.

"Only for people who try to fit me in the wrong place," she shot back.

Malone grumbled back into silence, eating his own food.

"You're the only one on this ship who puts up with me," she said. "Everyone else thinks I'm just a waste of oxygen. And food." She jabbed her spoon at her stew as she said it.

"They need you," she continued. "They don't think they need me. They think I'm a parasite."

Malone chewed for a moment before replying.

"Aren't I a parasite too?" he asked. "Like one of those fish things back on Earth – the little ones that always hang around sharks looking for a scrap of food. The *Dawn* is the shark, I'm one of those... what are they called?"

"Remoras," answered Cassandra.

"Yeah, that's the ones. See? We're the same!"

She shook her head.

"Remoras aren't parasites. Sure, they hang around looking for food, but the remoras deal with the parasites that affect the shark. Keeping the shark healthy keeps the supply of food coming. They mutually benefit, it's symbiotic. Same with you and the ship. The ship needs you to keep it running, you need it to... well, never mind your job, you just love tinkering with it."

"They call that essential maintenance, not tinkering. I tell you what, though, I'd love to go tinker with the remains of those fleets out there. Weird, though, they all look like they're part of the same fleet. Same design, construction. Wonder what the hell made 'em turn on each other. Guess I'll find out when they let me go do some of that essential maintenance on them."

"Was the moonshine still essential maintenance?"

"Damn right it was," he said.

They ate in silence for a while before he spoke again, while Cassandra tapped occasionally on her infopad as it processed different elements from the beacon download.

"Here's the thing, though, Cassie," said Malone as he finished the last of his meal. "Regs say we go to a contact situation, there has to be a translator aboard. They make no mention of having to have an engine monkey like me there. No mention of having to have a captain even. The regs just say science and medical teams, a diplomat if available – and a translator. I wouldn't be out here – none of us would – if you weren't on board. So out here, I'm still stuck being one of those remora things, swimming around in everyone else's wake. But you, Cassie? Out here, you're the damn shark. Go take a bite out of something."

He pushed his chair back to rise – and that's when Cassandra's comlink bleeped.

"Cassandra," came the captain's voice, "we need you up here."

"On my way," she replied quickly, before turning to Malone. "Something's wrong. You'd probably best be down in the engine room just in case."

"Wrong?" he asked, "how do you know something's wrong from just that?"

"The words we use matter," she said. "He called me Cassandra. He never calls me that. Now get going."

***

The bridge was abuzz as Cassandra entered. A holographic display showed a representation of the system outside. Captain Washington was busily shouting orders at the communications officer, Hoban, while the helm officer was snapping off readings from the navigation array. All told, a half dozen different crew members were busily at work on the bridge, not one taking notice of her.

She stood there quietly a moment, trying to work out what was happening. On the display, the *Arcturus Dawn* was the centerpiece, while around it, various other points were highlighted by the AI – including one triangular shape moving from one of the larger hulks. It was headed towards the *Arcturus*.

The communications officer was holding one hand up to the

captain, seemingly calling for quiet as he listened intently to his headset.

Cassandra took advantage of the moment's pause.

"Reporting, Captain. What do you need?"

Captain Washington looked at her, noticing her for the first time in the hubbub of activity. He jabbed a finger at the triangle on the display.

"Our Go Team is coming back early – and their broadcast is messed up somehow. Hoban here can't get a clear signal, and everything coming through the AI translation matrix is gibberish, like a ton of words all jumbled together. Hoban's trying to get through to the crew. See if you can make head or tail of what they're broadcasting. Probably a malfunction of some kind, but we've got a crew of six over there on the Go Team and I want to know they're okay as soon as possible. Get on it."

Cassandra nodded and settled at her terminal, calling for Hoban to dump the broadcast files into her software. The communications officer didn't move, still listening intently to his headset, so she spliced into his terminal from hers and copied the information across.

She didn't pick up her headset yet – the ears could only process information at the speed you could listen, and there was a lot more she could do before that. The first thing she did was to check the text translation coming across. The AI might not be able to handle everything, but it had its uses. Her screen filled with an upward scroll of words – but it came across as some kind of broken, pidgin language. And a disturbing one at that.

Her finger traced across the screen for one passage that leapt out to her. "Calling targets all destroy approaching incorporate vessels or remain neutralize at control safe merge distance annihilate unknown opposition vectors greater detected good danger unity alert."

It was gibberish, certainly, but the vocabulary used was unsettling. She flipped the translation mode off to scan the raw estimated pronunciation, to see if that would bring any clue.

She'd been looking at the files from the beacon for some time now – and at first glance, she couldn't see why the AI would be having a problem with this sequence. It appeared to have the same slightly guttural pronunciation to it. It looked faster, though. The screen was filling up quickly. Cassandra instructed the computer to return a 60-second sequence and ran a word count on it. A little shy of 300 words in that one sequence.

She needed to multitask. She dumped the data into her tablet and instructed it to keep monitoring the number of words translated per minute by the AI. On her terminal, she flipped to looking at an audio waveform of the incoming transmission. The peaks and troughs it displayed were... well, normal, she would have said.

"Computer," she said, "run the waveform against the Go Team crew, tell me who it is."

The screen split into seven displays of wavelengths – the one at the top representing the incoming data stream, while two columns of three showed the voice patterns of each of the crew members on the shuttle.

NO MATCH, displayed the computer screen.

No match? How could that be, Cassandra wondered.

"Overlay them one by one," she said, "are any of them close?"

The computer did as instructed, eliminating readings until only one remained – that of the security officer on the Go Team, Mason. But the reading was only the closest, that she could see plainly as the two waveforms sat side by side. The top one was jagged, full of little sharp spikes and drops, unlike the smoother, rounder curves of Mason's voice file.

"Got anything, Cassandra?" called the captain. "The shuttle's looking ragged on approach – any idea why?"

She shook her head, then glanced up to see him looking expectantly at her, wanting more.

"There's some kind of distortion going on – is the signal clean?" she asked.

The captain looked across at Hoban for an answer, but the communications officer was still bent over his console, listening intently to his headphones. He called Hoban's name, once, twice, but the officer didn't respond, leaving the captain to answer for him.

"Hoban said it was a pure signal – no change from it going out. What we're getting is what they're transmitting."

Cassandra frowned. "Okay. The thing is, we're receiving too much data. We're getting more than twice the amount of translations as words actually being spoken – I don't... I don't understand yet what's going on here. Let me have a listen. Hoban, copy the audio channel over to my terminal."

Again, the communications officer would not stir.

"Hoban," she said, with more snap to her voice this time, "copy it over now. I need full access. Now."

Still, no motion – except from the captain. Frustration on his face, he rose and marched over to Hoban, gripping his shoulder and spinning the communications officer around.

And for the first time, Hoban moved. He surged up from his desk, his hands grasping the captain's shoulders and pushing him to the ground. Captain Washington fell with a cry, trying to throw Hoban off, but without success.

"Captain!" shouted Cassandra, shocked by the sudden attack, her voice bringing the attention of the rest of the bridge crew.

Hoban was on top of the captain now, and pressing close to his face. It looked like he was trying to bite him.

"What the hell?" cried Cassandra, dropping her tablet and rising to run to the Captain's assistance. The big Russian at the sci ops desk, Kostina, was faster, though. He stepped in and, without subtlety, swung a heavy boot into Hoban's side. The com officer clung tightly onto the captain, hands locked around his head.

At that moment, the ship itself rocked. Cassandra looked up at the holographic display.

"The Go Team!" shouted the helm officer, Lopez, "They're firing on us!"

Kostina had lurched to one side with the movement of the ship, but he returned with a massive kick to Hoban's side, enough to throw him off the captain this time. Kostina knelt over the crazed man and hefted one massive fist before swinging it twice. Hoban stopped moving, unconscious.

The ship lurched again. Cassandra dashed to the captain's side, but he seemed dazed, his lips moving but no sound coming out.

"What shall we do, captain?" called Lopez.

"The captain's out of action," Cassandra shouted back. "We need to get him to the medbay. Where's the damn first officer?"

Lopez looked around. "She's off shift, but we're..."

Again, the ship rocked, and this time a batch of alert sensors went off too.

"We're under attack from our own crew – what should I do?"

Lopez was panicked, Cassandra could see. Things rarely went so badly in a contact situation that you didn't see the problems coming. This was... what was this? Sabotage? Mutiny?

She calmed her breathing. No one else was taking charge, so why shouldn't she?

"Defend the ship, Lopez. Take evasive maneuvers, and if you have to, open fire and disable them."

"Open fire?" he asked, "on our own ship? You don't have the authori..."

Cassandra cut him off. "You want to waste time waiting for the first officer while we're being fired on? Stop them before it's more than just the captain needing the medbay!"

Lopez nodded. He turned to his controls and a flare of weapons shone on the display, marking one, two hits on the shuttle, which began to spin aimlessly.

"Got it," he said, his voice shaky, "heaven forgive me, I got it."

"Then keep watch on it and make sure nothing else happens," said Cassandra. "Kostina? We need to get these two to a medbay right now."

The Russian nodded and slapped a communicator to summon the medical team to respond.

***

When the med-team arrived, first officer Abrahams was at their heels

Abrahams demanded to know what happened, but in truth Cassandra wasn't sure herself. She told the first officer how the communications officer had attacked the captain for no apparent reason and how it coincided with the Go Team's ship opening fire. With that, Abrahams had dismissed her, paying more attention to what Kostina and Lopez had to say. For once, Cassandra didn't mind being overlooked. It meant she could get on with trying to figure it out for herself.

The med-team carried both the captain and Hoban off the bridge, taking them down for treatment. Just to satisfy her curiosity, Cassandra popped open a monitor window on the screen to show the activity in the medbay. Her eyes flicked occasionally to the screen as she saw the team first sedate Hoban and then concentrate on identifying what was wrong with the captain, who since being attacked had been listless and... vacant. There was something about the look on his face that bugged Cassandra, but she couldn't quite pin down what it was.

Abrahams had taken the chair and was barking out orders – but in truth, there was less urgency now. The shuttle lost power when it was damaged – so out went its propulsion, its communications and, most importantly, its weapons. Lopez had done a good job – not that it saved him from Abrahams demanding to know why he opened fire without authority.

That debate was one that Cassandra happily tuned out. Her data was far more interesting than petty power games.

Yet for all the data she had, it proved a challenging puzzle. The AI had ground its way through all the transmitted data, and yet it still remained nonsense. Cassandra compared the information to her only other available reference – the voice data from the auto-recordings logged by the beacon, but the language there was very different. Different peaks, different stress points. If there was interference, then it wasn't coming from those transmissions.

The idea lingered, though. Ideas have a way of doing that. Cassandra let the idea grow. If it was interference, where was it coming from? And how could she find out more? Still on her screen were the harmonic waves of the transmission and the Go Team security officer, Mason. That's it, she thought.

"Computer," she began, hesitantly, a little unsure of how to ask for what she wanted. "Eliminate the points of similarity from Mason's waveform compared to the transmission."

The two waveforms overlaid on one another and, in a moment, it changed, becoming a spiky pattern. Mason's voice had been eliminated from the pattern – and yet something still remained, something clearly recognizable as a pattern of its own. That should not be, Cassandra thought.

She instructed the computer to eliminate Mason's input from the entire signal. A moment's processing and there it was, an entirely separate waveform, displayed on her screen.

In the corner of her screen, she noticed the captain was stirring in the medbay. Good, she thought, he's coming round. With luck, she might have some answers for him by the time the medics let him back out – and she knew he wouldn't want to be waiting around in the medbay long with the Go Team still hanging in the wind.

She looped back through her data. The passage that caught her eye earlier did so again. She matched the time sequence of the communication and instructed the AI to re-process it for translation without Mason's waveform. The AI took only a few moments to do so, and Cassandra chilled when she saw the result. In stark, simple words, it appeared on her screen.

Targets. Destroy. Incorporate or neutralize. Control. Merge. Annihilate opposition. Greater good. Unity.

She gasped. There was no way there should have been coherent words here. But... here they were. Yet that explained why there were so many words in the translation – there were two voices in one, one layered underneath the other. The top voice was Mason's, matching just as before. But somehow there was a second voice with it. A voice that, as Cassandra continued to scan the rest of its translation, spoke of destruction, control, incorporation, merging. Annihilation.

She looked at the central display, that showed the remnants of the alien fleet hanging in space. Broken. Shattered. Annihilated.

The harmonics on the waveform were so low that they would barely register to the ear of the listener, she could see, apart from spikes that would sound sharp, like some kind of static. Yet the listener would hear them. They would thrum on the eardrums, the signal carried through to the brain. Subliminally, the listener would hear the message, whispered across the dark, even as they thought they were listening to something else.

"Officer Abrahams," she began, tentatively. "I think I've..."

"What is it?" snapped the stand-in captain impatiently, "Can't you see I'm busy? We've got to recover the shuttle – and I can't say as you've helped any."

"But I think I've..."

Again, Abrahams interrupted, tutting and standing up, moving away from the command chair and coming to lean over Cassandra's console.

"This had better be good."

Cassandra pointed at her screen.

"It took me a while to see this – but there are two voices, no, wait, that's not right, there are two languages in the signal. One voice, but two messages being spoken at once. And the underlying message-"

Abrahams raised a skeptical eyebrow. "This is what you wanted me to see? Now? This can wait."

"But wait, the underlying message is important. It-"

Both of them were interrupted this time, by the feed from the medbay monitor. Captain Washington suddenly burst into life, leaping up and grabbing the nearest medic, and pushing him against the wall. The others present first reacted with shock, then tried to pull him away. The captain was relentless though, pressing his face close to the medic's and, well, doing something, Cassandra wasn't sure what. She peered closely, but still was unsure. The medic collapsed, though, and the captain turned on the next, knocking aside the sedative that was in one hand.

The third medic was trying in vain to pull the captain off, but he brushed her aside, as he concentrated his efforts on the second one.

Cassandra looked closely to see what the captain was doing. When she realized, she gasped. She grabbed the first officer's hand and turned to her, her voice level and demanding.

"Seal off the medbay. Seal it off now. Or we lose the ship."

Abrahams pulled her eyes away from the screen long enough to see the intent in Cassandra's eyes, and nodded before calling to the computer to seal off access to the section and place it under quarantine.

***

"You'd better be able to explain this, Jelani," Abrahams said.

The first officer had summoned the whole of the senior staff, and they had moved from the bridge to the conference area. All eyes were on Cassandra. Including, she noted with thanks, Malone's. Possibly the only friendly eyes in the room.

"I can," said Cassandra. "I think."

A dismissive sigh ran around the room.

"I want more from you than 'I think', Jelani," Abrahams replied. "Get on with it. We've got crew down on both the shuttle and in the medbay and you're the one who thinks you know why."

Cassandra took a breath, then stood, sliding her holographic projector into the centre of the table, ready to display her findings.

"Okay, it's more than I think. I know. You see, we've been invaded."

At this, the senior staff burst into life, some responding with disbelief, some demanding to be allowed to go and get on with real work. Malone held her gaze. As much as she could, Cassandra tried to pour her sincerity into that meeting of eyes. Here she was, a translator, trying to convince a friend without using words. After a few moments, he nodded, almost imperceptibly. He got to his feet and brought one meaty hand down hard on the table, silencing everyone around it. He said just three words. "Let her talk."

With that, the debate ended. And Cassandra spoke again.

"The transmissions were the key," she said. "The signal coming back from the Go Team was odd – the AI kept producing too much translation. Normally, we only speak at around 130 words a minute, give or take, higher in times of stress. But the AI was producing double that in the translation. You see, there were two languages coming through at once."

"The signal was mixed with another?" asked Abrahams.

"No," said Cassandra, "it was all in one voice. It was Mason. But even as he was speaking, there was another voice underneath, as if he was saying two things at once. There was a whole second set of low harmonics there – with a completely separate message from what Mason was saying as far as Hoban could hear."

She punched up the translation from earlier, now supplemented by the AI's expanded translation of the whole transmission with Mason's ordinary waveform removed.

"You see? This is what that voice was saying. Over and over, it talks about destruction or merging. Incorporation or annihilation. That message ran over and over through the transmission. Hoban thought he was listening to Mason – but he was also listening to this."

"And that made him attack the captain?" asked Abrahams.

"No," said Cassandra, punching a few controls to change the display. "Watch."

The image changed from the translation to the recording from the bridge cameras of the moment that Hoban pushed the captain to the floor, the moment when Cassandra thought he was biting him. She zoomed in.

"You see? He's not attacking the captain. He's talking to him."

The crew peered intently at the image, looking as Hoban appeared to be whispering intently in the captain's ear.

"Now see this," said Cassandra, and cut the image to the fight inside the medbay. Again, she zoomed in on the captain as he leaned close to first one, then another of the medics. In each instant, the crew could see the captain whispering into the medic's ear.

"The AI couldn't recognize it as a separate language because it was translating all the data – its job was to churn it all into something we could understand, it couldn't deal with the fact that two languages were being spoken at once. So it returned nonsense, all while Hoban was being subjected to it in the transmission."

"Call it a virus, if you will, a linguistic virus. Language can change you. Language can give birth to new ideas, new concepts. In this case, it is the carrier for this message, that works its way into the brain, that makes the host want to further the message, to spread it. To incorporate. Or annihilate."

She flicked the display again, this time to an external view of the spacescape outside.

"Look at those ships. Something Malone said to me earlier made me think. You said these ships all seemed to have the same design, Malone?"

Malone nodded.

"I think these were from the same race. All of them. And they tore themselves apart because of this... this lifeform. It may just be a virus of some form, but it operates on a sentient level. It got into their heads. It made them fight one another. It made them destroy themselves. Then we arrived. It got into our Go Team. It got into Hoban, then the captain, and now..."

Again, Cassandra changed the display. The image that hovered now in holographic form between them all was the view of the medbay.

The captain, Hoban and the three members of the med-team stood side by side, gazing into the camera. They didn't shift, they didn't waver. They simply watched, and waited.

A silence fell on the assembled crew as they looked at their shipmates – now perhaps no longer quite the shipmates they had long known.

"So..." began Abrahams at last, breaking the silence. "So what do we do?"

"We have two options," said Cassandra. "We can destroy the Go Team's shuttle. We can evacuate the air from the medbay. Like with an infection, we can sterilize the affected areas, in this case our crew. We can stop it right there, put up a warning beacon to avoid the area, mourn our losses and leave."

"Just kill them all?" asked Kostina. "But they're our-"

"Were our crew," interrupted Cassandra. "We don't know what they are any more. Not yet."

Malone's soft voice was the next to speak.

"You said we had two options," he said. "What's the other?"

Cassandra straightened, her hands moving to brush down her uniform.

"We carry out our mission. We've found an alien lifeform, right here among us. Now it's up to me. I've been studying the language already. I think I may even have found the way to say the word for peace."

She pointed at the display, where the captain and the infected crew stood waiting.

"I'm going to go and make contact."

THE END

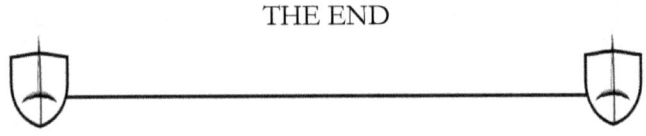

About Leo McBride

Leo McBride is a journalist and author. Born in Northern Ireland and now living in The Bahamas, he writes speculative fiction – that umbrella that covers fantasy to science fiction and everything in between, even a dash of horror. He is a co-founder of Inklings Press, and has been published in a number of anthologies from that imprint, along with collections published by Starlight Press, Rhetoric Askew and more. You can find him tweeting at @AlteredInstinct and blogging at Altered Instinct.com, where you can find more stories to read for free and links to his other work.

Shepherd of Memory
By Rob Edwards

My name is Doctor James Wilson. I'm a mission specialist for the GSA, and I am the first human being to have contact with a sentient alien life form. I just don't always remember it...

And where do I go from there? It's a bit late to start 'Dear Diary' after that...

Hell with it, I didn't want to write a journal anyway.

***

So apparently, that's not an option.

My counsellor, the devil in a bright blue suit, insists on it. I need to "express how the experience made me feel", I should be "frank, open and comprehensive." All so I can "process an emotional response" to it.

The thing is, I don't want to think about it. I don't want to find out if I remember it right. That's the worst bit. Sometimes it's clear as snow melt, other times, it's like... like I remember talking about it, but have no memory of... of the thing I'm talking about. Does that make sense?

The counsellor insisted it would help though.

So.

I remember landing on PhiLUp, Phi Lima Upsilon I should say. It's the normal kind of memory, the sort that's fuzzy around the edges, and built of memories of remembering it, coupled with the many times I've reviewed the mission logs. Normal, safe, memories.

Mission E X four twenty. Planetfall: June 16th, 2238. Crew of four: myself, Julia Minakova, Toby Mbataku, Captain Gaby Lopez commanding.

We deviated from projected LZ by four point oh two clicks at the recommendation of Mission Specialist Mbataku, geo plats indicating more favorable terrain and access to water table. Captain Lopez green lit the alternate, and we deployed habs per protocol. By 1400 Actual, we...

"Not like that."

Fine. "Frank, open and comprehensive."

***

With a twist of my fingers in the primary sensor array, I pulled up the life sciences overlay for workstations one and two. The virtual keyboards and monitors painted themselves across the white walls and desk, specialist tools and data arrays replacing the geology template that Captain Lopez used for her work.

Doctor Toby Mbataku slid into the chair at W2, while I took my seat at primary.

"Moment of truth," he said, and locked his monitors to the holding pen, and Specimen PLU217 within. Two-seventeen, or "Phil" as Julia insisted we call it, was a herbivorous quadruped, two feet long, covered in blue fur and with a distinctly porcine appearance.

On the W1 array, I pulled up video feeds of the lab rat and its holding pen. "How is Phil doing?"

Toby parted his thumb and forefinger, zooming in on Two-seventeen's biometrics. The skin sensor we'd tagged him with when the drone captured him fed basic diagnostics to the screen: skin temp and pH, something we thought was a heart rate, everything we could gather non-invasively. "All readings nominal. He fed two hours ago, he'll be at the tail end of the torpor phase. Ready to make history in the most boring way imaginable?"

"You may have done this a hundred times, but it's only my third."

Toby bowed in his chair. "Then by all means, Doctor Wilson, make history."

"Doctor Mbataku, I shall." I slid my finger along the desktop and the hatch in the rat's pen opened. The rat twitched its nose at the change, but didn't immediately approach it. "And now we wait." The problem with working with live specimens: you must take them at their own speed or risk contaminating the data.

The atmosphere on Phi Lima Upsilon has the right chemistry to be breathable for short periods. We collected soil samples, water samples, analysed them in every way we know how, before progressing to collecting flora and fauna. The stuff we found was safe. By every test in the book, and Toby wrote the book, everything registered as biohazard neutral. But the introduction of creatures from different biomes: we can computer model it until we're blue in the face, but without doing it, there's no way to be certain what will happen.

Eventually, the rat investigated the tunnel, and I closed the hatch behind it.

Toby leaned forward, eyes flicking from one scan to another. "Come on, Phil, don't disappoint us."

Phil wasn't sure what to make of the rat, and the feeling was mutual. They kind of edged around each other. I don't think either one liked the smell of the other.

We kept exposure time to a minute. No forced interaction. We had no agenda here beyond seeing if Terran and PhiLUp life could share atmosphere. It's a long way from declaring the planet safe, but it's a point on the graph.

I reopened the hatch, and deployed the rat's treat. It was trained, knew to expect it, and when it caught the scent, it twitched its nose again and left Phil alone. I sealed the hatch behind it, watched it scuttle up the pipe back into quarantine.

"Well that was an anti-climax," I said.

Toby put his hand on my wrist. "What. The. Actual. Hell?"

On the W2 monitors, Phil was running around his pen at a speed I'd never seen any of his species use. He struck one wall, bounced off, spun, and repeated it against the opposite wall.

"What are the biometrics showing?" I asked, half rising from my chair, peering over Toby's shoulder.

"Skin temp and heart rate both elevated, but that may be the exercise. Everything else, no change."

"Did they touch? I didn't see anything…"

Toby pulled up the recording of the interaction, and flicked it over to W1. He didn't take his eyes off Phil on the monitor.

I sat back down and skimmed through feed at triple speed, keyed the diagnostic to measure minimum distance between the subjects. They never got closer than 60cm. "Nothing. Atmospherics, then?"

Toby flicked those scans over to me, too. He just stared at his monitor, one hand raised towards it, reaching out. "What is it doing?" he said. "It started at the exact moment you closed the hatch behind the Terran specimen. It can't be a coincidence. Can it be a coincidence? Suggestive, certainly, but we can't assume a correlation…"

A sickening crack came from his video feed. Phil staggered back from his latest impact, legs failing him, he toppled over. Fluid leaked from a fracture in his skull. Hind leg twitching, he bled out, and there was nothing we could do, but capture it in every detail our sensors read.

"A hundred times, and I've never seen that before," said Toby, and there was a distinctly unscientific note of glee in his voice.

"Toby, please. I know there's a risk to both specimens in these tests, that's the point, but this was…"

"It was different, Jim. Different and new! It's a huge galaxy, but different and new is rare." Toby rubbed his hands together, then rewound his diagnostics to the start of the interaction. "Something happened here. Let's see if we can find any clue as to what. How's the rat doing?"

Toby's feeds were covering mine. I pulled them back down to get a look at the rat. It sat in the middle of its pen, unmoving, its treat in front of it, untouched. For all the world, it seemed to be looking straight at the camera.

"That's freaky," I said. "Wait, its eyes…"

And then I fell unconscious.

***

When I woke, I was in a quarantine of my own. Not often used, but standard on any off-world expedition, because you never knew. A sparse, small space, white like most of the hab. There was a bed built into the wall, a chair and small fold-out table, and complex medical scanners built into the ceiling. One wall made of what looked like glass, but was lined with every kind of filter known to science. Only a narrow band of visible light could penetrate it.

Captain Lopez was sitting on the other side of the glass, facing away from me. "Jim?" she asked, her voice sounding tinny from overhead speakers, deliberately low quality.

"Yeah, what happened?"

"That's the question of the hour. What can you tell me? Toby says you said 'Wait, its eyes' and then fell out of your chair."

I put a fingertip to my forehead, yeah there was a bruise forming there. "Its eyes? Really? I don't remember. We'd just finished the interaction test with Phil. It went sideways, but I guess you've seen that."

"Yes."

"The last thing I remember was checking on the rat. It seemed oddly still. I was about to tell Toby, and then… here."

"I see." She still wasn't looking at me. "And how do you feel in yourself now?"

I ran a mental checklist. "A bruise on my forehead, sore ribs, I guess I caught those on the chair arm as I fell? But otherwise okay. Embarrassed?"

"Not raging to be released? Swearing vengeance on all who dared entrap you?"

I chuckled. "Hardly. I know the protocol: 'Any unexplained phenomenon affecting a crew member is a mandatory 48-hour quarantine'. I can see how this qualifies."

"Good." She nodded and stood. "Glad you're back with us, Jim. You missed about three hours. Food will be delivered through the hatch on the left in about an hour, but I can hurry it up if you're hungry?"

"I'm fine, Captain. Don't worry about it."

"Comes with the title, Jim. And also coming with the title…" she turned and stared me square in the eyes. I stared back.

We held it an awkward thirty seconds, then she shrugged. "I'm not feeling any urge to shout 'The eyes' and fall over, so I guess we operate on the assumption that I've not caught whatever affected you."

I gave a rueful shrug. "Here's hoping."

"Right, well I need to get back to it. Some damn medical emergency has left us short-handed so I can't hang out here. Toby will be down to see you soon, I'm sure. He's very excited by the whole thing. Kind of obscenely so, in fact."

"Thanks, Captain."

"Feel better."

***

In fact, my first visitor was Skye.

She sat in the chair that the Captain had vacated, and gave me a little wave. "I'm sorry about this," she said.

"It's okay, Skye. It's pretty comfortable in here, and it's only for 48 hours. No problem."

The GSA takes all sorts, but Skye was exotic even by our standards. Attractive, but in an androgynous way. She had long dark hair like Julia's, which she often wore over one eye, which was a

216

shame, as her eyes were a distinctive indigo-blue. Her skin tone was not as dark as Toby's nor as light as mine, but somewhere in between. I used to tease her about her accent, I remember, I could never quite place it. "I came to English late," she would say.

"Still," she said "I'm sorry. Is there anything you need?"

"I'm fine, truly. Tell Toby to hurry his ass up, and bring me some files to work on. Boredom's my only danger right now."

"Okay." She fidgeted with the cuffs of her overalls. I never understood how she got hers so bright. We all washed clothes the same way, but our uniforms all came out non-descript grey. Hers were always as blue as her name. "What do you remember?" she asked. "Can you tell me? It might help, to remember."

I sat down on the bed. Closed my eyes, tried to recall. "We completed the interaction test, and separated Phil and the rat. Everything was textbook. Toby could have written it beforehand. But then it went sideways when we separated them. Phil went crazy. And the rat... the rat just sat there, no interest in the food, just staring at the camera with its bright blue eyes."

I jumped up. "That's it! I saw its eyes!"

Toby stood in the doorway; he looked nervous. "You're not going to keel over again, are you?"

"Toby?" I said. "No, I'm fine. I was just telling Skye. I remembered! The rat's eyes turned blue. And then there were explosions of blue light across my field of vision, that's when I fell unconscious. Wait... where is Skye? She was right here."

Toby still stood in the doorway, looking, if anything, more nervous. "Jim, who's Skye?"

***

Julia rigged a mobile screen on their side of the glass. She kept me company, working away at her own tablet. As the team Systems Engineer, she needed to keep an eye on all the hab systems, as well as our shuttle and the command ship in orbit. They were all taking turns "keeping me company".

The filters over the window made the image on the screen less than perfect, but that was their job, to reduce the bandwith of information passed through the window in either direction to minimize contamination risk. We couldn't be sure the filters worked until we knew what we were dealing with, but it was a compromise I was willing to work with. The alternative was sitting on my hands for 72 hours; the quarantine period extended courtesy of my new symptoms.

I'd rather be working.

I watched the footage from the rat monitor over again. The rat stared, I collapsed, the rat moved again. At no point were its eyes anything other than a pinkish-red. I saw no visible change. I slowed it right down, clicked through frame by frame.

"Nothing," I said.

Julia looked up. "What's that?"

"No blue eyes. Nothing strange at all, I mean it sits stock still after returning to its pen, and stays that way until I have my thing. That looks a little odd, and the timing is suspicious, but it's not totally outside the scope of normal behavior."

She came closer to the glass, risked a peek around at the monitor, the image of the pink-eyed rat frozen in place. "What did it look like?"

I rubbed the back of my neck. "That's the thing, I don't remember. I remember telling Toby that's what I saw, and I have a vivid, pin-sharp memory of remembering it. But I don't remember it. I don't have the words."

"No, I think I get it. You remember you had the memory, but not what the memory was. Like, remembering you had some really comfortable shoes, but not remembering what it felt like to wear them?"

I laughed, despite it all. "Something like that, yeah. Oh this is useless." I clicked off the monitor, fell back on the bunk.

"And what about this 'Skye' woman you imagined? Why her? Did she look like anyone we know?"

I stared at the ceiling, trying to recapture the image of Skye. "I don't know. It's the same phenomenon. I remember telling Toby about my conversation with 'Skye', but I don't remember her. She had... hair?"

"Well, I'll feed that into the facial recognition software and see what pops." Julia laughed. "But, seriously, what did it feel like, did it freak you out? A vivid hallucination like that, kind of weird?"

"No. Not at the time. It's unsettling after the fact, certainly, but at the time, it seemed normal. I knew her, I expected to see her. I didn't just hallucinate her, I hallucinated a history with her. A connection, a relationship."

"Weird."

"That, certainly."

***

The next morning, Toby took his turn to keep me company. He walked with a heavy step, and all but collapsed into the chair. Dark rings under his eyes made him look ten years older.

"You look awful," I said, helpfully.

He nodded. "And yet you're the one in quarantine. I had a bad night, didn't sleep much. How are you doing?"

"I feel fine. Bored, but fine."

Toby grunted. "Let me check that the med scanners in there are all working properly. Wouldn't want to miss anything."

"Don't get up, Toby, you need the rest. Julia checked them all last night, they're fine."

With a visible effort, he pulled himself out of the chair. "With all due respect, Jim, she's a technician, not a biochemist. I'll check she's not missed anything."

The tell-tales went dark in the ceiling, as Toby took down the scanners to run a diagnostic on them. "She had a talk with me last night," he said.

"Julia? What about?"

"No, not Julia, Skye."

"What?"

"I was programming some drones to send out for more specimens, and she was just there. And she had always been there with me."

"You've been working too hard," I said, but was worried it was more than that. He'd been with me when my problems started, he'd clearly been infected too.

"I don't think we're dealing with a mental aberration, Jim, not an illness at all. I think we're dealing with a life form."

I looked at the ceiling, the diagnostics were still cycling, all the recording devices were off.

"Toby, you're not well, let me call the Captain."

"Hear me out first, then you can."

"Alright."

"I don't remember what she said. I don't remember what she looked like. But she convinced me not to send the drones out, Jim." He stepped to the middle of the window, shoulders slumped, hands in pockets, but his face was alive with enthusiasm and energy. "I still think I need to send the drones out, to see if we can replicate what happened with Phil. I remain sceptical about Skye, and her motives… but… I didn't send the drones. That means that whatever she said was enough to convince me, with all my doubts, that I shouldn't."

"Toby, what if…"

"No, Jim, I've looked at it again and again, I spent the whole night chasing an explanation, and it's the only one I have that fits. Skye is not an illness, she is a life form with independent agency, the ability to reason, make logical arguments, enough to change my mind."

"You may have just dozed off, forgotten to send the drones. Perhaps you changed your mind. You're stressed, overworked."

Toby slammed a hand against the glass. "No, Jim, don't think I haven't thought of that. She shows independent agency, is capable of response to stimuli. While I don't know if we discussed their reproductive cycles, by all definitions I know, she is alive. Don't you see how important this is? Intelligent alien life. The first we've ever encountered. Our names will be forever linked with this."

"You've talked yourself into this, because you think you'll be famous? You're Dr Toby Mbataku, you've flown more missions than anyone in the GSA, ever. You wrote most of the protocols that we follow. Everybody knows your name, how much more famous can you get?"

"I was born too late to see the start of what we do; I wrote the books, sure, the protocols we use, but that just makes me a god-damned accountant of science. People remember Columbus, not the person who helped outfit his ship."

"Toby, listen to yourself, this is… you need to talk to the Captain… take some time…"

And as the tell-tales overhead blinked on, he said "Jim. Jim, she's not real, Skye can't have talked to me, she's not real, don't you remember?"

"What? I don't understand."

"It's okay, Jim, you just rest, I'll talk to the Captain. But it might be better if you stayed in there a little longer." He put a hand on the glass. "I'm sorry, Jim, right now, you're a danger to yourself and the mission. It's not your fault. It's not. We'll get you help, you'll see."

Of course. The part of the conversation where he confessed, the cameras were off. If I spoke to the Captain now, I'd sound like I was raving.

Toby gave me a sad, tired smile. "You'll be okay by yourself for a bit, won't you? I'll talk to the Captain now."

I watched him go, he'd boxed me in more thoroughly than the quarantine room.

Or... had I imagined his confession?

If I was imagining crew members who didn't exist, was it so impossible that I'd imagined that too? How could I trust anything I saw or heard?

But as the minutes passed, I grew more certain. The memories of Skye were fleeting and elusive, but the memory of Toby's betrayal was still clear, and hot in my chest. It was not the same. It wasn't.

All I remembered about Skye;

the way she picked out the chocolate chips from muffins to eat them at the end...

the time she'd convinced Julia that Saturn only had four moons...

how kind she'd been to me when I got the news from home about my parents' dog dying...

the sound of her laugh...

I blinked. "Hello, Skye," I said.

"Hello, Jim."

She sat in the chair on the other side of the glass, a warm smile on her lips. The vibrant blue of her eyes, matched by her uniform.

"Are you a hallucination?" I asked. "Or a life form, like Toby thinks?"

She laughed her familiar laugh. "Is there an answer I can give that would convince you?"

"I suppose not."

"Can we pretend I am a life form, just for the moment? If I were, what would you ask me?"

I thought about it. If she were real, there were a lot of questions I'd want to ask. But the one I wanted to ask most was "How did you learn English so quickly?"

"You have an interesting mind, Dr Wilson. The short answer is, I didn't. The longer answer will take a bit of explaining."

I gestured around us. "I'm not going anywhere."

She looked over her shoulder, pulled her hair away from her face, I watched the long strands slide along her fingers. An astonishingly human gesture, a visceral experience. Was my imagination so detailed?

"Fine," she said. "I think we have a little time. The problem is, English doesn't really have the words, but I'll try my best.

221

"My people are a co-species with Phil's. We have no physical form, existing only as a kind of mental construct. Phil's people host us, because we provide their herds with... continuity, I guess? We remember things for them, the best food sources, where the water is safe to drink, how to avoid predators. We don't control, we shepherd."

"And what do you shepherds get out of the relationship?"

She crossed her arm, shuffled uncomfortably in the chair. "Listen, I know how this will sound to you, but before you apply judgements, I want you to remember, this is a symbiotic relationship, not a parasitic one. They get as much from it as we do, just differently."

"I will try to keep an open mind."

She nodded. "Okay. We drain... leech... suck... there really isn't a positive word in your language for this. In exchange for what we do, we siphon a little of their mental energy."

"I see."

"That sounds quite judge-y, Jim."

"No, no, it's not. Not much. Just, if your host died, but you are still alive, where are you draining mental energy from now?"

She didn't answer, not right away. "I'm so sorry about Phil. I wasn't expecting that reaction when I left him to investigate your rat. Normally, we can exist separately without difficulty for short periods, but Phil was always prone to panic. I shouldn't have left him in such unfamiliar surroundings. I will miss him, terribly." She sounded genuinely sad.

"But to answer your question. I passed from Phil, to your rat, to you, and I've been moving between your crew mates ever since. I've not always made my presence known, but I have visited each of them.

"I'm not sure I like Toby. I had to convince him not to take up more of my people. They aren't all as... diplomatic as I am. I don't want any trouble, and it's best that we handle this between us, as scientists."

I put my hands to my head. "So, right now, you're in here somewhere, draining me of mental energy?"

"Hmm. Not quite. You are remembering this conversation, you aren't having this conversation. If you remember it, I am with you, but the conversation is already over. Which kind of brings us back to your first question. How I learned English so fast. I didn't. I've never learned English. But the way that you experience our interaction is in memory. And your brain interprets that interaction in English, with me, looking like this."

I shook my head. "I don't understand."

"I'm sorry. We're out of time. I will try again later. And I will stay with you as long as I can, so you can retain the memory of what I said. But you will forget it again, when I move on. It's like, you can only see Toby when he's in the room. You can only remember me, when I am with you."

The door behind her opened. I looked up to see Julia. In the moment my attention shifted, I lost the sense of Skye being there, but I retained the memory, so, she was still there?

I was getting a headache. Hopefully, if she was in there, it would hit her too.

***

Julia popped her head around the door again later that afternoon. "Sorry to leave you stewing, Jim, but Gaby has us working double-time. She wants me to run an analysis of the soil samples you didn't get to. Any tips?"

"I'll do them, Julia, not a problem. Connect this terminal to the network, and I can run them from here."

"No, no, that's fine, I'm happy to do them, just, hoping you might have some suggestions."

"Really, Julia, I'm bored as hell down here. Give me something to do, just hook me up, and I'll get on with it. You're all busy. I can sort this in no time."

"Jim…"

I sagged. "Oh. But Gaby has asked you not to connect this terminal, hasn't she?"

"Yeah. Sorry, Jim. We still don't know what, if anything, you have, but if you did catch it from the rat, that happened over the network, so…"

"Well… put the data on a cube, no need to connect up the terminal. I'll look through the data, tell you what I see…"

Julia retreated. "Sorry, Jim, I better get on with it, thanks anyway."

Of course, they couldn't trust what I saw either.

"It's not a disease, you know," I told the empty air. "It's a life form. Skye is real, and she's roaming around the hab while you have me locked away in here.

"Let me out!" I slammed the glass.

Damn it.

"Let me out! Let me out! Let! Me! Out!"

***

The crew, my friends, left me alone after that. I didn't blame them. If they watched the video of my outburst, I wasn't surprised.

I didn't see Skye for two days, either, but my memory of her ebbed and flowed. Sometimes I would remember her clearly, at other moments I would only remember remembering her. Part of me hoped that it wasn't a sign of my illness deepening, but I had decided, for better or worse, that I believed Skye. That I didn't have an illness. That I had made contact with sentient alien life.

It would be exciting if it wasn't so damn frustrating.

And then as I lay on my bunk feeling sorry for myself, there she was again. She was always light-footed. I remembered that time during flight training, she'd surprised me in study hall, just appeared out of the blue behind me. I all but jumped out of my skin.

Except of course, that memory wasn't real. Even if it was such a clear memory, every nuance sharp and vivid.

"Hello again, Jim," she said. "Sorry I've not been by much. They are really busy out there in the hab without you. It's been fascinating to watch."

"Hello, Skye. I'm glad you're having fun."

"Sweet of you to say so, Jim."

I contemplated the white ceiling, and the blinking lights and tell-tales of the med scanners. "I need to get out of this quarantine. Can you help?"

"If you can suggest something I can do, I'll listen, of course."

I swung my legs around and sat on the edge of the bed. "Let Gaby have a memory of you. She's sharp. A keen, logical, mind. I'm sure if you present a case, she…"

"Toby told me not to."

"Toby? I thought you didn't like Toby. Thought you didn't trust him?"

"Oh, I don't. He sees me and mine as an opportunity, a resource to be exploited. But for now, our… how did he put it, 'our ambitions align'."

That caught me. "Skye, what ambitions do you have?"

"I want the same thing you do, Jim. I want to see the galaxy, to seek out new life and civiliza…"

"Toby made you watch Star Trek."

"Only a couple of episodes, but I skimmed his memories of the rest. But I told you, among my people, I am a scientist. And this represents the greatest chance at new knowledge my people have ever had."

I stood and walked to the window, looked down at her, remembered looking down at her in the chair. "You're planning to come back to Earth with us."

Skye grinned, a dazzling smile, her eyes sparkling blue, her enthusiasm radiating off her. "You bet your ass I am. And sooner than you think. Toby has convinced the Captain…"

"… that the risks here are too great," said Captain Lopez.

My head spun.

Gaby paced up and down in front of the glass, Skye was gone, and my memory of her evaporated in a moment. What was Gaby saying?

"I'm sorry, Gaby, I zoned out for a moment. What were you saying?"

She paused her pacing, and frowned, her concern for me written all over her face. "We can't treat you here, Jim, and we think your condition is getting worse. We run the risk of further infection the longer we stay here. Toby has suggested, and frankly I agree, we must scrub the mission, and get you back to Earth, where you can be properly treated."

"I'm fine, Captain, truly," I said. I was, of course, but it sounded hollow to me, when I said it out loud.

She ignored my interruption. "It's not a decision I take lightly, but it is a necessity. We will flag Phi Lima Upsilon as dangerous, though Toby is talking about bringing a medical team back to study this phenomenon in a couple of years, once he can work out safety protocols."

"Right, of course, so Skye can return home with her findings." I was past caring how I sounded.

Gaby put her hand up against the glass. "I'm so, so, sorry, Jim. We'll get you home. We'll get you help."

***

I have had a lot of time to think, on the return trip. I've not seen Skye since that last time, but the memories come and go, so I know she's around. I thought I saw her once, as my quarantine pod was rolled across the tarmac at Huntly's spaceport. A woman in blue with long dark hair, but when she looked my way, she wasn't Skye. Was she?

Did I imagine it all? Which is worse? Am I losing my mind, or did we bring an alien home, and me the only one who cares?

The memories seem sharpest in my counselling sessions, so, maybe they are helping. Maybe they are necessary. Maybe I do have some kind of affliction from the conditions on Phi Lima Upsilon.

Maybe the only life in Skye is in my memories. But there's the rub, that is what I remember her saying she was. A living memory. Life in memory.

What did she hope to achieve by coming with us? Something Toby said to me, what did we know about their reproductive system? Had we brought back one alien, or potentially, an invasion force?

She's gone, but to where? There's nobody else here. Is there?

As my counsellor said to me this morning...

What did my... she...
I don't remember.
I don't remember.
Her suit. I... her suit it was...
What color was her suit?

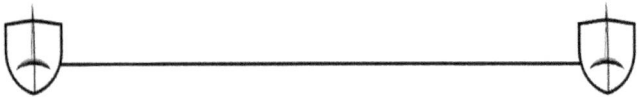

About Rob Edwards

Rob Edwards is a British born writer and podcaster, currently living in Finland.

He was first published at the age of 11 in a Royal National Institute for the Blind anthology called Stories for a Prince in honor of the birth of Prince William. Since then his work has included RPG scenarios for Wizards of the Coast's convention-based Star Wars campaign and articles for a games website.

In more recent years, he has returned to writing fiction, and has short stories in the anthologies *Tales from the Universe*, *Tales from Alternate Earths* and *Tales of Wonder*, published by Inklings Press. He has also appeared on RB Wood's Word Count Podcast.

Rob's own podcast, StorycastRob.co.uk features readings from his short stories as well as chapters from his urban fantasy novel, *Writ in Blood and Silver*.

For updates, follow him on:

Twitter - @StorycastRob

Sci Fi Roundtable

The Sci Fi Roundtable is a cooperative association of writers, editors, readers, and artists dedicated to supporting and promoting the Independent Author and Indie Publishers. With a substantial Facebook presence and active websites, it has become a vibrant collection of people who love to craft stories and those who enjoy reading them. The Sci Fi Roundtable works to develop indie authors and artists by helping with brainstorming, editing, marketing, and building members' social media presence.

Sign up to our Newsletter for the latest updates: